SOPHIE PRICE IS VAIN

Fisher Amelie

http://www.fisheramelie.com/

First Edition: December 2012

Printed in the United States of America

For Bruce,

You lived the kind of life we are all meant to live.

You took your hands and dug them in the dirt. You knew that serving others was your calling and you answered with a resounding and immediate yes, devoid of doubt, devoid of "what-if's". I was blessed to know you, to call you dad...

And we'll miss you more than you could possibly imagine.

P.s. Pura Vida!

Read Fisher's other contemporary works...

Callum & Harper
Thomas & January

Read Fisher's Paranormal work...

The Understorey

Stay tuned for the first chapter of *Callum & Harper* at the back of *VAIN*.

PROLOGUE

Vanity's a debilitating affliction. You're so absorbed in yourself it's impossible to love anyone *other* than oneself, leaving you weak without realization of it. It's quite sad. You've no idea what you're missing either. You will never know real love and your life will pass you by.

But you will see.

One day you will blink and the haze will dissipate. You'll discover that what once defined you has wilted into graying hair and wrinkled skin. Frantic, you'll glance around yourself, in hopes of finding those you swore adored you, but all you will find is empty picture frames.

CHAPTER ONE

Six weeks after graduation and Jerrick had been dead for three of them. You'd have thought it would've been enough for us all to take a breather from our *habits*, but it wasn't.

I bent to snort the line of coke in front of me.

"Brent looks very tempting tonight, doesn't he?" I asked Savannah, or Sav as I called her for short, when I lifted my head and wiped my nose.

Savannah turned her glassy eyes away from her Special K laced O.J., her head wavering from side to side. "Yeah," she lazily slurred out, "he looks hot tonight." Her glazed eyes perked up a bit but barely. "Why?"

"I'm thinking about saying hello to him." I

smiled wickedly at my pseudo-best friend and she smiled deviously back.

"You're such a bitch," she teased, prodding my tanned leg with her perfectly manicured nail. "Ali will never forgive you for it."

"Yes, she will," I said, standing and smoothing out my pencil skirt.

I could've been considered a dichotomy of dressers. I never showed much in the way of skin because, well, my father would have killed me, but that didn't stop me from choosing pieces that kept the boys' tongues wagging. For instance, everything I owned was skin tight because I had the body for it, and because it *always* got me what I wanted. I loved the way the boys stared. I loved the way they wanted me. It felt powerful.

"How do you know?" Sav asked, her head heavily lolling back and forth on the back of the leather settee in her father's office.

No one was allowed in that room, party or no, but we didn't care. Sav's parents went to Italy on a whim, leaving her house as the inevitable destination for that weekend's "Hole," as we called them. The Hole was code for wherever we decided to "hole up" for the weekend. My group of friends was, at the risk of sounding garish, wealthy. That's an understatement. We were filthy, as we liked to tease one another, double meaning and all. Someone's house was always open some random weekend because all our parents traveled frequently, mine especially. In fact, almost every other weekend, the party was at my home. This isn't why I ruled the roost, so to speak. It wasn't even because I was the wealthiest. My dad was only number four on that list. No, I ruled because I was the hottest.

You see, I'm one of the beautiful people. That truly sounds so odd to have to explain, but it's the truth nonetheless. I'm beautiful, and it's not because I have a healthy dose of self-esteem, though I have plenty of that. It's obvious in the way I look in the mirror, yes, but even more obvious in the way everyone treats me. I rule this roost because I'm the most wanted by all the guys, and all the *girls* want to be my friend *because of it.*

"How do you *know?*" she asked again, agitated I hadn't yet answered.

This made my blood boil. "Stuff it, Sav," I ordered. She'd forgotten who I was and I needed to remind her.

"Sorry," she said sheepishly, shrinking slightly into herself.

"I *know* because they always do. Besides, when I'm done with their boys, I give them back. They consider it their dues."

"Trust me," she said quietly toward the wall, "they do not consider it their dues."

"Is this about Brock, Sav?" I huffed. "God, you are such a whiny brat. If he was willing to cheat on you so easily, he wasn't worth it. Consider it a favor."

"Yeah, you're probably right," she conceded but didn't sound truly convinced. "You saved me, Soph."

"You're welcome, Sav," I replied sweetly and patted her head. "Now, I'm off to find Brent."

I stood in front of the mirror above her dad's desk and inspected myself.

Long, silky, straight brown hair down to my elbows. I had natural blonde highlights throughout its mass. I'd recently cut my bangs so that they fell straight across my forehead. I ruffled them so they lay softly over my brows. I studied them and felt my blood begin to boil. The majority of girls at Jerrick's funeral suddenly had the same cut and it royally pissed me off. *God! Get a clue, nimrods. You'll never look like me!* I puckered my lips and applied a little gloss over them. My lips were full and pink enough that I didn't need much color. My skin was tanned from lying by the pool too much after graduation, and I'd made a mental note to keep myself indoors for a bit. *Don't need wrinkles, Soph.* My light gold eyes were the color of amber and were perfect, but I noticed my lashes needed a touch more mascara. I did this only to darken them up a bit, not because they weren't long enough. Like I said, I was practically flawless.

"He won't know what hit him," I told myself in the mirror. Sav mistook this for speaking to her and I rolled my eyes when she responded.

"You play a sick game, Sophie Price."

"I know," I admitted, turning her direction, a fiendish expression on my unblemished face.

I sauntered from the room. As I passed the throngs of people lined against the sides of the hall that lead from the foyer to the massive den, I received the customary catcalls and ignored them with all the flirtatious charm that was my forte. I was the queen of subtlety. I could play a boy like a concert violinist. I was a master of my craft.

"Can I get you boys anything?" I asked as I approached the elite group of hotties that included Ali's Brent.

"I'm fine, baby," Graham flirted, as if I'd *ever* give him the time of day.

"You look it," I flirted back, just stifling the urge to roll my eyes.

"Since you're offering so nicely, Soph," Spencer said, "I believe we could all use a fresh round."

"But of course," I said, curtsying lightly and smiling seductively. I purposely turned to make my way toward the bar. I did this for two reasons. One, to make them all look at my ass. Two, to make them believe I'd only just thought of the next move on my playing board. I turned around quickly and caught them all staring, especially Brent. *Bingo*. "I'll need some help carrying them all back," I pouted.

"I'll go!" They all shouted at once, clamoring in front of the other like cattle.

"How about I choose?" I said. I circled the herd, running my hand along their shoulders as I passed each one. Spencer visibly shivered. *Point, Soph.* "Eeny, meeny, miny, *moe*," I said, stopping at Brent. I followed the line of his throat and caught a glimpse of him swallowing, hard. "Would you help me, Brent?" I asked nicely without any flirting.

"Uh, sure," he said, setting down his own glass.

I linked my arm through his as we walked to the bar. "So how are you and Ali doing?" I asked him.

He gazed at me, not hearing a word I'd said. "What?" he asked.

Exactly.

Three hours later and Brent was mine. We'd ended up sprawled out on the ancient Turkish rug in Sav's parents' bedroom, our tongues in each other's throats. He threw me underneath him and hungrily kissed my neck but stopped suddenly.

"Sophie," he breathed sexily in my ear.

"Yes, Brent?" I asked, ecstatic I'd gotten what I wanted.

He sat up and gazed down on me like he'd never really seen me before. I smiled lasciviously in return, tonguing my left eyetooth. "Jesus," he said, a trembling hand combed through his hair, "I am such a fool."

"*What*?" I asked, sitting up, stunned.

"I've made a horrible mistake," he told me, still wedged between my legs. No need to tell you how badly that stung. "I've had too much to drink," he said, shaking his head. "I'm sorry, Sophie. You being the most gorgeous girl I've ever met's clouded my judgment, badly. I've made a terrible mistake."

At that most fortunate of moments, we heard Ali calling out Brent's name in the hall outside the door and he tensed, his eyes going wide. I could only inwardly smile at what was to come. Before he'd had a chance to react to her calling to him, she'd walked into the room.

"*Brent?*" she asked him. She saw our position and the recognition I'd seen in all the others before her was so obviously written all over Ali. She wasn't going to fight it. "I'm sorry," she said politely, like I wasn't in a compromising position on the floor with her boyfriend. *She's so pathetic*, I thought. She closed the door. We heard her pounding the floor to the stairs, running toward Sav no doubt. Sav would have to pretend she had no idea.

He threw himself to his feet, abandoning me haphazardly on the carpet and immediately began chasing her. *Well, that's a first,* I thought to myself. Usually they went right back to business, but I suppose we hadn't gotten far enough. *Yeah, that's why he left you lying here, half-undressed, chasing after his girlfriend, Soph.*

I balked at my own idiocy and stood up.

I walked to Sav's parents' bathroom and leaned over her mother's side of the double sinks. I fixed my bristled hair and ran my nail along the line of my bottom lip, fixing any gloss smudges. I tucked my formfitting black-and-white V-striped silk button-up back into my pencil skirt and stared at myself.

A single tear ran down my cheek and I grimaced. *Not now,* I thought. I was my own worst enemy. That was my secret weakness. Rejection. Rejection of any kind, in fact. I hated it more than anything.

"You're too beautiful to be rejected," I told the reflection in front of me, but the tears wouldn't stop.

I ran the tap and splashed a little water on my face before removing the small bag of coke I'd hidden in my strapless. I fumbled with the little plastic envelope, spilling it onto the marble counter and cursed at the mess I'd made. I scrambled for something to line it with, finally stumbling upon her father's medicine cabinet. I removed the blade from her father's old-fashioned razor and made my lines. I remembered her mom kept small stacks of stationery paper in her desk in the bedroom and I went straight for that, rolling the paper into a small tube.

The tears wouldn't stop and I knew I wouldn't be able to snort with a snotty nose. I went to her parents' toilet and tugged at a few squares of toilet paper, blew my nose, then flushed it down. I swiped at the tears on my cheeks and bent over my lines just about the time a policeman came rushing in, catching me right before the act for the second time that night.

"What are you doing? Put your hands on your head," I heard a man's deep voice say.

I languidly stood from my unfinished lines and stared into the mirror. Sharing its reflection with me was a young, rather hot cop. *Shit.* I dropped the rolled-up stationery that smelled like old lady lavender potpourri and lazily put my hands over my head.

"Turn around," he said, fingering the cuffs on his belt.

I turned around and faced him, his eyes widened at the full sight of me. He stumbled a little, a hitch in his step, as he progressed my way. He brought my right hand down slowly, then my left and swallowed just as Brent had earlier. *Gotcha.*

"What's your name?" I whispered, his face mere inches from mine. Beats Antique's *Dope Crunk* rang loudly from downstairs. *No wonder I hadn't heard them come in.*

"That's none of your concern," he said, but the hesitation in his voice told me he thought he'd like it to be.

"I'm Sophie," I told him as he clicked the first ring around my wrist.

He kept narrowing his eyes at me, but they would drop to my breasts then back up.

"N-nice to meet you, Sophie."

"Nice to meet you, too...," I drug out, waiting for his name.

"What are you doing?" he asked me, throwing

glances over his shoulder, no doubt worried if more officers would be joining us.

"Nothing. Cross my heart," I appraised, taking my free hand from his and crossing my heart, which just so happened to be at the crest of my cleavage. His gaze flitted down and he started breathing harder.

"Casey," he told me.

"Casey," I said breathily, testing out his name. He fought a drowsy smile, apparently liking the way I said it, and I smiled.

"L-let me have your hand," he said.

I gave him my unconstrained hand without a fuss. He took it and restrained it with the other.

"All tied up now, Casey," I whispered, raising my fisted hands just as he closed his eyes, almost drifting forward a bit.

"Come with me," he said, pulling me from the counter. His eyes glanced down at my lines and he shook his head. "What makes you do that shit?"

"Because it feels good," I told him, turning his direction and seductively running my tongue along my top teeth.

"Don't even," he said, "or I'll get you on propositioning an officer as well as possession."

"Suit yourself," I told him, shrugging my shoulders. "It might have been nice," I leaned forward and sang in his ear.

"I'm sure," he said. I could see the surprise on his face at his unexpected and candid response. I decided to run with it.

"I bet if you handcuffed me to the closet bar just beyond those doors, I'd be quiet as a mouse until you came back for me," I said, letting the double meaning sink in.

"Stop," he said. The breath he'd been holding whistled from his nose.

"How old are you, Casey?" I asked, leaning into him.

"Twen-twenty-two," he stuttered.

"Huh, I just happen to be into twenty-two-year-olds. They're currently my thing," I lied.

His eyes came right to mine and held there.

"Really?" he asked, skeptical, yet inadvertently leaned into me. The grim line that had held his face before turned into a slight grin. *Seal the deal, Sophie.*

"Mmmhmm," I said. I pushed farther into his chest, my breasts mashed against his armor plate.

I tentatively kissed the pulse at his neck, knowing full well that if he really wanted to, he could definitely get me on propositioning.

I just couldn't go to jail. Not again. I'd already been once for possession when Jerrick died, and the judge told me if I showed back up in his courtroom, I'd be toast. This was worth the risk.

"Jesus," he murmured.

I threaded my fingers through the belt loop at his waist and brought him closer to me. He fiercely took my face in his and kissed me like he was dying. *What an amateur,* I thought. *Thank God I got a dumb one.* His hands grappled all over my face as he had no grace whatsoever. If the guy wasn't so sexy, I don't think I could have put up the charade as long as I did.

"Officer Fratelli!" we heard come from downstairs and he broke the kiss. "Fratelli!"

"I'm-I'm up here," Casey said, flustered. He adjusted himself and wiped his mouth.

"Uncuff me," I said, almost panicked.

"I can't," he said.

"Yes, you can, Casey. Do it and I'll repay you exponentially."

He groaned but looked at me apologetically. "When you get out, come find me," he said quietly as the other officer entered the room.

"The rest of the upstairs is secure," Casey said as if he hadn't just kissed my face off. "She was the only straggler."

"Fine," the older officer said. I thought he was going to leave but instead came through and examined the bathroom around us. "What the hell is this?" he asked Casey.

"What?" Casey asked.

"This," the older man said, gesturing to the lines of coke.

"Uh, yes, she was attempting a line when I found her," Casey told his superior.

Fuck.

"I'll bag this up," the man said and waved Casey on.

"I'm sorry," Casey said when we were out of the room. "I had to tell him. He'd have known I was lying."

"It's okay, Casey," I said with saccharine ooze. I kissed his mouth, then bit his lip playfully. "It would have been the best ride of your life," I whispered. His eyes blew wide.

"Wait, what? We can still see each other," Casey desperately plied.

"Sure we can," I lied again.

"I wasn't going to tell him about the drugs," he said again, his voice quivering. "I had only planned on getting you on the party. That would have only been a ticket, a misdemeanor."

"I know, sweets," I told him, "but you still messed up."

Casey led me down the winding staircase and I felt as if time was standing still. All my friends, cuffed themselves, looked up at me as I descended over them. I smiled down at them bewitchingly and they almost cowered in my presence. I'd been the one who brought the coke, and my smile let them know that if they brought me down, I wouldn't be going down with the ship on my own. If they squealed like the pigs they were, I would make their lives miserable. There's a fine line between friend and foe in my world.

Casey placed me into the back of a squad car when we reached the winding drive and buckled me in.

"Tell me," I said softly against his ear near my mouth, "what exactly am I being charged with?"

"Sarge will probably get you on drugs, but if it's your first offense, you should be able to get off lightly."

"And what if it isn't?"

"Isn't what?" he asked, glancing over his shoulder.

"My first offense."

"Shit. If it's not, there's nothing I can do for you."

"Oh, well, there's nothing I can do for you then either," I said coldly, the heat in my seduction blasted cold with a bucket of ice water at the flip of a switch. Casey's mouth grew wide and he could see that he'd been had. I turned my face away from his, done with my pawn.

Casey got into the front seat and I could see through the rearview that his face was painted red with humiliation and obvious disappointment in himself that he fell for my game. He stuck the key in the ignition and drove me to the station.

I was booked, processed and searched. I scoffed at the women who had to search me before placing me in my cell. Stripping naked for anyone of the female persuasion wasn't exactly what I'd had planned for the evening. They looked down on me, knowing my charges, like they were somehow better than me.

"My lingerie probably costs more than your entire wardrobe," I spit out at the short, stocky one who eyed me with disdain.

She could only shake her head at me.

"Well, it'll go nicely with *your* new wardrobe addition," the dark-haired one said, handing me a bright orange jumpsuit.

This made both the women laugh. I slipped the disgusting jumpsuit on and they filed me away into a cell.

I shivered in my cell, coming down from my high. I was used to this part though. I only did coke on the weekends. Unlike most others I knew, I had enough self-control to only do it at the Holes. It was just enough to drown out whatever crappy week I'd had from being ignored by my mother and father.

My parents were strangely the only I knew of who married and stayed that way. Of course, my mother was fifteen years younger than my father, so I'm sure that helped and she stayed in incredible shape. If you pitched a pic of her then and now, you wouldn't be able to tell the difference, and she'd gifted those incredible genes to yours truly. That was about the only thing my mother ever bothered to give me. My mother and father were so absorbed in themselves I don't think they remembered me some days. I was born for one reason and one reason only. It was expected of my parents to give the impression of a family.

My mom was a "housewife," and I use that term loosely. My father was the founder and CEO of an electronics conglomerate, namely computers and software. His company was based in Silicon Valley, but when he married my gold-digging mother, she insisted on L.A., so he jetted the company plane there when he needed to. It was safe to say that one, if not two or three, of my father's products were in every single home in America. I'd had a five-thousand-dollar monthly allowance if I'd kept my grades up during prep school, and that's about as much acknowledgment I got from my parents.

I'd just graduated, which meant I had four years to earn a degree of some kind then move out. I would retain a monthly allowance of twenty thousand a month, but I had to earn my degree first. That was my father in a nutshell.

"Keep appearances, Sophie Price, and I'll reward you handsomely," my father said to me starting at fifteen.

And it was a running mantra in my home once a week, usually before a dinner I was forced to attend when he was entertaining some competitor he was looking to buy out or possibly a political official he was trying to grease up. I would dress modestly, never speak unless spoken to. Timidity was the farce. If I looked sweet and acquiescent, my father gave the impression he knew how to run a home as well as a multinational, multibillion-dollar business. If I did this,

I would get a nice little thousand-dollar bonus. I was an employee, not a child.

"Sophie Price," someone yelled outside the big steel door that was my cell. I could just make out the face of a young cop in the small window. The door came sliding open with a deafening thud. "You've made bail."

"Finally," I huffed out.

When I was released, I stood at a counter and waited for them to return the belongings I had walked in with.

"One pair of shoes, one skirt, one set of hose, one set of...," the guy began but eyed the garment with confusion.

"Garters," I spit out. "They're garters. God, just give them to me," I said, snatching them out of his hands.

He carelessly pushed the rest of my belongings in a pile over to me and I almost screamed at him that he was handling a ten-thousand-dollar outfit like it was from Wal-Mart.

"You can change in there," he said, pointing at an infinitesimal door.

The bathroom was small and I had to balance my belongings on a disgusting sink.

"Well, these are going in the incinerator," I said absently.

I got dressed sans hose, returned my ridiculous jumpsuit and entered the lobby. Repulsive, dirty men sat waiting for whatever jailed fool they bothered to bail. They eyed me with bawdy stares and I could only glare back, too tired to give them a piece of my mind.

Near the glass entry doors, the sun was just

cresting the horizon and I made out the silhouette of the only person I would have expected to come to my rescue.

Standing more than six feet tall, so thin his bones protruded from his face, but with stylish, somewhat long hair, reminiscent of the nineteen-thirties, clad in a fitted Italian suit, stood Pembrook.

"Hello, Pembrook," I greeted him with acid. "I see my father was too busy to come himself."

"Ah, so lovely to see you too, Sophie."

"Stop with the condescension," I sneered.

"Oh, but I'm not. It is the highlight of my week bailing you from this godforsaken pit of bacteria." He eyed me up and down with regret. "I suppose I needed to get the interior of my car cleaned anyway."

"You're so clever, Pembrook."

"I know," he said simply. "To comment on your earlier observation, your father *was* too busy to get you. He does want you to know that he is severely disappointed."

"Ah, I see. Well, I shall try harder next time not to get caught."

Pembrook stopped and gritted his teeth before opening the passenger door for me. "You, young lady, are sorely unaware of the gravity of this charge."

"You're a brilliant attorney, Pembrook, with millions at your disposal," I said, settling into his Mercedes.

He walked around the front of the car and sat in the driver's seat.

"Sophie," he said softly, before turning the ignition. "There's not enough money in the world that can help you if Judge Reinhold is presiding over your case again."

"Drive, Pembrook," I demanded, ignoring his warning. *He'll get me off*, I thought.

My house, or I should say, my father's house, was built a year before I was born, but it had since been newly renovated on the outside as well as the inside so although I may have grown up in the home, it barely resembled anything like it did when I had been small.

It was grotesquely large, sitting on three acres in Beverly Hills, California. It was French Chateau inspired and more than twenty-eight-thousand square feet. I was in the left wing, my parents were in the right. I could go days without seeing them, the only correspondence was out of necessity, usually to inform me that I was required to make a dinner appearance, and that was usually by note delivered by one of the staff. I had a nanny until fourteen, when I fired her for attempting to discipline me. My parents didn't realize for months and decided I was capable of caring for myself after and never bothered to replace the position.

Freedom is just that. Absolutely no restrictions. I abandoned myself to every whim I felt. Every want I fulfilled and every desire was quenched. I wanted for nothing.

Except attention.

And I got that, I'll admit, not in the healthiest of ways. I won't lie to you, it felt gratifying...in a sense. I was rather unrestrained with my time and body. I wasn't different from most girls I knew. Well, except the fact I was exponentially better looking, but why beat a dead horse? The only difference between them and myself was I kept them wanting more. I used many, many, *many* boys and tossed them aside, discarding them, ironically, like many of them did to so many other girls before me.

This is what kept them baited. I gave them but a glimpse of my taste and they tasted absinthe. They were hooked by *la fée verte* as I was so often called. I was "the green fairy." I flitted into your life, showed you ecstasy, and left you dependent. I did this for fun, for the hell of it, for attention. I wanted to be wanted, and my word, did they want me. Did they ever.

CHAPTER TWO

Pembrook wound through the cobblestone drive of the palatial estate.

"Drop me off at the service entrance," I told him. I wanted to avoid running into my father if possible.

He snorted. "I have to see your father."

"Oh," I said.

Pembrook had his own parking space in the last of the twenty ports off the carriage house. That's how often he visited our home. As much as it pains me to say it, Pembrook was like an uncle to me. Whenever I filled out paperwork for visiting physicians, as it was considered beneath us to visit an office, under the tab "who shall we contact in case of an emergency," I always, always, *always* put Pembrook.

He was the only reliable one. He was my father's attorney and yet the only adult in my life that had any interest in what I did with that life. He was Pembrook.

Pembrook was English, but had lived in America for close to thirty years. He specialized in international law as well as got me out of my minor legal tiffs. Standing freakishly tall at six-foot three, he was lean, bordering anorexic-looking. If I were to guess, more than likely hadn't had more than maybe an ounce of fat on his entire body at any given moment of his life. His cheeks were a bit sunken and he reminded me so often of one of the rare, gaunt and goth creatures who attended my prep school, but his look was natural. I suppose that's what leant him additional intimidation factor as an attorney. I believe he played it up when possible. I also believe he was a virgin. For one reason: He lived and breathed his job. For another, I couldn't imagine a single woman taking pity on the poor man. Then again, he was rich, who was I to say?

"Pembrook, who do you visit when you return to London?" I asked, suddenly struck with the interest to know what went on there when he left here.

He eyed me strangely. "You are odd."

"Pembrook, answer me."

He rolled his eyes at me. "I visit my sister and her family."

I checked my shocked expression as best I could. "You have a sister?" I asked in disbelief.

"Why is this so hard to imagine, you daft girl?"

"I'm not entirely sure, Pemmy. I cannot conjure a female version of you, I suppose? What does she look like? Another Bram Stoker character inspiration?"

He sarcastically looked at me with pity. "What an astute observation coming from someone who couldn't hear the sirens blaring down the street of her latest conquest."

"Point, Pemmy. Point."

"You are sorely in need of guidance," he said more to himself than to me.

"I am fine," I spit back, folding my arms across my chest as the gravel crunched beneath our shoe-clad feet.

"Clearly," he added sarcastically.

We approached the service entrance nearest the carriage house and Pembrook opened the door for me.

Inside were members of the staff. Gerald, our head chef, stood at one of the giant Viking ranges experimenting with sauces no doubt, but the remaining crew sat strewn about the large industrial kitchen. The kitchen, aside from our everyday, more personal one, was where the food was prepared for more formal dinners and I knew then just why my father was truly disappointed in me.

I looked around me wondering why there wasn't more fire beneath their asses. The staff sat reading, listening to music or just staring into space. I suppose it was too early to do prep work. They paid no immediate attention to me either as I was often seen entering my father's abode at that hour. I used the service entrance to access my wing of the house in order to avoid my parents. They wouldn't say anything to my father and neither would I. It was an unspoken agreement we all had. They looked up briefly for confirmation, but when their gazes swung to the figure behind me, they began scrambling around. Pembrook was certainly not expected and I almost burst out laughing.

"Oh, cease this incessant buzzing," Pembrook told the seemingly aimless help, his hands raised above his head, giving him a luring feel. I waited for fangs but none came. "Calm yourselves, fools. I am not your boss, and I couldn't care less if you st with a knife in your hand or a magazine." But the staff continued on as if they'd not heard a word. "Very well," he sighed, gesturing for me to continue.

"Carry on, Gerald," I said, saluting the head chef. He smiled and waved me on.

Gerald was the only member of our staff I could stand and that was more than likely because he was mute.

When we reached the grotesquely large foyer, I made a move for the winding stairs.

"Ah, ah, Sophie," Pembrook said and I cringed into myself. "Come with me."

"You never said I had to accompany you to see my father."

This was highly unusual and made my heart beat wildly in my chest.
"I never said you didn't. Come," Pembrook said as he made his way toward my father's office several doors into the first floor west wing. He expected me to follow, so I did.
Knock. Knock. Pembrook's bony fingers rapped on the door of my father's office.
"Come in," I heard my father say.
When I walked in, my father was nose deep into a stack of paperwork on his desk as well as on the phone.
"No! How many times have I told you?! That is unacceptable, Stephen! I refuse, *refuse* to acknowledge their desperate attempt to hold the upper hand. Tell them I said the offer stands until midnight tonight and when it expires, the offer will not present itself again." His crony must have been acquiescing and my father nodded curtly once as if the man could see him and promptly hung up.
He looked upon me and I very nearly vomited onto the carpet at my feet. I was scared of very few things but of those few things, my father stood atop the list.
"Ah," he said, drinking in my appearance. "I see you're alive."
I nodded once succinctly. I was standing in the doorway and Pemmy prodded me forward. I glanced behind me briefly to scowl before fixing my expression ahead. Pembrook was on the verge of laughing. *Sod off!* I wanted to yell, to borrow a phrase from his people's vernacular, but I kept my

mouth shut instead not wanting to wake the dragon before me any more than he was already awake.
"Let's see," he said, settling into his creaky, leather office chair. He began to stuff his pipe. "A second drug offense, Sophie Price. I'm not exactly sure how I plan to keep this out of the media this time. PR has their work cut out for them, it seems. I can barely stand to look at you, so this will be brief. You are required to attend a formal dinner tonight. I expect you to get some sleep, remove those hideous bags from underneath your eyes, dress properly and entertain the son of Calico's CEO. Do you understand?"
"Yes, sir," I squeaked out.
"Do you? By entertain, I mean show the boy the house, make conversation. I do not mean offer him anything illegal."
"I would never—" I began, but my father cut me short.
"Wouldn't you?" He eyed me harshly.

I sank into myself and inadvertently backed into Pemmy. "Ugh!" I heard him say before righting me and setting me beside him. He rolled his eyes.

"Dinner is at seven, Sophie," my father continued, ignoring Pembrook and ,me.

"Yes, sir," I said, parroting my earlier acknowledgement.

I turned and barely contained myself from fleeing.

"Oh! And one more thing," my father said, making me turn to face him. "If you're caught again, I'll disinherit you. Close the door."

I closed the door, my chest pumping in air at an alarming rate and nearly sprinted for my wing of the house. I knew enough about my father to know he was in earnest. I also wasn't a stupid girl. I knew there were things I needed more than coke, and his money was one of them.

When I reached my room a few minutes later, I opened the fifteen-foot double doors and closed them behind me. I started to strip, pulling off my garments and tossing them at the foot of my bed. I needed a shower. I was on the verge of one of my breakdowns and needed a place to hide away.

But first things first.

I went to the wall nearest my bedroom door and pressed the intercom, still undressing.

"Yes, Miss Sophie?" A staticky voice came on. It was Matilda, the house coordinator.

"Yes, 'Tilda." I glanced at my nightstand clock. Eight a.m. "Can you ring Katy at home and let her know I'll need her services at four this afternoon?"

Katy was lovely. Tall and slender, blonde hair and only a few years older than I. She was the beautician I used when I had one of my father's soirees to attend. Katy never came alone though. She always brought Peter, her masseuse, and Gillian, her makeup artist.

"Of course, ma'am. Anything else?"

"No, thank you." And with that, I headed toward my bathroom, securing the door behind me.

The bathroom was almost as large as my bedroom. On the far back wall was an estate-sized fireplace. It's French-inspired marble mantel reached halfway up the wall. Situated in the center was the focal piece, the oversized, burnished cast-iron tub and swathed in polished stainless steel for a mirrored effect. The entire floor was bathed in three-inch octagonal tiles of Carrara marble. The Carrara marble continued on the walls in subway tile. Oval undermount sinks were fitted into the Carrara marble tops with custom washstands. The room was almost a duplicate of one I'd seen when I was thirteen on a trip to Paris.

I stepped into the tiled shower and started the water. Piping hot. I closed the glass door and decided it was safe. I let go of all the unhappiness that took unending residence in my heart and soul and stomach. I sobbed into my hands and let the water wash away the salt. My heart was in a perpetual state of sadness and the only relief I could find were in those cathartic cries. I lived a fragile existence. I knew it even then but feigning I didn't was easier than embracing something so altogether daunting. If I faced what I'd truly created for myself, a life of debauchery and seedy fulfillment, I knew I couldn't have lived another day and self-preservation was very much still alive in me. I loved myself too much to say goodbye. So, I would go on living just as I had been because it was the only life I knew.

I bawled for at least half an hour before washing and conditioning my hair and shaving my legs and even then the tears continued, but I had a job to do that night and damn if I was going to have bags underneath my eyes. My dad would faint, or the male equivalent, anyway. I needed sleep.

Life will continue on. Everyone will continue their worship of you. Just keep up appearances. Just keep up.

When I was done and sufficiently under control of my emotions, I shut off the water and stepped onto the heated marble beneath my feet. Reaching for my robe, I wrapped it around my body and grabbed a towel for my hair. I sat at the edge of my vanity in my room and moisturized my entire body with the five-hundred-dollar-an-ounce moisturizer my mother insisted I used.

By then, sleepiness was attempting to claim me. I was too tired to dress in pajamas so I just slipped under the covers donning my robe and the towel still wrapped around my head. Sleep came easily. It always did. It was a true safe haven from the hell I'd created for myself.

Knock! Knock! Knock!

I woke startled to the sound of rapping at my door.

"Miss Price!"

"Come in!" I shouted.

The doors bellowed open and in poured Katy and her entourage.

"Oh, I'd forgotten you were coming," I told her.

"Thank you. Nice to see you, too," she teased.

"Just a moment," I told them.

I relieved myself and brushed my teeth then met them in my room. Peter had already set up his portable massage chair, modified so Katy could do my nails while he did his thing. I almost sat before realizing I'd yet to put undergarments on. I ran to my dressing room and slipped them on before joining them again.

I sat down and Peter started in with the massage. "Any place in particular I need to focus on today, Miss Price?"

"No, Peter. Just the standard."

"Very well, miss."

I'd already closed my eyes when I felt Katy at my feet, removing my polish. "And what are you wearing this evening, Miss Price?"

"I'm unsure. Let's just do a French. That's all encompassing."

"Of course."

Very well, Miss Price. Of course, Miss Price. I very nearly yelled at them to quiet the ridiculous platitudes but checked myself. It'd be good practice for this evening.

When my nails were dry, they sat me in the leather chair stool in my bathroom in front of the mirror. I studied myself, ensuring my skin was still flawless, my hair still long and beautiful, my eyes still shining. I would never have admitted this to anyone, but I panicked if I hadn't seen a mirror in a few hours, affirming I still had the only thing that made me so adored.

Katy and Gillian worked their magic and within two hours I was plucked, polished, buffed and readied to entertain the only son of Calico, a company I knew nothing about. *Shit.*

"Peter," I called out to my room while Katy finished up my hair.

"Yes?"

"Bring my laptop in here, will you?"

I heard shuffling in my bedroom and then Peter entered the bathroom with my computer. I pried open the monitor and put in my password. My father would kill me if I wasn't schooled on the boy's father's company. I Googled Calico.

Ah, plastics. And a durable product at that. In fact, their plastics were damn near indestructible. It made sense my father wanted in. Impervious electronic products would make him unstoppable. *Okay, let's see.* Founded by Henry Rokul, married to Harriet Rokul. One child by Harriet named Devon. Devon Rokul is a twenty-year-old Harvard student studying, what else, business. I further Googled Devon Rokul's picture and stumbled upon his social media. I familiarized myself with Devon's Twitter updates and almost gagged at how mundane they seemed to be.

Took the dog for a walk today.

Studying for an exam.

Meeting Sam for a film.

Blech! Boring! But he wasn't a bad-looking boy, and that made me not dread the evening as badly. I'd also discovered he was tall and would be able to wear heels, thank God, unlike my last charade where the guests were terminally short. I was forced to wear flats that night.

"Done!" Katy said, obviously proud of herself.

When I looked up, I saw that I looked as I always did. Impeccable.

"Thank you, Katy," I said drily. "Settle with Matilda, I'll ensure she includes a generous tip."

"Oh, of course, Miss Price. Thank you."

I stood, not bothering to see them out, and entered my dressing room. My closet was compartmentalized according to color and event. If I didn't do that, I'd never find anything. The thousand-square-foot room was filled with clothing from floor to ceiling save for a small step to the massive wall mirror. My shoes were housed below the large island in the center and the counter held my jewelry and hats.

"Let's see here," I told no one. I made for the not-too-formal section of my wardrobe and chose a couture Chanel gown. Black and white. *Gasp.* Shocking, right?

I dressed and was downstairs in half an hour, awaiting the guests in the library where my father brought all his guests before dinner.

My mother walked in five minutes later. "Sophie," she said, barely acknowledging me. She leaned over the mirror beside the door and examined her makeup.

"Hello, love," my father laid on thickly for my mother when he entered the room. He kissed her with such fervid mania, I had to clear my throat to alert my presence. *Disgusting*. The lust poured off them. "Sophie," my dad spit out, still looking at my mother.

"*Asshole*," I said under my breath, but he didn't hear.

Finally, the doorbell rang and I heard the clamor of feet in the marbled foyer. Our Steward, Leith, lead the Rokul family into the library. "The Rokul family," Leith formally announced before swiftly exiting.

"Henry! Harriet! Devon!" My dad said jovially, hugging each like he wasn't the giant prick we all knew he really was. "This is my lovely wife, Sarah, and my daughter, Sophie."

I plastered the most genuine smile I possibly could and made my way their direction, taking each hand after my mother did.

"What a lovely family you have, Robert," Henry complimented.

"I couldn't agree more," he told Henry, grabbing us each by the waist.

I absently recognized that that was the first physical contact I'd had with my father in more than six months.

Harriet and my mother sat together on the tufted fainting couch and the men, except for Devon, observed the grounds from the window. This left poor Devon shifting near the door.

"So, I hear you attend Harvard?" I approached and asked him.

He seemed to soften at my question. "Yes, I study business."

"What else?" I asked, not realizing how rude that was until it was too late.

A soft smile reached his lips.

"I'm so sorry that was incredibly boorish of me." I needed to patch it up before my father found out. "I meant that it would only make sense you'd study business seeing who your father is. An unerring sense of business must be inherited."

"And she recovers flawlessly," he teased, making me smile genuinely.

"Dinner is served," Leith said, interrupting the room.

Devon offered his arm and I took it. My dad winked at me in approval and I wanted to gag. Dinner was served in the more intimate dining room, as there were only six of us. Devon pulled a chair out for me at the end of the table then sat next to me, two full seats separating us from our parents.

"Thank you for this," I secreted in his ear.

"My pleasure," he flirted.

Devon was a complete gentleman throughout dinner and I found myself unbelievably attracted to him. I mean, of course, all the boys in my circle were utter gentlemen. It was a product of their breeding, but Devon seemed genuinely interested in being courteous just for the sake of being courteous.

When dinner was over, coffee and cake were to be served in the library and I followed my parents out of the dining room, but Devon pulled me away, out of range.

"Our parents are a drag. Why don't you show me your garden instead?" he asked.

"Of course," I told him before leaning into the library. "Devon has an interest in seeing the gardens. Is it okay if I show him?" I asked for show more than anything.

"I don't mind. Do you, Rokul?" my father asked.

"Of course not. Have fun you two," Henry added.

"Come with me, Devon," I smiled sweetly, taking his arm once more.

As much as I was attracted to Devon, I knew my father would kill me if I was anything but what he thought a lady should be and I had already made plans to keep my cool with him. Not to mention I wasn't exactly in the mood after the day I'd had.

It was also kind of nice for a guy to pay attention to me because he was just polite, no ulterior motive. I wasn't used to it.

The gardens were a garish feature of our home and had been since I was small, but my mother loved them with their winding boxwood geometric designs, so they stayed and were impeccably kept up.

"It's very beautiful here," Devon chimed in after a quiet turn around the main garden.

"Mmm, yes," I agreed politely.

"Not as beautiful as you though."

Gag.

"Thank you," I told him, trying my damnedest not to burst into tears laughing.

We rounded the boxwoods and entered the garden maze.

"Perhaps we should return to the house..." I started before Devon shoved me into the prickly bush maze behind me.

"Or we could just stay here," he roughly bit out, kissing me so harshly I wasn't able to speak.

I shoved him off me. "What the hell, Devon?"

"Oh, come on. You know you want to," he continued, handling me as if I hadn't just thrown him off.

"Excuse me?" I said, shoving him back again, but he only came back twofold.

"Please, Sophie. I know you're reputation, and you could do a lot worse than me."

My chin dropped to my chest. *The gall.* I purposely fixed my gaze.

"You're right, but we can't do it here so close to the maze entrance, someone might hear."

He backed off me for a moment. "Lead the way, Miss Price."

"Follow me," I flirted over my shoulder. "This way."

I led him through the winding maze and purposely toward a dead end but near a bench so I could enjoy the show. "No one will find us here," I told him. I grabbed the front of his jacket and settled him in front of me as I sat myself on the bench, reclining on one arm. "Go ahead."

"Wh-what should I do?"

"Undress, of course," I playfully teased.

"You're a kinky bitch."

What a lovely compliment. "You know it."

I watched Devon shed each expensive layer of clothing until there was nothing left but the moonlight on his skin. He smiled devilishly at me. I won't go into how ironic his name suddenly became to me.

"Here I am," he said, spreading his arms wide.

I stood slowly and walked seductively his direction. I bent slightly to retrieve his tie from the pile and sauntered around him. I placed the tie around his eyes and began to tie a knot.

"Wait, what are you doing?" he asked.

"Just a little game I like to play," I sang into his ear before kissing his neck. This visibly relaxed him. "Now, I want you to count to ten then come find me," I hurriedly said while gathering all his belongings down to his shoes.

"Wait, I don't think..."

"Don't think. *Feel*," I teased.

He grabbed for me blindly and I sidestepped him, making a beeline for the exit of the maze I'd used to visit every day as a little girl. It's where I used to hide from my nannies. *What a fool*. I made my way from the maze and finally let myself smile genuinely for the first time that night. I threw his clothing in the fountain in the center of the boxwoods and turned around when I heard Devon call out my name. He was quicker finding his way out than I'd anticipated.

"What are you doing!" he grated as I tossed in the last shoe.

"Oops."

"You bitch!"

I climbed my way up the gravel walk and into the house not bothering to look behind me. I continued up to my room determined not to think of the consequences of what I'd done.

"Nobody messes with Sophie Price," I said out loud. "I don't care who you are."

CHAPTER THREE

My father burst into my room without knocking. I attempted to hide my shock at seeing him on my side of the house.

"What the hell happened tonight?" he demanded.

My mother came into the room and silently stood beside my father.

"Nothing," I said, leaning over my vanity, removing my makeup.

My father met me at my chair and swung me harshly by the arm away from my task.

"I have put up with a lot from you, Sophie."

"Really?" I asked, surprised at my own words. "The last time I checked neither you nor my mother bothered to endure anything to do with me unless absolutely necessary or if it was a publicity risk. I was raised by strangers. You have not put up with anything from me save for the occasional call to your attorney. So you can spare me the lecture. You missed the opportunity to be my father a very long time ago."

He slapped me across the face and I stumbled back into my vanity chair, stunned silent. My hand went to my cheek and held there.

"You spoiled, selfish little whore," he told me through gritted teeth. "I pay for your life and all I've asked in return were a very few things. Stay out of the limelight and support the image we are a healthy family in company. But apparently even that was too much to ask. You've done irreparable damage this time, Sophie, and there's only one thing I can think to do with you."

He whipped his cell from his jacket's inside pocket, dialed and held the phone to his ear.

"Pembrook? Sorry to wake you. Yes, as we've discussed," he said and hung up.

My parents left my room abruptly and shut the door behind them. My hand trembled from my cheek and fell into my lap. I tried not to think what the subject of conversation had been, tried not to take my dad's accusation that I was a whore to heart, regardless how true it was, tried not to think too much into the fact that my mother let him accuse me

without so much as a peep from his side.
I stood and slinked out of my Chanel, letting the garment fall into a heap at my feet. I slept in my underwear and bra, uncaring of anything around me. It's easier to pretend. So much easier.

In the morning, I showered and forewent breakfast, something I did often as I rarely ate. A girl has to keep her figure. I'd planned on visiting Sav, to get away from my tension-filled home, but when I approached the carriage house, my SLS was gone.

"What the hell?" I asked no one. I searched the entire garage, but it was nowhere. *Ah, I see. He thinks to punish me.*
I took out my cell and rang Sav, but it went straight to voicemail.

"Fine, you don't feel like answering, you piggish trout?"
I dialed Spencer and he picked up the first ring.

"La fée?"

"What are you doing right now, love?"

"I'm taking you out, I hope?"

"You've read my mind," I flirted back. "Pick me up at my place in, say, an hour?"

"Right."
I hung up and went straight to my room to pack a bag. I wouldn't need much. I planned on spending most of my time warm in Spencer's bed.

Spencer was right on time just as I expected as no one kept me waiting, ever. On my way out the door, Sav rang me.

"Sav," I spit out.

"I'm so sorry, Sophie. I—"

"Save it, Sav. I've no need of you. Goodbye."

I hung up.

Spencer leaned casually against the passenger side door and looked incredible. Just under six foot. Spencer's wardrobe spoke trust fund but his face screamed of how handsomely rugged he was, not at all babied-looking and I appreciated that about him. His face would be screaming something else within the hour if I had anything to do with it.

I'd just hit the last of the steps when he lifted his finely sculpted body and sauntered my direction.

"Hello, beautiful," he whispered into my ear when I reached him. He yanked me by the waist toward him and lightly kissed my ear. "I was wondering when it would be my turn."

My stomach clenched at the memory of my father's words, but I stuffed them back down.

"Seems you were a fine wine, Spence. You only needed aging."

He grabbed my bag and opened the door for me. I settled inside, wrapping my seat belt around myself just as Spencer joined me after placing my bag in the trunk.

"I have to crash for a few days," I told him, examining myself in the vanity mirror.

"That shouldn't be a problem," he said, smiling at me.

His teeth were white and perfectly straight. He was equally as flawless as I was.

He started the engine and it purred like a kitten, but I'd heard Aston Martins did that.

"Why?" he asked.

"Well, after Sav's party—," I said, but there was no need to finish.

"Ah, well, I might have a few things in mind to pass the time," he flirted. "I was going to meet Brent for lunch, but I can reschedule if you don't feel like it."

I definitely didn't feel like it. Anyone else and I would have agreed.

"No, Spencer. We'll be too busy to lunch with Brent," I teased.

Spencer's home was modern in architecture but equally palatial to my parents'. The entire home seemed to consist of nothing but windows and never-ending levels. I almost felt sorry for his staff, almost.

We parked in his space and he killed the engine. He leaned over and placed his hand high on my thigh. A rush trilled through me at how hot his hand was. "Good news. My parents left this morning for Africa on holiday."

I rolled my eyes. "How cliché."

"Tell me about it."

He got out of the car and came over to my side, opening the door for me. He kissed me suddenly and my stomach dropped in hesitation for a moment like it always does but as always, I worked through it and put up my barrier. The same barrier that allowed me to what I did with all the boys.

He broke the kiss and grabbed my hand then retrieved my bag. "Who goes to Africa anymore?" I asked him as we ascended the steep and sharply staired walkway.

"My parents?"

We both laughed.

"I gave the staff the day off today," he mentioned absently when we reached the top, dropping my hand and bag to fish his keys from his pocket.

When the door opened he threw my bag over the threshold. He kissed me on the doorstep and we went toppling toward the white plastered exterior of his doorway. We hit the wall hard and my head reverberated slightly from the force. *Ow*. "Sorry," he murmured, but continued to kiss me. I worked through the pain and kissed him fiercely in return.

He wrapped one big arm around my waist and lifted me from my feet, continually kissing me. He walked us into the foyer and slammed the door shut with his foot. He began unbuttoning my shirt and tugging it out of my skirt, never breaking contact. He tossed it behind me. My arms felt heavy and my heart felt a mess. *It's not working! Why isn't this working?*

I doubled my efforts and he took this as invitation to remove my skirt, undoing my side zipper slowly. "Oh, God, Sophie," he exclaimed, making me want to vomit. "You taste incredible."

I ignored him and the feeling and kissed him harder. My skirt fell to my ankles and I stepped from it as we made our way to his parents' sofa. He stopped suddenly and held me at arm's length.

"Jesus," he hissed, sucking in a breath. His gaze raked my body and stifled a shudder. I stood in front of him, in full lingerie with garters and ankle-strapped heels. He approached me deliberately, his hands running through my hair, then down my shoulders and back before palming my ass. "You're more beautiful than I could've imagined, Price."

"Thank you," I said, wishing I could just run.

Work through it, Sophie. You're just a little off your game.

He kissed languidly up my neck to my chin and across my jaw line. "You smell like," he inhaled, "cherry bark and almonds."

"It's my shampoo."

"I love it," he told me.

He laid me on the leather sofa nearest the fireplace and the morning sun was streaming in at seemingly impossible angles. It was beautiful. Too beautiful. I felt ill at all it was revealing to me. "So much light," I whispered, not realizing I'd said it out loud.

"We can move to my bedroom," he said. "It's darker in there."

"Please," I said, needing to remove myself from exposure. I felt desperate.

He picked me up, tucking one arm under my knees and the other around my back. He brought me back to his room and laid me on his dark sheets. The room had shutters and dark curtains that kept out every inch of light.

"Better?" he asked.

"Much," I answered.

"Now, where were we?"

He crawled over me and kissed me feverishly, his hands roaming my body. He lay on top of me and cupped his hand around my knee, bringing it around his waist.

That was when I broke. I don't know why I did it, what I was thinking, why my usually stalwart barrier was so weak, but silent tears began to cascade down my face and Spencer pulled away.

"Sophie? Are you *crying*?"

"No," I insisted, swiping at my face in the dark, hoping he couldn't see me. *How humiliating*.

I'd never cried in front of anyone. Ever.

"Oh, Soph," he soothed. "You are."

"I'm so sorry," I said, pushing at his shoulders to flee.

"Wait," he said, pulling me back to his embrace. "Stay with me for a second." He laid back and tucked me into his side, smoothing my hair behind my ear. "We don't have to do this, Soph." I waited for it, but he didn't retract his words. Instead, he continued. "You forget I've known you since we were small." I couldn't help but laugh at the image of a simpler time when Spencer and I used to giggle and play in the gardens at my home. "You're thinking about our games."

I nodded against his chest. "I'm still sorry," I grated out again.

"You know, I'm going to confess something to you," he said, ignoring me, taking a deep breath to steady himself. "I've wanted you since I was old enough to discover I could want someone." My body tensed beside his, but he just held tighter. "Shh, stop. Listen to me.

"I can't lie to you. You're goddamned beautiful, Sophie, and I'm so turned on right now I can't even think straight, but I won't have you, not like this. I thought you wanted this."

"I did," I began truthfully but he shushed me.

"No need, Sophie. Just lay here with me while I try to calm the hell down."

"Okay," I sniffed.

It was then I realized that Spencer was a good friend, a real friend, probably the only one I really had.

We both fell asleep and I woke to Spencer snoring softly. I peered down at myself and realized I was practically naked. Shame heated up my face and body and I slid out from under his hold to retrieve my clothing from the main living area. The room was dark as the sun had set not long before and I began gathering my skirt and blouse from the blonde wood flooring.

I'd just bent to retrieve my purse when I heard the front door swing open. I froze in absolute fear as

Spencer's father stood in the space just outside the threshold. I held the loose clothing against my body.

"Well, well, well, what do we have here?" he asked, strolling in at a snail's pace. He removed his keys from the lock and threw them on a nearby table. He looked more closely at me and realization struck him. "Ah, the Price girl."

"I'm sorry," I began, but he cut me off.

"No need to be sorry," he said, oozing creepiness. "I'm not." He perused my body with obvious appreciation and I turned to bolt back up the stairs to Spencer's room.

"Wait," his father called out, grabbing my elbow. "If he's finished, I'd like to have a turn."

"Excuse me?"

"It looks like you're finishing up, aren't you?" When I couldn't answer him he continued, "My wife flew ahead of me. I had an emergency at work and had to fly back from Atlanta. I told her I'd meet up with her later. She's not here."

"What the hell does that have to do with me?" I asked, bewildered.

"I can give you things my boy can't," he slimily offered with what I'm sure he thought was a charming smile. All I could see were serpent's teeth.

"What the hell is wrong with you?"

"I'm assuming Spencer's asleep because you've worn him out." I balked at his presumption. "I, uh, know of the trouble you've recently gotten yourself into." *Uh-oh.*

"What exactly are you saying?"

He ran a finger down my upper arm and I visibly convulsed at his touch. His eyes became hard. "I'm saying if you want me to keep this indiscretion quiet to your father, you'd best accommodate me."

I shook my head and he ripped the clothing from my hands before gripping my shoulders. I trembled, having no idea what I was going to do. I knew I could scream for Spencer, but if he walked in, he'd just assume I had volunteered. After all, I had a reputation.

"Let go of her!" I heard behind me.

Spencer's father stiffened at the sight of his son and released my arms.

"Spencer."

"Oh spare me."

He descended the remaining stairs unbuttoning his shirt and throwing it over my shoulders. "You won't say a fucking word to her father, or I'll tell mother what I just witnessed." Spencer gathered up my skirt and top and he led me back to his room, closing the door behind us.

He ran the palm of his hand over his mouth. "Jesus, Soph, I'm so fucking sorry."

"It's okay," I said, but my trembling body said otherwise. "I'm just glad you showed up when you did. I'm the one who's sorry. I-I'm just no good for anyone, am I?" I joked.

Spencer narrowed his eyes at me. "You really feel that way, don't you?" he asked me.

"Hmm?"

"You really, truly believe that."
I offered a hesitant smile and tried to shake my head no, to play it off, but he ignored me.

"Sophie Price, you are a mess. Come on, get dressed."

"Where are we going?"

"I believe we've earned a stay at the W, love. My treat."

CHAPTER FOUR

Sunday night, while Spencer and I were at Lucques for dinner, I received a call from Pembrook. This was not unusual if I was gone for days at a time as he would ring me to confirm I was still breathing so I denied the call, planning on calling back when dinner was over.

"So Brown, eh?" I asked Spencer.

"Yup," he said, perusing his menu but briefly looking up to make a silly face. "So Yale, eh?" he teased.

I sighed in reply.

"How do you suppose we'll withstand the weather?"

"I plan on racking up thousands of frequent flyer miles. I don't want to leave, to be honest."

"Damn, Spencer, that breaks my heart a little."

"I know, but Brown is my family's institution and," he dropped an octave, "*no son of my father's will attend anywhere else*."

"Will you get supremely pissed if I tell you how much I can't stand your father and that if it were me, I'd defy him just to screw him, no pun intended?"

Spencer's facial expression hardened and I regretted insulting his father. That is, until he said, "No one can stand my father, including my father. He's a terrible person and I hate him."
His expression didn't change and I realized how deep that resentment toward his father really went.

"Don't go to Brown then," I simply told him.

"I can't do that," he said, exhaling sharply and staring out the glass into the street.

"Why not?"

His face softened. "I need his money."

Spencer looked at me and I couldn't help but stare back. We were all in the same boat, prisoners to greed. Suddenly, my stomach dropped out from under me.

"I don't want to be like them," I candidly admitted as much to myself as to him.
Spencer leaned over and took my hand in his, squeezing my fingers in earnest.

"Neither do I."

"How do we break the cycle?"
He sighed heavily and sank into the plush booth,

releasing my hand. "I don't think we can, Soph. It's done."

"Don't say that," I desperately argued. "Don't say that," I repeated as if that could change it.

"Why not?" he asked me, furrowing his brows in frustration. "We're dependent on them, utterly. I could no more live in a studio with barely enough cash to feed myself any more than you could." A single tear fell from my face at the truth of that declaration and Spencer wiped it gingerly away. "We're stuck, Price."

"I can't believe that."

"Well, try. Look at us, Soph. We party harshly at the Holes on the weekends. I think we've all had sex with one another at least once, apart from you and I. And I'd still do you if you'd just admit that you like me as much as I like you." I cringed into myself a little. When I didn't respond, he continued, turning to study the nightlife outside our window again.

"The only difference between us and our parents is that we're younger, we do coke while they drink, but we'll graduate or simmer to that, depending on how you look at it, as they did. We're not married but soon we will be and to each other, but it won't matter because we'll trade partners like we do now. We're addicted to the lifestyle. I can't see a way out of that." He leaned over me. "And need I remind you, that you rule us all?"

"That won't be necessary, Spence, but thank you. I'm well aware my standing in our group."

Unexpectedly, I wanted as far away from Spencer and my life as quickly as possible, but how could I remove myself from the toxicity when I was the main component in the vile concoction that was our lives?

On our way back to the W, I took the opportunity to ring Pembrook.

"Pemmy, it's Sophie."

"Sophie, you'll need to be at the courthouse at seven in the morning tomorrow. Do not arrive late. Court is at eight and dress appropriately. I don't think it's necessary to remind you to keep a lid on your illegal activities this evening. Do try and be sober."

And with that, he hung up.

My hands began to shake from their normally composed cool and I brought them to my mouth.

"What's wrong?" Spencer asked.

"I have court in the morning."

"How is that possible? It was only Friday you were arrested."

I stared out the window at the cars around us. "My father did this."

"Why would he bother?"

I thought back to the image of a floating jacket in our fountain. "Because I ruined something for him and this is my punishment."

"Bastard." He glanced at me. "You don't have to go home, you know. I can drop you off tomorrow."

"That's really sweet, but I have nothing appropriate for court tomorrow."

He gave me a sardonic expression and extended his hand toward the row of shops lining the street we were traveling.

"Buy something."

"Fine, turn left here. I'll just charge the long posy dress I saw in Temperley's window last week."

"I didn't interpret anything you've just said besides turn left here, thank God."

I could only playfully roll my eyes at him.

He dropped me off and found parking in the rear while I waited for him at the door. I needed his presence to keep me calm. If I were being honest with myself, I would have admitted that I was terrified at what was going to happen the next morning. If your father pulls political strings to get your criminal court date moved to the front of an already astronomically busy queue, I can't imagine what he could stand to gain from that. Except revenge. Which meant he had no intention of making my life easier. I could feel Luques beginning to surface when Spencer opened the door to Temperley's for me. I took deep breaths to calm my nerves. I was sincerely nervous for probably the very first time of my life.

"Which one?" he asked, this savior in do-me clothing.

"The soft pink one hanging in the window."

He left me to browse while he took care of my purchase for me. I knew this little act just confirmed everything he'd accused in our dinner conversation, but I still strove to hold on to the slightest thread of hope that I would never turn out so pathetically acquiescing as my mother or as cold-hearted as my father. *But isn't that who you already are, Soph? You certainly cast your friends aside easily to screw their boyfriends, don't you?* I shook my head. *Build the wall,* I ordered myself and just as easily, my facial expression eased and my thoughts turned an entirely different direction.

"Size, miss?" I heard behind me, turning my head.

"A four, please," I told the clerk and she quickly scurried off.

"It that all you'll need?" Spencer asked from beside me after they'd adjusted the garment for a quick tailor. "I spied a shoe store nearby. I wouldn't mind."

"Thank you, Spence. That's fine. Shall we walk?"

"Of course." He turned his head toward the back room. "We'll just be next door as you do the alterations," he called out.

The clerk emerged and nodded discretely. "Give me half an hour," she said.

Spencer led me to the shoe store next door and we perused the windows as we passed by. "What are you going to give me for buying these for you?"

"A swift kick in the junk?"

He laughed wholeheartedly. "I had to try."

"Yeah, yeah," I teased.

Inside, I immediately spied a pair of buttery-soft leather peek-a-boo's in the corner. "Those," I told him succinctly.

"Damn, you don't waste any time."

"I know what I want when I want it."

"One can hope..." he trailed off.

"Really, Spence?"

"I'm sorry, but I keep getting flashbacks of yesterday night. You were goddamn hot in nothing but your lingerie."

I sighed loudly.

"No, no, I know. I'm just frustrated is all."

"I'm so sorry about that," I told him sincerely.

"Not as sorry as I am, but it'll do." He winked in jest. "Anything else, then? Purse, scarf, a frenzied escape across the southern border?"

"Please, Spencer, if I wanted to flee, I'd fly. I'm not a wanted felon, for chrissakes."

"Ah, but you'd be so hot on the posters. Bounty hunters across the states would mortgage their homes to be the one to bring you in."

"You're seriously starting to chafe me. I'm nervous as it is."

"I'm sorry," he said, kissing my temple. I could feel his chuckle against my skin. "Would you like me to come with you?"

"It's going to be humiliating enough. I don't believe your presence would be soothing."

"Damn, Soph."

"I apologize, old habits die hard."

"Fine, but as soon as you're done, you'll call me?"

I bit my bottom lip to keep it from trembling.

"The first."

Seven in the morning is made for people who deserve nothing but death. If I were a judge, I'd schedule all my court dates after eleven in the morning and end them at three in the afternoon. I mean, my God, they went to school practically their entire adolescent and adult lives, probably rising before it was even light, only to graduate and begin working as a toiling law firm crony or in a political office position they'd had to commit no less than fifteen years of their heart-clogging lives toward only to reach for aspirations of waking at the crack of dawn to deal with the lowliest of the low? No, thank you.

But we all really know why they did it. Prestige and power. *That's* why they did it. And who could blame them?

"You look incredible, Soph. Convict-less."

"Thank you, I suppose."

Spencer pulled up front and I got out, nervous as hell.

He rolled down his window as I began the ascent into the courthouse. "Don't forget to call me!" he shouted.

I turned and nodded once before meeting Pembrook at the top of the steps.

"On time. Thank you."

"Something about my father getting the courts to agree to this has made me less than comfortable. I thought being on time would be, oh, I don't know, wise?"

"Ah, so today I get facetious Sophie. How delightful."

"I'm sorry, Pemmy," I sighed out.

"It's fine. Follow me," he bit.

Pembrook led me through the security checkpoints and into a cavernous marble lobby to a set of elevators. I counted the floors as we passed each one. *One...Surely the lesson is in the threat...Two...He wouldn't risk the publicity...Three...He's doing this because he loves me...Four...He does love me...Five...I know he does...Six...He has to...Seven...Doesn't he?*

The ringing bell announcing our floor startled my anxiety-ridden body, stiff from tensing my muscles as if in anticipation of a beating. And that was what that morning would promise me. I knew it. Pemmy's short answers and minimal sarcasm told me that better than words ever could.

"Through here," I barely heard Pembrook mutter. He opened the door for me and I entered the sunken room.

The smallest sounds resonated throughout. The creak of the door, the taps of our shoes on the cold marble floor, the intake of every labored breath.

"Sit here," he said, pointing to a bench reminiscent of a church pew just outside of the fenced-in chamber in the public gallery.

I sat and the wood protested underneath me, warning me, begging me to act, to run. Pembrook easily threw open the swinging half doors that separated the courtroom and approached the prosecutor's table. I took in my surroundings and noted I wasn't the only defendant in the courtroom, which was confusing. A singular man sat in the corner opposite my side of the room. This was typical for most minor criminal court cases, but for some reason I thought my father wouldn't want the potential spectacle or would be willing to risk my being seen and would have arranged for a private hearing.

"You," a burly guard with bright red hair said pointing to the lone man. "You've been reassigned. You should be in Courtroom C now." *Of course.*

"Oh, so sorry," the man offered. He stood and gave me a half smile.

I wanted to vomit at the butterflies that gave me. *Worry*. You could see it in his eyes. Thick strain seemed to bulge the walls in all its sensationalism. It crawled over my body and settled heavily on my heart.

Pembrook called me to his table and sat me in a leather swivel chair. The animal skin ground against my own, cold and stiff to touch. The cumbersome weight of unease in the room settled over me with a finality that choked.

"All rise," the bailiff said, surprising me from my thoughts. I looked up just in time to see Reinhold walk into the room. *Doomed.* "This court is now in session, the Honorable Judge Francis Reinhold presiding."

Judge Reinhold refused to look my direction. "What's

on the docket today, Sam?" he asked the bailiff. He meant "chopping block." Reinhold knew.

"Your Honor, case one this morning is Price vs. the city of Los Angeles."

Reinhold finally met my face with zero expression, but his eyes were calculating, measuring, assessing.

"Are you ready?" Reinhold asked my attorney and the prosecutor.

"Yes, Your Honor," Pembrook said.

The prosecutor nodded her head with a single, "Yes."

The door to the courtroom groaned open in that moment and in stepped three people I would have paid not to have step through. My father and mother moved to sit on the bench I had sat just minutes earlier, giving off the impression they had somewhere else they really needed to be but the real jest, it seemed, was Officer Casey in all his youthful, handsome glory and his countenance spoke volumes of hate, lust, anger, and want.

He earned a brief glance from me and that earned myself a cruel smile in return. I kept my gaze on him, leaned imperceptibly his direction, lightly touched the tip of my tongue to the top of my teeth, smiled effortlessly and winked. This startled him and his own smile faltered, stuttered and fell off his face. I turned back to Reinhold, no one in the room the wiser but for Casey and his thundering heart.

"I understand an agreement has been made?" Reinhold asked the attorneys.

An agreement?

"Yes, Your Honor," the lawyers said in unison.

"Miss Price, please stand," he ordered.
I obeyed, my booming heart clamoring to stay steady, and stood from my chair.

"I promised you the next time I saw you in my courtroom you would not leave as easily and yet here you are. Now, I've agreed to this plea bargain *only* because I feel it can teach you the value of your life far better than any amount of incarceration, rehab or community service."
I wrapped my hand around the other to keep them from visibly trembling. I didn't dare anger Reinhold's already ice thin patience by asking him what the plea actually was. I turned to stare at Pembrook who stood beside me but he didn't return the glance. I turned Reinhold's way once more.

"Sophie Price," he said with finality, making my stomach clench. My eyes closed tightly in preparation. "You are hereby sentenced to six months in Masego." And with that, Reinhold slammed his gavel home, sending an icy shiver through my body.
I stood standing, mouth agape at the tabletop below me as the remaining people in the room stood when Reinhold exited.
And just like that, it was over.

When the room cleared, I turned to find my parents, but they had already begun to leave. My father barely acknowledged me with a nod. Casey loitered near the swinging doors and I turned his direction wondering what he could possibly want.

He leaned toward me. I could only blink where I stood. "Good luck, princess."

He left chuckling under his breath.

Pembrook. "Pemmy, what—," I coughed back the choking sensation that had taken up residence in my throat. "What is 'Masego'?"

Pembrook sat in his chair and gathered all the seemingly unnecessary paperwork he'd strewn about the table before the short sentencing. He busied his hands and refused to acknowledge me with his eyes. "Masego is an orphanage in Uganda belonging to a very dear friend of mine I've had since primary. I expect you to work hard, Sophie. I expect you not to embarrass me. You leave in a week. The physician will be at your parents' home tomorrow at three in the afternoon to administer the necessary inoculations. Be there, or suffer the court's wrath. Also, here is a card your father has designated for you to purchase the necessities. Buy sturdy shorts, boots and things of this nature to weather the harsh Ugandan climate." Finally, he looked up at me and took a deep breath. "I'm risking myself for you, Sophie. I wouldn't do this for anyone else. You need a hard dose of reality and Charles will be able to deliver that to you."

"You think to change me, Pemmy?"

"You need to change and soon, or you will be beyond salvaging."

"Nothing can prevent me from becoming what I already am," I proclaimed, honest with myself for the very first time.

"True," he said, setting his leather satchel on the table. "But people can change, my dear, and I know you're capable of being better than this girl you've created for yourself. I never speak ill of your father if it can be helped, for obvious reasons, but you have been treated poorly by him and for some unfathomable reason I feel it my responsibility to fix it.

"I've known you since you were small and sweet and innocent, Sophie." He breathed deeply and palmed the handles of his satchel. "I cannot undo the things you've done, but I'll be damned if your future is as bleak as your past."

Pembrook kissed my cheek lightly and took a few of the tears I'd unwittingly shed with him. He abandoned me there in that cold room. I was alone.

I didn't know much more than I had that morning. The only slight additional awareness I owned was that in one week I would be on a plane to Uganda to see an old friend of Pemmy's and to help out at his orphanage. Such a simple idea with such huge consequences.

I pinched the stupid card my father had left me between my thumb and forefinger, rubbing the new foiled number. I'd always considered them little plastic hugs instead of seeing them for what they truly were. To my father, they were obligations. And if my father did one thing, he always fulfilled his obligations.

CHAPTER FIVE

I dazily walked outside and down the steps, not really knowing where I was going.

"No call," I heard Spencer tease beside me. "Typical Sophie Price."

I looked his direction and the joshing smile on his face fell when he read my expression.

"Come on, it couldn't have been that bad. A few hours of community service, tops."

"Not quite, Spencer."

Spencer looked visibly nervous. "What'd you get?"

"Six months in Africa."

Spencer laughed out loud. "Hilarious, Soph, a jab at my parents. Funny. Now, seriously what'd you get?"

"I'm not kidding. I've been sentenced six months working in an orphanage in Uganda."

Spencer's face fell, his brows narrowed. "You're fucking with me."

"I'm really not. I wish I was."

Spencer took me by the hand and we sat at a stone bench in front of the courthouse. My back laid flat against the rest and Spencer angled himself toward me, his arm strewn across the top.

"Where?" he asked.

"Uganda."

He sank back a bit. "I wish I had any idea if that was dangerous or not."

"Me too," I stoically added.

"When," he said, before clearing his throat, "do you leave?"

"Next week."

"Holy shit, Sophie."

"I know," I said, squeezing my eyes shut. I opened them and turned toward him.

"Make this week for me, Spence. Make it so damn fun it'll hold me over for six months."

"Of course, Sophie."

The club he'd taken me to was new, so new I'd never been there and that was saying something, but it was packed, sardines packed. I could tell even though we hadn't even stepped a foot inside.

Spencer's Aston Martin pulled up to the curb outside the door and I could practically feel the stares of the club patrons in line, heavy and full of wonder. The impossibly sexy Spencer casually stepped from his car and handed the keys to the valet. A second valet attempted to open the door for me but Spencer waved him off and came to my side, swinging my door open softly and reaching in for my hand. I heard the cottony sighs of the girls in queue when they saw Spencer and it made me wonder why I couldn't get into him the way he was into me.

My hand gripped his as he culled me from my seat. My hair blew away from my face and I got a good glimpse of the glinted eyes of admirers for almost half a block. My heel hit pavement and the collective groans from the men in line at the sight of my leg made Spencer wink discretely. He lifted me and closed my door behind me. In the seconds it took to turn, a secret thrill blew through my chest at the envy emanating from their faces, but our expressions would have never conveyed such. No, we were trained from birth to assert disinterest. We were the ultimate snobs and realizing this, that secret thrill quickly dissipated into shame. *What is wrong with me?*

The doorman opened the door for us and ushered us inside and the people in line didn't question the move, assuming we were more important than they were and that made me think further into why society accepted such nonsense, but there I was, letting it happen anyway. I was turning into a massive hypocrite and all I wanted was to go back to how I was.

"Can we make out a little, Spencer, and not have it turn into anything?" I asked him, knowing that was such a bitch move but needing a little of my old life to come back in order for me to feel sane again.

"Are you kidding, Sophie Price? I thought you'd never ask."

"That was diplomatic."

"I wasn't being tactful. When Sophie Price asks you for a kiss, you perform. Now, if you need any other, uh, performing, I'd be happy to oblige as well."

This stopped my heart. "Maybe making out is a horrible idea."

"No, no, forget everything I just said." He hurriedly led us to our private table and whipped me toward him. "Dance with me."

I threw my small bag in the booth in answer, knowing security in VIP would cover it since Spence handed the guy a hundred and I let him pull me toward the floor. I took the lead and wound my way through the crowd with Spencer just behind me and found a spot two people could fit comfortably. Darkness surrounded us other than the dancing lights that touched the top of the crowd but bounced off just as quickly.

The first song was slow and sexy. Spencer laid his hands on me and I let him. They perused my body in appreciation as I used him. We swayed with the erotic tempo and his mouth found mine, answering my earlier question. The warm feel of his tongue soothed away any raw feeling of moral contradiction that had taken residence so obnoxiously in my heart. I groaned in response and his arms found my rib cage, encircling me tightly before giving me a slight squeeze and lifting me slightly from the floor.

I kissed Spencer like my life depended on it. I hoped every exhale into his mouth shed a little of my newly found struggles.

"Hold me tighter," I whispered against his teeth. He clutched me closer, yet not tight enough. "More," I demanded.

Spencer drew me firmer against him and I felt every ridge of his body. "Is that close enough?" he laughed into my throat.

"Perfect," I told him. I didn't feel as alone anymore.

Spencer kissed me again but softer, as if he knew I needed that. He read my body well, giving when I drew back, drawing back when I gave. All I could think was he was going to make some girl *very* happy one day. He ran his hands through my long curls, gripping my waist just above the hip before enfolding me against him once again.

And just as suddenly, the very heated kiss turned lighter, tapering off into a desperate embrace. I felt it in that moment as did he. It was glaringly obvious to us standing there in the middle of the crowded dance floor. I needed to be needed by him and he needed to be needed by me. We clung to one another, not sure exactly what it was we required from one another but acknowledging it all the same.

When the song ended and a more upbeat tune replaced it, Spencer pulled away.

"Let's just get the fuck out of here," he told me.

We went back to my house but parked his car in the employee lot just in case my father was on the lookout, though I doubt he was. My room had been serviced since I'd left it last so I tossed the covers back and tumbled inside, whipping my clothes off under the covers. Spencer tossed his jeans on the chair in the corner along with his shirt, tucking himself with me in only his boxers.

We held each other the entire night, no words spoken but the still, silent night uttered so much.

"Miss Price?" A voice woke me. "Miss Price?" the voice asked louder.

My eyes barely opened and I took in my position, sprawled over a softly snoring Spencer. *Brilliant.*

I turned over and peered into the eyes of Dr. Ford and his nurse Cassandra. *Just splendid,* I thought. He was going to report this little incident to my father. I could see it in his face.

Cassandra was too distracted by the exposed chest of Spencer to give me her usual eye roll.

"Good morning, Dr. Ford."

"Afternoon," he corrected me.

I glanced at the clock and saw it was indeed three in the afternoon.

"You're right on time," I sarcastically spat at him.

"Miss Price," he began, ignoring me, "would you prefer it if Cassandra and I left the room for you to dress?"

"Not necessary," I told him.

Spencer woke and stretched beside me, causing Cassandra's eyes to bulge from her round face.
"Don't most of these go in the posterior region anyway?" I teased, making Dr. Ford close his eyes in disapproval. Spencer tried to hide his laugh behind a closed fist, but it wasn't fooling anyone.
"I'll just use your shower, Soph." Spencer slid from beneath the covers and strode across the floor in his boxers without any sense of shame. Winking, in fact, toward Cassandra and causing her to choke on nothing.
"All the same, Miss Price, I'd prefer you in at least a robe."
"As you wish, Dr. Ford."

Cassandra grabbed the silk number that hung at the end of my door and brought it to me. Dr. Ford turned his head and I stood, sinking my arms through the sleeves of the robe Cassandra held out for me.

"Yummy, isn't he?" I whispered low, teasing Cassandra.
Her face flushed and she narrowed her brows at me in obvious disdain. I smiled.
"You smile now," she caustically bit, "but you have

no idea what you're in store for today." She smiled in return and my own fell.

I swallowed hard and stared at Cassandra's mean expression, shocked at myself for being unable to show no emotion. The truth? I *was* scared, terrified really because I had absolutely no idea what I truly was in store for. Not concerning the shots and certainly not Masego or whatever the hell they called it.

"Miss Price," Dr. Ford said, "if you'll sit down. I have several forms here for you to sign."
He handed me a stack of papers.

"What are all these?" I asked him, perusing from one form to the other.

"Liability wavers."

"Ah, so what exactly do you need liability protection from?"
Spencer walked in at that moment and sat beside me on the bed, drying his wet hair with a towel.

Dr. Ford sighed and pulled my vanity stool closer to me. He opened his leather satchel and inside, strapped tidily within a pouch, was an ungodly amount of syringes. I sucked in a breath and Spencer tucked his hand around my shoulder.

"Adacel," he began, reading from a list on his lap, "which prevents tetanus, diphtheria and acellular pertussis. Hep A and B I've given you several months ago."

"Why?" I asked curiously, just now wondering why I never asked questions before.

"Because of your," Dr. Ford said, clearing his throat and glancing at Spencer, "increased activity as of late."

"I see," I said simply. Spencer laughed and I elbowed him. "Continue."

"I'll give you a revamp of the flu shot. Let's see," he said, glancing down at a few different sheets of paper. "A meningococcal booster dose, MMR or measles, mumps and rubella. Uh, pneumococcal, very important, polio you have, rabies," he said, looking over a chart, "you'll need a refresher on. You'll need typhoid but varicella you've had." He looked up at me. "Yes, that's it."

"That's it!" I exclaimed, grasping Spencer's hand.

"Calm yourself, Miss Price. You'll need to follow strict food and water precautions while abroad. Consume only canned or commercially bottled drinks. Avoid using ice cubes, though I doubt they'll have refrigeration where you're going, which is also why you should only eat fruits and vegetables you peel and wash yourself. Avoid cold cuts, salads, watermelon, puddings."

Dr. Ford looked up at me.

"It goes without saying, Miss Price, but do try to avoid casual sexual contact. I cannot stress that enough." I rolled my eyes at him. "Never use needles or syringes used by other people. Avoid sharing a razor or toothbrush. No tattoos or piercings while there. Remain in well-screened or air-conditioned areas when possible. Wear clothing that adequately covers your arms and legs and use DEET-containing insect repellent on both your skin and clothing. Refuse blood transfusions unless in a life or death situation and try to ensure they've been properly screened first."

"Yes, if I'm dying and in desperate need of blood, I'll be sure to ask if the blood's been properly screened first." *Deflecting your fear through sarcasm. Nice, Soph. He's only trying to help you.*

Dr. Ford's face became deadly serious. "You do not understand, Miss Price. This is no joking matter. You are visiting a highly-diseased area. The things I am trying to protect you from can be the difference between dying a painful, horrible death...or not." *Right, thanks for that visual, doc.*

"Cassandra will be bringing by an immunization record to keep with your travel documents. Don't lose it. They may not let you back in the country if you can't prove you've taken preventative measures."

"You're shitting me," Spencer piped in.

"Hardly," Dr. Ford replied, now rolling his own eyes. "Shall we get started?" Dr. Ford asked, turning to me.

"You will be feverish and sore in the injected areas but Tylenol should help you there. Get some rest," Dr. Ford added after the shockingly painful administrations, right before closing the door behind him and Cassandra.

"You should probably take those pain meds now," Spencer said. "My mom always made me take them right before my shots as a kid so I'd avoid getting ill later."

"They're in my bathroom. Shelf," I said, lying down.

Some of the shots I'd gotten hurt tremendously. I'm not joking. The needles were huge and the injections felt warm and invasive.

Spencer brought me a glass of water and a fever reducer. I drank it down quickly. We both laid down on the bed facing the ceiling after I turned the stereo on low.

"Well, that was enlightening."

"I'm frightened beyond belief, Spencer."

He sighed loudly. "I know, Soph. I can tell."

"It's a good thing I haven't used my father's stupid card yet."

"Why's that?"

"Because I would have gotten short shorts and tank tops had I not known I needed to wear longer sleeves and pants."

"Christ, Soph. This is scaring the shit out of me and I'm not even going. I'm panicked for you."

He dragged me over to him and culled me into his body, spooning me and smoothing my hair behind my ear. It was the first time a guy had ever done anything like this with completely innocent intentions and I fought the tears burning to shed. He was so nice to me and I didn't really know why. I mean, yeah, he did want to sleep with me. What guy didn't, if I was being honest with myself, which was my own fault but Spencer wasn't asking me to do anything. He was offering himself as comfort without any expectations in return.

I turned over and wrapped my arms around him. He hugged me fiercely in return. After a few minutes, I drew back and looked into his eyes.

"You're a good man, aren't you, Spencer?"

He laughed at me. "No, I'm not, Soph."

"You're a liar."

"I'm not a good man."

"Then you just aren't aware of it, but you are."

"Fine, fine. I'm a friggin' saint, yada, yada. Can we get you your shit before all the stores close? I want this Africa shit done and over with so we can finish out the week in total debauchery."

He made me laugh, but he wasn't fooling me. Somehow, growing up in the house he did, with the father he had, Spencer had the unbelievable potential to become a very great man. He amazed me. I suppose the choices you make really are what define you.

Why can't you get into him then?

I took my father's card and maxed it out. I bought all new sturdy canvas luggage because my soft leather designer bags weren't going to cut it, obviously. Spencer took me to the store his mother visits when she goes on safari and the clerk there was exceedingly helpful, informing me what would work best in mid-Africa and what I could get away with. I only bought a few things but still took their advice to my own favorite shops. The hell I would look like a slob if I could help it.

I bought fifteen pairs of badass jeans and a lot of formfitting button-ups as well as a few knee-length riding boots to wear over my jeans. It wouldn't define me, that fashion sense, but it would keep me safe and I had to admit I wouldn't look like a total slob. I tried on a complete outfit for Spencer and paraded around him in the store.

"You look transformed. I'm not used to seeing you so casual." My shoulders slumped a little in disappointment and my signature pout came to the forefront. "Oh, please," he continued, "you look sexy as hell as if I needed to say it. Your ass is the sweetest I've ever seen, *especially* in those jeans."

I smiled devilishly at him. "Thank you," I told him, sashaying off, swinging my hips from side to side. His audible groan sent that secret thrill through my stomach again, but it was short-lived by that nagging sense of guilt. *What is wrong with me!?*

When Spencer took me home and helped me load all my purchases into my bedroom, we came across a massive pile of things resting on top of my bed along with a letter from Pembrook.

Pemmy told me to go with the impression that I wouldn't have electricity ever, as Masego only had it sporadically and for maybe a day at that. All that translated to me when he wrote that was I wouldn't be able to fix my hair and I had nothing but cold showers in my future. He included a huge bed net to protect me from insects at night, a massive medical kit containing things I'm fairly certain only a doctor should have a license to handle, various over-the-counter medicines as well as prescription antibiotics from Dr. Ford, which, by the way, looked like they were lifted directly from the pharmacist's shelf. The bottles obviously held hundreds of pills. It made me nervous just looking at them.

Pemmy closed his letter telling me that he loved me like a daughter and he wished me to be careful. I didn't know what to think of that, but I'd be lying if I told you it didn't make me smile...just a little.

CHAPTER SIX

I woke at three in the morning shaking. Dr. Ford had told my father about Spencer's sleepover and that had been the last night Spencer was able to stay much to my dismay. If ever I needed a warm body by my side, it was through the long nights before my departure. Nights of quiet. Nights of speeding thoughts and concocted scenarios of danger and disease.

I stood in the shower for close to half an hour, attempting to let the steam soothe my fears, but it did no good, no good at all. I stepped from the water and wrapped a towel around myself. I stood in front of the mirror and took a good hard look. I was as bare as I could make myself, no makeup with wet, stringy hair. I hated to look at myself in this state. I didn't feel real. I felt too exposed and that made me exceedingly nervous, but I made myself look that morning. I memorized that girl. That girl *was* the real me. Frightened. Worthless. A terrible friend. Terrible daughter. Well educated but so limited in ideas worth having. Beautiful yet repulsive...

And finally honest.

Spencer picked me up that morning for my flight at seven in the morning. He rang me from inside the house and I met him in the foyer standing next to Pembrook, no sign of my mother or father.

"Sophie," Pembrook smiled, "here are all your necessary papers. An emergency card, as well as cash. Keep these close to your body. You're flying to Germany first, then Dubai, staying the night. The hotel arrangements are in your travel documents. A car has been arranged to pick you up there. From Dubai you will fly to Nairobi, Kenya, where a small plane has been chartered to take you to Kampala, Uganda. Look for a boy named Dingane to pick you up. I've taken the liberty of outfitting your case with a satellite phone for..."

"Emergencies?" I asked, smiling back.
Pembrook's shoulders visibly relaxed and he wrapped his long, lanky arms around my shoulders.

"Do be careful, my dear," he whispered against my hair before speeding off down the hall.
I sighed as I watched him make way for the kitchens.
I turned to Spencer and smiled again.

He held his hand out to me and I took it. He squeezed it softly. "It'll be okay," he reassured, but I didn't believe him.

I looked around me, at how empty the foyer was and felt a little disappointed that Sav and the rest of my friends hadn't shown up. I'd texted them the night before, but I suppose there was no reason to say goodbye to someone they cared very little for.

I met Spencer's eyes once more. "They didn't come," I told him matter-of-factly.

"No, they didn't," he stated.

"No need to dwell. I'll just be a moment," I told him and headed toward my father's office.

I knocked on his door and heard a faint "enter." I obeyed and turned the handle. Billowing cigar smoke enveloped me before dissipating behind me. The cleared smoke revealed my father, busy as usual, and on his phone.

"No! No! I never agreed to that!" My father turned my direction. "Just a minute, will you?" he asked the receiver. "What is it?" he asked me.

"I'm-I'm off."

"Good luck."

And just like that he was immersed in his phone conversation and I closed the heavy wooden door behind me. On the way back to the foyer, I passed one of our maidservants Margarite carrying folded towels to one of the guest suites.

"Have you seen Mrs. Price this morning, Margarite?"

"Yes, she has gone to town for a morning of shopping."

"Ah, I see. Tell her that you saw me?"

"Of course, miss." Margarite's eyes softened. "Is there anything else you'd like me to convey, miss?"

"No."

"As you wish, miss," Margarite said before going about her business again.

I followed suit but could feel her eyes look back at me as if she pitied me. I cringed at the thought that my maid felt sorry for me.

"I'm ready," I told Spencer.

"I've loaded your bags already."

"Thank you, Spence."

The ride to the airport was eerily quiet. I contemplated the almost twenty hours of flying I had in my future, not including my overnight stay in Dubai. My hands began to visibly shake and Spencer stilled them with his own. Regina Spektor's *All the Rowboats* began to play and I couldn't help but let the haunting melody seep into my skin. The words felt prophetic, although the subjects of her song were entirely objects, but when I really defined myself, that's what I was, a mere object and it was all by my own doing. I was those breathing objects, desperately aching to escape, to live, and suddenly a calm washed over me.

All the talk of danger, disease and devastation frightened me, but I was ready for a change, just as desperate and just as aching to escape, to live, really live, as the songs and paintings in her words.

We pulled up to the unloading zone and Spencer opened my door for me. He looked deflated.

"No worries, my very good friend."

He smiled but the grin never touched his eyes. His hands dug into his pockets. "And that's all I'll ever be to you, I think."

My shoulders sank into the car door a bit. "Spencer, please..."

"Shh," he said, pressing the pad of his thumb at my lips. His fingers grazed my cheek slightly when he pulled away. "Absolutely no worries, Sophie Price." He smiled in sincerity then and my heart dropped a tad for him.

"I'll miss you very much," I admitted to the only real friend I'd ever really had but only very recently realized.

"As I'll miss you. I've just discovered you're as lost as I am and now you leave."

"By court order," I jested, making his grin wider.

"I'll give you that." He sighed. "We were supposed to find our way together though."

"I'll still be as lost when I come back. We can pick up from there, Spence."

Spencer grabbed my bags and laid them on the cart the porter had brought over.

"I'll see you in six months," I told him.

"I'll be right here," he said, pointing toward the pavement. "Waiting."

I grazed his cheek and squeezed my eyes painfully. "Don't wait for me, Spencer," I whisper ordered.

Spencer pulled me from him. "I'll do as I damn well please, Price. Now get."
I smiled at him and followed the porter. When I turned back around for a final wave he'd already gone.

Twenty hours of flight, despite a night of sleep in The Palm in Dubai still feels like twenty hours of flight. When I arrived in Africa by way of Nairobi, I didn't get a chance to absorb the continent as I only had twenty minutes to catch my Cessna, but when my little chartered plane landed, barely, and the stairs were brought out, the door opened, I looked out onto a most wonderful sight, a breathtaking sight. A sight of green lush vegetation, dirt red with iron and the expansive blue and breathtaking Lake Victoria. My breath sucked into my chest as I took it all in. It was *incredibly* beautiful.

I descended the stairs and was met with my luggage at my feet and a happy African young man with dark mocha face and gleaming white teeth.

"Welcome to Africa, miss," he greeted me with cheer. "I understand this is your first visit?"

"Yes, thank you."

He smiled the largest smile I'd ever seen and I wondered what had made this guy so happy. "Follow me, miss."

I fished around in my pouch for a ten-dollar bill. A guy in Dubai had told me they prefer American currency so I never exchanged the hundreds Pembrook had given me. We approached the airport itself and all I could think when I looked upon it was the nineteen-seventies had died and gone to heaven on this little inlet. My skin went cold when I thought on that. Before I'd left, I'd read up on Uganda and discovered the very airport I'd flown into was also the site of a most dangerous hostage situation involving terrorists in that same era. I shivered thinking on the details and the very close call it was. It reminded me *where* I was and what my real purpose for visiting entailed.

When the enthusiastic porter set my bags down inside, he beamed at me and I almost laughed at his optimism.

I couldn't help myself. "You're quite animated, and why are you so happy today?"

"I am happy every day, Miss. I am alive and working. I have a roof. I can feed my brothers and sisters. I am very, very happy."

My heart clenched and I dug in my pouch for another ten, thought twice, and grabbed a fifty before settling the cash in his hand. His eyes blew to impossible proportions and I shook my head at him, silencing the protest forming on his lips.

"Think nothing of it," I snapped and cleared my throat. "Excuse me," I told him and grabbed my bags hurriedly before walking with purpose down the corridor toward what I assumed was the front entrance.

I tried not to think of what fifty dollars meant to that boy and his family. I also tried not to think about the silly bracelet tied around my wrist that cost five hundred. I stopped where I was and gathered myself, remembering my notebook and sliding it out of my pack. I flipped through the pages and looked for the name Pembrook told me not to forget but did anyway because it was such an unusual name.

"Dingane," I repeated out loud. "What kind of name is that?"

"It's Din-John-E," a deep voice interrupted and my head shot up.

Struck. Speechless.

A deep, punching sensation washed over my entire body and I almost fell to my knees at the powerful impression. My breaths became labored and I fought for a clear head. A balmy, scorching but unbelievably ecstasy-ridden awareness swam through my body. An exhilarating, pleasant haze settled over me and it...Burned. So. Good. This was a feeling of realization. I stood there, relishing the effects.

I remember Sarah Pringle telling me once about a boy she had met while on holiday in Europe. The way she painted him made me doubt her sanity.

"I can't describe him, Sophie," she'd said, her hands covering her cheeks in desperation. "It was like my body knew instantly that he was mine and that I was his."

"Awfully *primitive* of you to admit that, Sarah," I'd mocked, making everyone around us laugh.

But *now* I knew what she meant. *Now* I understood what she was trying to convey to me.

The boy who stood before me was on the cusp of becoming a man. All taut, lean muscle, narrow where a boy needed to be and broad where a man should always be. I'd never known a person could be this drawn to another human being, especially a complete stranger. His face captivated me without the ability to speak. I felt my chest grasp for air but was unable to accommodate its feverish demand, so I stupidly sat panting there like a dog after a brisk run. He leaned over me, hands tucked into the front pockets of his jeans, pulling the fabric of his shirt stiff against the muscles of his arms and shoulders and sending me deeper into immediate obsession.

I gulped down my lack of breath and studied him. He was the complete opposite of what I'd always imagined I'd be the most attracted to. Straight black hair met his chin but was tucked behind his ears, cerulean blue eyes stared at me strangely, his full bottom lip separated from his upper lip in question. He was looking down a straight Roman nose at me and his square jaw was clenched.

"Are you the one they call Sophie?" he asked stiffly, already exasperated with me it seemed.

"I am."

"I am Dingane," his thick accent repeated.

When he spoke, my eyes involuntarily rolled to the back of my head. His deep silky voice washed over me like warm water on a cold afternoon and I willingly leaned closer to him. The proximity was like fuel to my already out of control flame. I bent away from him to gain rational thought and shook my head.

"But you're white," I stupidly blurted, making me want to crawl underneath something.

"You are incredibly astute," he said tightly.

"I'm sorry, I was-I was just expecting an African," I stammered.

"My name is Ian. Dingane is a nickname, but I *am* African. My ancestors came to South Africa in the seventeen-hundreds from England," he explained although he seemed annoyed to be doing so, as if I deserved no such courtesy.

His accent sounded like a mix of formal English, Australian and Dutch. That's the only way I could describe it. I'd never heard its equal. It was so incredibly beautiful and unique. Every film I'd ever watched that featured the South African accent completely butchered it. Listening to him was like listening to velvet.

"Oh," I spit out intelligently. "What-what does Dingane mean?" I sputtered, still unable to remove my stare from his face.

"Don't worry about it," he said, apparently no longer humoring me and bending to pick up the luggage I'd only just realized I'd dropped.

"I can get that," I said stupidly, reaching toward the floor. *What is wrong with me?* I'm *the one who strikes men dumb! Not the other way 'round!*

"I already have them. Follow me," he ordered, standing to his full height.

I swallowed the embarrassing five-minute loss of sanity and began to follow him like a meek mouse. I didn't feel like myself, didn't feel like Sophie Price. *Wake up, Sophie.* I picked up my head, remembered who the hell I was and met every stride he strode. We were neck and neck and I could tell this surprised him by the way he spied me from the corner of his eye. I kept my face neutral. Eat that, *Dingane.*

He lead us to a white beat-up jeep and I stopped just short of visibly balking. He threw my bags with little care into the exposed back and began to strap them down.

I watched him work. "Are you expecting me to open your door for you?" he asked, his thick accent shocking once more.

"Do I look like I expect you to open my door for me?" I bit back.

He narrowed his eyes at me. "Then why stand there?"

"It would be presumptuous of me to just sit inside your jeep without you, don't you think? Possibly rude?"

His calloused hands unexpectedly rested over the now tight straps and he looked at me for longer than I considered comfortable, studying me, but just as suddenly walked to the passenger side door as if just remembering himself and opened it for me without a word. I climbed into the jeep and watched him close the door behind me before walking the front of the vehicle and hopping in.

"How old are you?" I asked, turning toward him after buckling in.

"Twenty," he said succinctly.

He was quiet as he started the jeep and sped through the almost impossible jumble of pushy taxis waiting for passengers. I admit I white knuckled it until we met open road.

"It'll take an hour to get to the city capital," he yelled over the rumbling engine and whipping wind. "Kampala is a busy city, Miss Price, and I'd rather not stop, but I suspect it will be our only opportunity to eat before the long journey back to Lake Nyaguo."

"I ate just before we landed," I lied.

If I was being honest, I was afraid to eat anything other than what was prepared at Masego. *Damn that Dr. Ford.*

"If you're game to go straight through then so am I."

And that was the last thing Dingane said to me almost the entire journey.

The silence afforded me astonishing views of an unbelievably attractive country. It also gave me time to come to terms with how much my life was going to change and just how dramatic that change would be.

Four hours is a very long time. Long enough to ponder my very physical reaction to my driver and what it was going to mean to live and work with him. I decided it was just a tenacious chemistry, that I was not without self-control. *Oh yeah, you're the queen of restraint.* I turned toward him and drank in his lean, muscular figure.

Oh. My. Word.

CHAPTER SEVEN

"That's Lake Nyaguo," Dingane said, startling me. "Masego Orphanage is just north of this lake. Charles owns the land we drive through now."

"How much does he own?"

"Approximately five thousand acres. He owns the land north of the lake as well as south and his property lines go east from there."

"Why did he buy land in Uganda?" I asked, more to myself than to Dingane.

"Why not?"

"Fair enough," I conceded.

Dingane sighed in exasperation. "This is his life's work. He wanted the land to accomplish it.

Surprisingly, land in this part of Uganda is inexpensive." He smirked.

Half an hour later, we'd rounded the east side of the blue lake and were on a straight red dirt road. "Masego is just five minutes up this drive," he stated.

My throat dropped to my stomach and I tried to swallow the sinking feeling away. "What's it like?"

"It is beautiful. It is horrifying."

The breath I'd been holding for his response rushed out all at once.

"I feel I must prepare you," he continued.

I gulped. "Prepare me for what?"

"For the children here." An unexpected gleam came to his eyes and I could see how much he loved them just by speaking of them. "Some will be deformed."

"*Deformed?*"

"Maimed."

"I know what you meant but *why*?"

"Do you know nothing of our facility?" he asked impatiently, briefly narrowing his eyes my direction.

"I know nothing. I know only that it is an orphanage."

He breathed out slowly. "We are too close to begin explaining now. Charles or his wife, Karina, should explain it all to you when you arrive. I don't have time. I've spent the entire day driving to fetch you and I need to catch up on a mended fence at the northeastern edge of the property line."

"Thank you...for *fetching* me," I oozed out.

He squirmed in his seat and I could tell I'd made him uncomfortable. Very uncomfortable. He wanted as far away from me as he could possibly get and that confused the hell out of me. He didn't know me at all.

In the distance I spied a long, tall fence surrounding what I assumed was Masego. As we approached a very sturdy, heavy-looking gate, I recognized the word Masego on a shabby, falling sign.

"What does Masego mean?" I asked.

"Blessings."

I studied him. "You're a man of few words, Dingane of South Africa."

This surprisingly made him fight a smile and it shocked me. He quickly shook it and mumbled under his breath and out of the jeep to open the gate. His muscles flexed beneath his shirt as he dragged the heavy wooden barrier and I sat up a bit in my seat to watch him. Night was quickly coming and the jeep's headlights magnified just how beautiful he was. He was surprisingly tall for an African. Six-foot one, maybe two. Then again, what the hell did I know of Africans?

He jumped back into the jeep and steered us through before getting out once more and closing the gate behind us. I cursed the setting of the sun, wishing I could stare at him unabashedly once more.

When we drove the small distance to what looked like a clustered village, droves of little children with dark faces and white teeth came bounding up before the jeep had come to a complete stop.

"Dingane! Dingane!" they all shouted as they raced around to his side of the jeep.

My door was clear of children and I could remove myself easily, but Dingane had a tougher time of it. He began laughing, further bewildering me. When he could free himself, he began shouting in a bizarre tongue. I studied his face and saw perfectly straight, perfectly beautiful teeth shining in the most perfect smile to the crowd of children around him.

That's when I saw them, noticed what Dingane was trying to prepare me for. Children, all ages, missing arms, eyes, parts of their faces, even legs. I held back my gasp and met Dingane's eyes. They were warm and full of understanding but for the children only. He looked at me sternly and his eyes conveyed what he wanted me to do.

I looked down on them, half-smiling, trying so very hard to look sincere when all I wanted to do was run and lock myself away from their terribly shocking faces. I had never in my life thought humans could endure such physical damage and survive.

Dingane held his hand out toward me and introduced me to them, finally using a word I recognized: my name.

"Sophie, Sophie, Sophie," I kept hearing over and over as the children tested my name on their tongues.

"Hello," I greeted them shyly.

I was overwhelmed and incredibly and most surprisingly sad for them but had no idea what to say or do. They stared at me, smiling, when finally a young boy approached me and touched my clothing. I stood still. This was an invitation to all of them to surround me like they had Dingane and they enveloped me. They pulled on my clothing speaking animatedly in a language I knew nothing about. They forced me to their height where I could fully take them in. One little girl's right arm was missing below her elbow, another little boy was missing a leg below the knee, another girl had some sort of bandage wrapped around the left side of her face. The injuries went on and on, but they didn't seem to care or remember they had no arms or legs or faces. They carried on, smoothing my clothing over with their tiny hands or running their fingers over my hair. One little girl told me in English that they all found it to be soft.

I fought tears and tried to keep in mind that if I started bawling in front of the small creatures before me that they would have no idea what it was for.

I was swallowed by children but could still hear a booming man's voice come from the direction of the largest dwelling on the complex. I say dwelling, but it was far from that. It looked like a large open run-down building made from very old wood.

"Dingane, where is our prisoner?" the man's voice cracked across the grounds making the children scurry from my side and glue themselves to his. "Yes, yes, you're all very excited to see our newest member, but let's all calm ourselves." I stood. "Now, where is she?"

The man was tall but not as tall as Dingane and he was middle-aged. His salt-and-pepper hair laid flat against his head but was rather full for someone I pegged for being around sixty.

"Ah, our latest victim!" he jested, yet the words still made me more nervous than I already was.

He approached me and threw his arms around me, picking me up in one motion and swinging me playfully from side to side before setting me right again. "You must be the infamous Sophie Price! I've heard many things about you, child!" he said in an accent similar to Pemmy's.

"All good I hope?"

"No, not all good," he stated honestly, making me blush. I peered Dingane's direction for his reaction, but his face was stoic. "But that is neither here nor there. It has brought you to us and that is all that matters. Second chances. I'm all about second chances."

I could tell Charles was the type to find the good in everything. I wasn't quite settled on whether or not I would like him. I was peculiarly leaning toward liking him and that amazed me. I looked to my left again and noticed Dingane had already started making his way toward whatever fence he claimed needed mending.

"Ah, she's here!" a female's soft voice exclaimed.

I looked to my right and noticed a woman with burgundy, shoulder-length hair. She was also in her sixties and she was beautiful. I could tell she was the type of woman who, in her prime, would have had all the boys running around like imbeciles. A kindred spirit.

"Hello!" she said, extending her hand.

I grabbed it and she tossed me into her arms for the kind of hug I'd never once gotten from a woman but was so desperately in need of. It was the kind of hug a mother gave her daughter. I know, I'd seen Sav's mom give her them many a time.

"It's so nice to meet you, Sophie!" she sang in a lovely English accent, London if I were to have guessed.

"It's nice to meet you too, Karina."

I silently thanked the almost mute Dingane for mention of her name earlier. It would have been so embarrassing not to be able to say her name after such a warm hug.

"I suppose I'll help Din with that fence then. Let the ladies get acquainted."

"Yes, yes," Karina said, shooing Charles with her hand and leading me toward a cluster of buildings just to the left of the main building. She stopped and turned to her left. "Kate! Kate! Please see that *all* the children wash before bed?"

"I will," a dark, beautiful African woman answered before gathering children's hands and singing them to their destination.

Kate was tall and exquisite. She looked like a supermodel, to be frank. If I had seen her in Paris, I'd assumed she was there for the catwalks. It astounded me that she worked in the orphanage when there were so many outside opportunities to be had for her.

"This is to be your bedroom," Karina said pulling me from my thoughts and pointing to what I thought earlier was an outhouse. I almost blurted, "you can't be serious," but stopped myself immediately, remembering the missing arm of the little girl from minutes before. "It's actually separated into two rooms," she continued, swinging the door open to the room on the right. It was about as big as the toilet room in my bathroom back home. I peered inside and took in its contents.

Though it had a roof and floor, it didn't have much else. There was a sink basin to the right but no faucet and a simple bed, smaller than a twin, and no real floor. Essentially, it was uneven planks of wood on the floor, walls and ceiling and a makeshift door.

Karina took in my face and smiled. "It's not the Ritz, I admit, but it is a roof, my dear," she added sweetly. "I'll have Samuel bring your bags in for you. If you have no net, I can provide one for you." She swung me out onto the red dirt path and pointed to the door next door. "You share a wall with Dingane, but he's rarely there. Besides, both of you will be so busy and by the end of the day you'll be so exhausted, your room will be used for sleeping and not much else. Any noise won't bother you. You'll get used to the night noises here as well. "

I gulped, not really sure I could get used to any of it: rooming next to someone who obviously found me repulsive, though I found myself a magnet to, "night noises" or the exhaustion part.

"Have you eaten dinner?" she asked me.

"Yes," I lied again. Too many butterflies had taken residence in my stomach anyway even if I had been hungry enough to eat.

"Are you sure?" she asked again, eyeing me like a mother hen.

"Yes, Karina."

Her eyes crinkled around a smile. "Come. I shall show you the showers."

Karina led me outdoors and back toward the gate where I spied two square hut-like objects. When we came upon them, I noticed they were crawling with five-inch bugs I'd never seen before.

"Oh my God!" I shouted, grabbing onto her arm. I stared at the extreme creatures with the same horror they presented themselves to me with. *A land of extremes.*

Karina giggled. "They won't bother you if you don't bother them."

"Are-are they always there?"

"Yes, love but don't fret. You get used to them."

Oh my God, I'm going to reek like a freak. I'm never going to shower.

"You must shower, Sophie," Karina chimed in, revealing psychic abilities. "This land is not kind.

You must wash regularly to keep yourself free of disease."

I swallowed audibly. "Of-of course."

"My dear, we bed early here as we hardly ever have electricity and we like to rise with the sun. I suggest getting some sleep now. I would love to tell you that the water is warm most days but it is not."

"I see." I studied the showers with a blank expression. I was essentially going to camp for six months.

When Karina led me back to my room, the sun had set completely.

"Goodnight, love."

"Goodnight, Karina."

I walked into my room and almost screamed. Dingane stood there dropping one of my bags to the floor.

"Samuel was busy," he said to explain his presence. He wanted it known that he didn't want to be there.

"Ah, well, thank you, Dingane."

"No problem," he said, squeezing through the tiny room toward the door. I sat there swimming in the scent of his soap. It made me delirious. *My Lord!*

He turned around and stood a foot over me, almost skin to skin. "You'll want to lock your doors so no animals try to get in," he said and left me to the Ugandan night with the creak of my door slamming shut.

It echoed through me and I sat on my bed, not looking before I plopped myself down right on top of something slippery and *moving*. Naturally, I screamed and jumped. Dingane came running back into my room. *Shirtless.*

"What's wrong?" he asked.

"I-I..." I began but couldn't finish. I could only point to the long black thing slithering its way on my mattress.

"Oh, it's only a millipede. Archispirostreptus gigas, to be exact. Take care if you come in contact with one, avoid touching your eyes and lips. They can be harmful."

"Get it out," I told him, eyes clenched closed. I heard the door open and shut and when I opened my eyes, Dingane stood there staring at me like I was a fool. "Stop judging me."

"Who said I was judging?" he lazily drawled. Broad, calloused hands rested on his narrow, exposed waist. I tried so hard not to look.

"I know when someone is judging me. I can read people with impeccable accuracy. You're thinking *this spoiled brat can't even handle a simple insect. How will she handle Africa?*"

"It is not an insect. It's an arthropod," he deadpanned.

"So you're a nerd then. Great, glad we've established that."

He narrowed his eyes. "Yes."

"What?"

"Yes, I was thinking that you were a spoiled brat who won't last two seconds here."

My eyes widened at his candid response. I was taken aback. My mouth gaped open.

"I'll show you," I threatened, but it lost steam by the last word as he stared at me harshly.

Dingane rushed me in that moment and the movement stole my breath away. He loomed over me and I fought to keep my mouth closed. "Girl, you are the epitome of spoiled. I can smell it in your expensive perfume, in the quality of your ridiculous clothing, in the bracelet wrapped 'round that delicate wrist." He closed the gap between us and all the air sucked from the room. "You won't last out here. You'll stay blind to the environment that surrounds you. You'll live in your clean, perfect bubble and return to your posh life come six months. You are....*you*. I know your kind. I've seen it all before. You will never wake up. Not really," he explained away before backing up and leaving me to my room once again.

I felt tears burn but I steeled myself. My hand clamped my bracelet-covered wrist brutally and I shoved it down my fingers and let it fall to the floor. I yanked the bag I knew contained all my bedding onto the top of the mattress and unzipped it, removing all the contents I needed.

One goose down mattress cover.

One goose down duvet.

One goose down pillow.

One high-quality netted canopy.

One thousand thread count Egyptian cotton sheet set.

I looked down at my bedding and felt the urge to sob seep out of me. I stifled it with a hand across my mouth. I shook it away and stood on the mattress, hooking my canopy net to the hook on the ceiling before shaking out the rolled up mattress cover. I placed everything as it was meant to be, threw off my clothing, put on my pajamas and got into bed. I remembered the lady at the shops telling me to tuck the net into the mattress so I did as she instructed me to. I laid back on the impossibly soft bed and closed my eyes but all I could see was the little girl with the missing arm...

And cried in earnest.

CHAPTER EIGHT

I slept horribly. Terrible thoughts swarmed through my head and it was cold. Horribly cold. Apparently Africa hadn't gotten the memo that it was August and fifty-degree nights shouldn't be possible. I tumbled out of bed after shaking out the bugs that had died in my net over the night. I peeked out my door and it looked like the sun was only just rising. I didn't think I'd ever seen the sun rise before and I watched as pinks and greens, yellows and oranges danced and disappeared over the incredible landscape.

I grabbed my shower caddy and robe and headed toward the showers just to the right of my little hut. I felt so incredibly alone there. I'd always felt alone. My entire life, actually, but this was a loneliness that felt unbearable. I knew I could always find solace in Karina, but I wondered if she'd be too busy to be the friend I needed though I didn't really deserve one. I knew that. Dingane was right. I was a spoiled, repulsive brat, but I'd never had anyone actually tell me so before to my face. It felt like a slap, but I also felt relief, strangely, something I hadn't been expecting. I'd never been told the truth so brutally before and it was releasing, not that I'd tell Dingane that. Regardless, he was rude to me and that pissed me off beyond belief.

No one was out then that I could see and I was grateful that I'd have some time to myself before I was thrown into whatever daunting situation I would inevitably be thrown into. I showered quickly and threw on my robe just as quickly, ready to haul ass back to my hut when I suddenly took notice there wasn't a single insect or *arthropod* in sight. *Huh*, was all I could intelligently piece together in that moment.

Back in my room, I dressed in jeans, boots and a fitted button-up, ready for work. I braided my hair in two French braids down the sides of my head, leaving my straight bangs to air dry over my forehead. I tidied as best I could, tucked in my canopy net and stood by the door, my hand clenched on the handle, frozen in absolute terror.

I don't know how long I stood there before I heard Karina's voice singing a sweet melody. I peered through the cracks of the wood in my door and watched her stroll my direction, in her hand was the hand of the little girl with the missing arm. I studied the girl, finally able to really look at her.

She was no more than three years old with big, round, beautiful brown eyes, perfectly white, straight teeth and a smile as wide as the Nile. They were singing and laughing together, throwing their hands back and forth without a care in the world. When they got close, I backed away, my calves catching on the foot of the bed letting me know I could go no further.

Karina knocked softly. "Sophie, sweetheart. Are you up?"

"Ye-yes!" I called out after a moment's hesitation.

"We're here to walk you to breakfast!" she said cheerfully.

"Oh okay," I said through the door. "I'll be right out."

I stepped in front of the small square mirror that hung loosely above the sink basin and checked myself. Simple makeup. Simple hair. I didn't think I'd ever looked so droll before. I wanted to laugh at myself. I wouldn't dare walk into public back home looking like that.

I opened the door and filed out in front of my audience of two.

Karina gasped. "Oh, dear Lord, Sophie. You scared me. I didn't expect you to be up and ready so early." She laughed. She eyed me and her hands came to rest on her hips. “Well, don’t you look a sight! My dear, you are a breathtaking girl.”

“Thank you,” I told her, knowing she was just being kind.

“Shall we?” she asked, grabbing my hand without asking. She started leading us to the second largest building on the property, just to the right of the main building, the center of the large half circle of buildings. To the right of the kitchens were the bathhouses. Just to the left of the main building and to the right of the remaining staff living quarters, was Charles and Karina’s house I deduced. I could tell because it was a bit more established-looking over the other residential huts, had a proper roof as opposed to the thatched roofs of the other buildings. To the left of their house was what I assumed was Kate’s and the other staff’s double hut and to the left of those was mine and Dingane’s. In the center of the property was the largest tree I’d ever seen in my entire life.

“What kind of tree is that?” I asked Karina, astonished that I was just then noticing it.

“It’s a baobab tree,” she smiled sweetly at me. It looked like a giant bonsai, thick trunk, easily twenty feet around the base, and reached to impossible heights before its canopy shot flat and spread out to a radius of a hundred feet easily.

“It’s beautiful.”

“I know,” she said, patting its trunk as we passed by it.

“It’s always been here. Always.”

"Stalwart, is it?" I asked.

Karina smiled at me. "Yes, much like my Charles."

I returned the easy smile and felt a little of my anxiety begin to melt away.

The kitchens were small and I wondered how they fed them all with such meager operations. I looked around me and saw tables overflowing with laughing children.

"How many are there?" I asked.

"Fifty-nine," she said succinctly. "We're only equipped to handle twenty."

"How do you manage?" I asked quietly, taking in the expanse of children.

"We just do. Lots of faith, my love. It always works out in the end. Somehow. Somehow we turn thirty beds into sixty. Somehow we stretch our food to impossible measures. Somehow we survive on our impossibly meager income. Somehow we love them all equally. Somehow."

I swallowed away my disbelief because there was proof in this pudding. Somehow they did it.

"Now," she began brightly, "breakfast will not be what you are expecting, I'm guessing, but it's food nonetheless and you'll get used to it." She looked at me then.

"I keep saying that, don't I?" She laughed loudly. "Poor dear."

"I'll be just fine," I told her sincerely as I watched a little boy with one hand try to steady his bowl.

Suddenly, Dingane came from out of nowhere. I hadn't been prepared to see him yet and my chest felt like it was hit with the atom bomb. My veins ran warmly all over my body and my face flushed. I watched as he placed what appeared to be a little scrap of rubber underneath the boy's bowl. It didn't budge from its place and the boy looked on Dingane with a brilliant smile. I felt an incredible urge to hug both boys, maybe Dingane a little closer than was socially acceptable. My blood ran hot in that moment. *What the hell is wrong with me?*

"Sit, my dear," Karina said, pointing to a chair at a table near the door. "That's where the adults sit unless one of the children needs us, which is nearly all the time," she joked. "I'll bring you your plate this morning. At lunch, just walk up to the window and Kate will hand you your meal."

"Thank you, Karina."

I sat at the table and the little girl with the missing arm came up to me. "Hi," she said sheepishly.

"You speak English?" I asked her, bewildered.

"Karina teach me," she answered brokenly.

"What's your name?" I asked her.

She touched the middle of her chest with her remaining hand and answered, "Mandisa."

"It's-It's nice to meet you, Mandisa," I told the baby girl, awkwardly tripping on my words. I was so unaccustomed to talking to children, let alone an amputee.

She smiled at me and picked up the hand I had resting on my leg. I began to pull the hand back but something in her eyes told me it was okay, that she was just a human girl, and a beautiful one at that.

I tentatively squeezed her little hand and she giggled, sending a warm, tingling sensation up my arm and into my heart.

"Have you eaten, Mandisa?" I asked her.

The smile dropped from her face and she ran off, disappearing behind the kitchen doors.

"What did I say?" I asked the air in front of me, stunned she'd fled.

"She doesn't eat," I heard a voice say from behind me. Dingane. My blood began to boil once more.

I turned toward him. "What do you mean she doesn't eat? How does she stay alive?"

"She drinks. For days after she first arrived we couldn't even get her to do that."

"Why?" I asked him as he sat across from me.

"We thought it was because she was recovering from the loss of her arm but later discovered it is because she misses her mother."

"What happened to her mother?" I asked, exponentially afraid to hear his answer.

His eyes met mine for the first time that morning and his lips tightened, his shoulders shrugged in answer and my stomach fell to my feet.

"We supplement milk with all sorts of proteins and vitamins, but she's still not gaining weight the way we need her to."

Dingane turned from me and spotted a child who needed help. I have no idea how he saw but he did. He stood and helped a little boy who couldn't reach his chair to sit with only one leg. I watched him. He didn't put the boy in the chair like I assumed he would but helped him discover how to do it on his own.

"What happened to them?" I asked Dingane when he sat down again.

"There is an incredibly evil man named Joseph Kony who roams south Sudan and northern Uganda in search of children to create his child army called the LRA or Lord's Resistance Army. He invades innocent villages, takes young women for obvious reasons, attempts to kidnap their children. If the children refuse to come with him, they chop off a limb to prevent them from being able to grow into a useful soldier that can oppose him later. He kills their parents and we're sent the orphans who survive, broken and damaged and all alone."

I swallowed down the lump that had grown in my throat. "Why does he do it?"

"I don't think he even knows. He claims to fight for peace and security in Uganda as well as for the impoverished. These are his proclamations, but he just works for the devil, in my opinion. He is the ultimate in evil."

I examined the tiny faces that surrounded me and felt so incredibly sad for them and their fates. I wanted to respond to everything Dingane had revealed to me, but I couldn't. There was nothing to say.

After breakfast, Dingane told me I needed to follow him.

"The children usually retrieve their school things right now. Karina, Kate and I teach them from eight to two in the afternoon while Charles and occasionally I make repairs or preparations for the day's activities. Wednesdays, I'm in charge of doing some sort of outdoor activity with them during school hours. Unfortunately, you've been assigned to me at Karina's insistence, so you'll be accompanying me all day every day."

"Yes, so unfortunate," I spit back sarcastically. Dingane stopped short between the baobab tree and our huts. "I don't like you. Is this such a surprise?"
"Frankly, yes, it is," I told him candidly. "You don't know me."
"Ah, but you see, I do. I know you quite well. I know you're here because you were caught with cocaine *twice*. I recognized immediately the type of person you were before you even arrived."

"I was caught with cocaine. I admit it, freely. I'm not proud of it, God knows, but I also knew coming in here everyone would be aware of why I was forced to be here—"

"Forced," he repeated, stopping me midsentence and closing in narrowly.

"Another reason why I'd be just as satisfied if you hopped right back on that plane. Every single soul here is present because they want to be. You're only serving a sentence."

My breath rushed in and out of me in heady anger. "All the same," I gritted. "I'd appreciate it if you got off your self-righteous pedestal and came back down to earth. I'm here to work. So let's work."

That's the moment I realized that my attitude about feeling like being sent to Masego was the most unfair punishment in the world had disappeared the second I'd laid eyes on Mandisa. It surprised me, shocked me, to be honest, but that didn't mean I was going to enjoy my work at Masego. It only meant that while I was there, I wouldn't feel as if a gross injustice had been performed against me. All I had to do was remind myself of Mandisa's story.

CHAPTER NINE

"Come with me," a pissed-off Dingane ordered. He led me to his side of the hut and I followed him inside.

His bed looked plain and barely able to contain him, but his walls were covered in an eclectic assortment of belongings from pictures the children had drawn him to an acoustic guitar.

He slid a large tub out from underneath his bed and grabbed a stack of papers I'd seen in the back of the jeep when he'd picked me up from the airport.

"What are those?" I asked.

"Worksheets. Any time I'm in town, I try to get as many as possible."

We walked to the classrooms and my heart started

to beat erratically. I was nervous, really nervous. I wondered if the kids would see right through me, if they knew what a fraud I really was, that I had no business helping them, as I was the worst person I knew.

The door opened and I saw twenty smiling faces, happy and giggling. They fell quiet as soon as Dingane and I entered the room. I gulped. Audibly.

"Students, you've met Miss Price—"

"Sophie," I interrupted. "They can call me Sophie."

Dingane narrowed his eyes at me for interrupting but continued, "You may call her Miss Price. Should we try to speak English today? To make her more comfortable?" he asked them kindly. *Oh, I see,* I thought. *They get Dr. Jekyll and I get Mr. Hyde.*

"Yes, Mr. Aberdeen!" they all chimed in wildly.

"Good. I've brought the new worksheets from town and I'd like to start on these first. Oliver?" he asked a little boy in the front row.

The boy got up quickly and began passing the worksheets around.

Dingane closed the distance between us and I couldn't help how much more nervous his proximity made me. Tried as I did, I could not get over how attractive I found him. "Think you can handle math?" he asked.

"I'll try my best," I sneered.

"Are you capable?" he asked again.

"Excuse me, but I attended the most elite prep school in my area and I graduated with honors, not that that's any of your business. So, yes, I believe I am *capable* of handling third-grade math."

"Fine. All I want you to do is circle the desks and make sure they're grasping the lesson."

"I'll try, your majesty." And that earned me an eye roll that simultaneously made me want to slap him and kiss him.

"Today we'll continue with equations and variables." I turned, expecting them all to groan and whine the way my classrooms back home would, but I looked at the little faces and saw nothing but excited anticipation.

They like *learning*.

I listened as Dingane taught them how to solve for "x" in a simple variable and tried so hard not to let myself get distracted by his hands as they moved fluidly over the chalkboard. When the lesson was over, he and I both awkwardly danced around the other in attempt to avoid being near each other as we circled the desks. I'd barely avoided him when I noticed a little girl twirling her pencil in her hand and blankly staring at her desk.

I bent and sat on my heels next to her. "What's wrong?" I asked too harshly. I cleared my throat. "What's wrong?" I asked as sweetly as I could.

"I do not understand," she stated clearly, no emotion in her voice.

"Here," I said leaning over her a little, "let's try together then."

She scooted nearer to her paper and readied her pencil. "Okay," I continued, "the equation reads, solve for 'r' when three times 'r' is twenty-four. Let's imagine 'r' is a number. What number multiplied by three will get you twenty-four?"

I could hear her saying her times tables under her breath and when she got to her answer, she blurted, "Eight!"

"Very good," I told her. "I wanted this to be simple for you to understand. Do you understand what they were trying to get from you now?"

"Yes, Sophie," she said, making my heart race at the mention of my name.

"O-Okay," I stumbled out, swallowing hard. "Now that we know what they were trying to get from us, let's apply Dingane's method. Shall we?"

"Yes."

"If we know that three multiplied by eight yields us twenty-four, then twenty-four *divided* by three gets us eight or twenty-four *divided* by eight gets us three, right?"

"Yes."

"And if three multiplied by 'r' is twenty-four, then we can take three from this side of the equation and divide twenty-four by it and that will yield us 'r.' What would we do if there was a division sign on this side of the equation?" I asked, pointing to the left side of the equation.

"We would multiply the number by the answer to get our variable."

"Oh my word, you're a genius!" I told her, squeezing her hand.

She beamed at me. "I understand now."

"I'm so happy!" I told her and I was. Happy. Truly. "What's your name?"

"I am Namono."

"It's so nice to meet you, Namono."

She surprised me by throwing her arms around my neck. A swelling sensation invaded my heart and I'd no idea what it was but it was a good hurt, a hurt that felt worthwhile. I smiled at myself before looking up. Dingane stood at the far corner of the classroom, peering my direction, but I couldn't read his expression. My face flamed a bright red and I turned slightly into Namono to hide my reaction. Although I could no longer see him, his eyes still felt heavy on my head and shoulders. What I wouldn't have given to read his thoughts in that moment.

The rest of the morning was full of math, math and more math. At lunch, I waited in line a few children down from Dingane. Namono held my hand while the other children bombarded me with questions.

"Where do you come from?" a little boy asked.

"California. Do you know where that is?" I asked him.

"No," he said, squinting his eyes as if he could imagine it.

"That's okay. I'll show you when we return to the classroom." He was satisfied with that answer.

"Do you have a mother and father?" another little boy asked.

"I do." I looked up and noticed Dingane had tilted his head, listening in.

"What are they like?" he continued, while the others' eyes were rapt with attention.

"They are nice," I lied.

"Are you married?" a little girl chimed in.

"I am not," I chuckled.

"Dingane is not married either," she added for good measure.

I almost fell over in laughter when Dingane's shoulders tensed.

"He isn't?" I asked. "Why not?" Dingane stopped breathing altogether and I stifled the snort threatening to escape.

"He says he will never marry," one little girl answered.

"Never marry. How interesting. Do you think it is because no girl will have him?" I teased.

He turned around then and shot me a look to kill, but I just shrugged my shoulders in question.

"No," she answered, "he is handsome enough." *No kidding, kid.* "I think it is because he doesn't think he deserves to marry."

"All right, that's enough!" Dingane said, parting through the line of children before us like he was Moses and they were the Red Sea. "I have to talk to Miss Price. Excuse us."

He grabbed my arm.

"He likes Sophie," the little boy who had asked where I was from proclaimed, making me want to squeal in happiness at Dingane's obvious want to squirm.

I looked up at him as he led me away, but he refused to acknowledge me.

"He does? I do not think so," Namono added.

"Yes, he stared at her in class all morning."

My mouth gaped open at Dingane and he closed his eyes tightly before focusing them on me.

"I did not stare at you," he whispered.

"When I said I thought her the most beautiful girl I've ever seen, I asked if he agreed and he nodded his head yes," the little boy added for confirmation.

Dingane led me to the front of the line. "Two, Katie," he asked and she handed over two plates of rice and beans. I took one and he forced me to a table by the door.

We sat down and I just stared at him as he began to eat.

"What?" he asked.

"Nothing," I told him, digging in myself.

"I was not staring at you," he told his plate.

I leaned over. "Did you hear that, Dingane's lunch? He was not staring at you."

He looked up at me crossly. "I was not staring at *you*."

"I never said you were."

"I was merely explaining that Henry was exaggerating. I did not stare at you."

"Okay," I stated, implying in my tone that he had done just that.

"I didn't. I-I wasn't."

"I believe you," I told him.

"I may have looked at you a few times to make sure you were doing your job."

"Oh, I see then."

"But I certainly wasn't *staring*."

"We've established that you were not staring."

He breathed deeply a few times, his eyes burning into mine. "Good."

He'd definitely been staring. The butterflies in my stomach fluttered and flew.

When lunch was over, I circled the children's desks while Dingane taught penmanship, which was both in English and what I'd learned was Bantu. He then taught geography, where I got a chance to show Henry and all the children where California was, science, and we ended the day with an hour of reading then discussing what they'd read.

All in all, I was impressed with the day's activities and knew those kids were actually learning valuable lessons they could take and create lives with. After school was out, all the kids congregated in the courtyard under the baobab tree and played football with a ball that had almost completely deflated. My heart hurt a little when I saw that. I saw a flock of girls building little dolls out of straw. They had obviously zero interest in playing soccer and that made me laugh.

Dingane caught my attention and pointed away from the children. “Kate, Joseph and Ruth will watch them before dinner. Come on.”

“Where are we going?”

“Our day has only begun,” he explained.

“Who are the others I saw this morning around Masego?” I asked as Dingane took me outside the fenced property.

“You’ve met Kate. Joseph does maintenance and guards at night occasionally when it’s needed. Ruth heads the kitchen and she and Mercy, who only works part-time, care for the laundry, which is quite a task. Ruth is married to Solomon, who does maintenance and helps guard as well. They have two kids, Sharon and Isaac. They have their own home just off property.”

Dingane stopped and cupped his hand over his eyes to see farther toward a grove of trees. “No, we’ll have to get my jeep,” he told me.

I followed him to his jeep and hopped in. “What are we doing?”

“We got a call yesterday that there were men loitering around that grove of trees,” he said pointing off into the distance, “near our swimming hole. We’re going to see if the rumors are true, to check for tracks.”

“Why would they be there?”

“If they’re Lord’s Resistance Army soldiers, they could be scoping us out, or they could have been men just looking for shade and water.”

“How can you tell?”

"The LRA wear boots that most here cannot afford. It's a good indicator."

We stumbled along uneven terrain and I had to keep myself from sliding into Dingane's hip several times. Finally, we came to a stop just inside the canopy of trees. Dingane reached over my lap and my blood began to boil before running ice cold when the gun he'd pulled from his glove compartment came into view.

"*What are you doing*?"

"These men, if they're still here, could be armed, Sophie. I can't take any chances." He checked to see if the gun was loaded and an audible clicking sound resounded around my head when it clicked back into place.

I gulped and got out, not too subtly siding closely to Dingane as we started to examine the outer perimeter.

"There," he said quietly five minutes later. Adrenaline shot through me at an astronomical rate and I grabbed his arm, pressing myself into his side.

"Wh-where?"

He pointed to a small cluster of plant life near the ground and a mud outline of a large boot print shone between.

"Jesus! What does this mean?" I asked him, my nails accidentally digging into his arm. He looked down at my hand but didn't say a word. I lightened my hold.

"It means they were most likely LRA." He sighed. "The men will have to take shifts over the next few days to watch for them. Hopefully they were just passing through and have no business with us."

"And what if they do?"

"Pray they don't," was all he replied.

CHAPTER TEN

"Did you see anything?" Charles asked as we exited the jeep.

Karina came to my side smiling and opened the door for me.

"Yeah, boot prints," Dingane explained.

Karina's smile fell but quickly picked back up.

"We'll have to set watch times then," Charles said, walking off with Dingane toward his house.

Karina slid her arm through mine.

"Kate and the others will be watching the children at dinner tonight. I thought we'd do something special for your arrival. I've made dinner for you myself."

"Thank you, Karina," I said, but kept an eye on Charles and Dingane talking animatedly on the front porch. "I look forward to it."

Karina brought me up her little porch and the men stopped talking. The tension was palpable but Karina forced me through it and we entered the door.

Karina's little house was beyond charming. It was fairly bare, but the few things she did have, you could tell, meant a lot to her. Lots of old quilts, an entire living room set that looked like it came out of the fifties but was in good shape, well maintained. She had at least a million pictures of beautiful, smiling faces. I studied them one by one.

"Who is this?" I asked her when I came upon one of a small boy with Charles and Karina who looked to be in their twenties. I was right, of course, she was unbelievably gorgeous.

"Oh, that's Isaac. He was our first boy here." She started laughing and shook her head. "He was so mischievous and we had absolutely no idea what we were doing." She picked the frame up and studied it. "He's like a son to me."

"Where is he now?" I asked quietly.

"America. We helped him, or rather Harrison helped him, get there. He educated himself and now he sends us a monthly stipend that helps feeds the children here."

"Oh my God," I whispered more to myself than to Karina.

"He is a very good boy. Married now, though I've never met his wife. They have a little girl themselves. It's all very lovely."

"It sounds it," I told her honestly. I thought on something. "Does Pembrook often help you get children over there?"

"I cannot count the number of times Harrison has either helped adopt them out or helped them emigrate."

I wondered why Pembrook had never talked about that before. I wondered if he thought me too selfish to bring the subject up at all. That thought sent me down a shame spiral I needed to sit from so I plopped myself on one of Karina's chairs. Charles and Karina's house was essentially one giant room. The living area was at the door. The little dining area and kitchen were at the back and shared a space with the living. The only rooms I could see not part of the main room were the bedroom and bathroom and I assumed those were off to the side through the only doors I could recognize besides the front door. All in all, the entire house looked to be a thousand square feet, about the size of my parent's pantry back home and yet they were the most happy people I'd ever had the pleasure of meeting.

I watched Karina, Charles and Dingane spill into the tiny dining area set next to the miniscule kitchen, smelled the wonderful aroma of whatever garlic-infused dish Karina was cooking and pondered over their simple yet incredibly complicated lives. One thing I could say for certain was they were infinitely more content than I'd ever felt my entire life.

Dingane, laughing boisterously, broke me from my revelry.

"Come join us, Sophie," Karina said, patting the chair beside her and opposite Dingane.

I hoisted myself up and stumbled to the chair feeling the day's work in my back and legs. I smiled at them as I sat.

"We were laughing at a very old story," Charles offered to bring me into the conversation.

"Yes, old but very sweet," Karina chimed in.

"It's the story of how they met," Dingane said, surprising me. My head whipped his direction and I watched his eyes light up as he looked on the two of them.

"What is it?" I asked.

Charles smiled at his wife. "Karina was desperately in love with me..."

"A lie!" Karina exclaimed, giggling like a schoolgirl. "You always make me out to be this silly creature and I wasn't." She turned my direction and sobered. "Charles exaggerates. I was not in love with him. In fact, it was quite the opposite."

"I admit it without hesitation. I was most decidedly in love with Karina Smith from the second I laid eyes on her," Charles added.

"Smith?" Dingane asked. "Was that your maiden name, Karina?"

"Yes, and I was a grade lower than Charles. He and I met at a church function for teens and he politely introduced himself. I had no idea he attended school with me, I just figured he was a local boy, but when he informed me we had chemistry together I was wracking my brain trying to remember him. I told him finally, 'You're not in my chemistry class.' To which he replied dryly, 'I beg to differ.'"

So Charles was witty.

"I pretended to be offended," she continued, "but secretly was dying to swoon on the inside. Every day he would meet me at the front doors of school, but I would diligently ignore him, even going so far as to take alternate routes, but he always found me."

"I was relentless," Charles added.

"Apparently," I teased.

Karina sighed. "I may have been attracted to Charles, but there was nothing I could do about it. I wasn't allowed to date. My father would have killed me, but Charles was so dogged in his insistence that one day I agreed to meet him at a nearby ice cream shop. I had planned to tell him that he was very kind, that I found him to be a sweet boy, but I could not date so he might as well fixate his obsession on another."

"To which he refused and probably pursued you with even more fervor," I stated.

"Of course."

"And you eventually gave in."

"Naturally. Look at him. Who could refuse?" she asked, smoothing Charles' cheek over with her thumb.

I watched Dingane smile at the older couple and wondered about his own parents. Mine would never be as sweet or as loving as Charles and Karina and I decided right then and there that I would be gobbling them up as long as I had the opportunity. I would learn from them. I would study them. I would endeavor to be like them.

Dinner tasted amazing and I hadn't realized just how hungry I'd been. I ate more than my fair share and then immediately felt guilty thinking about Mandisa. The conversation was lively between myself, Charles and Karina or between Dingane, Charles and Karina but the conversation between Dingane and myself was practically nonexistent. A "pass the blank" here or a "hand me that" there.

Karina cleared the plates and a hormonal rage built in my stomach as I watched Dingane fold his napkin on the table over and over and over, creasing each fold tightly with nimble fingers. I wanted to rip it out of his hands, clear the table and attack him with my mouth. How can someone bug the shit out of you so much yet simultaneously cause you to want to know them intimately with your tongue? He was driving me crazy.

We all said our goodbyes on the porch and Karina kissed my cheek after I thanked her for dinner.

As soon as my head hit my pillow, I dreamt of Dingane's ridiculous hands.

CHAPTER ELEVEN

I woke to someone shaking me.

"Get up," I heard someone whisper. "Get up," they said, shaking me more harshly.

I whimpered as I turned around. "Dingane?" I asked, sitting up and smoothing the hair from my face.

"I need your help."

"What?"

"I'll explain in the truck. We don't have time. Get dressed and meet me outside."

"What time is it?" I asked, throwing back my net.

"Just past midnight."

And with that, he left me to myself, my creaky door swinging shut behind him.

I stood and immediately began brushing my teeth while I dressed, spit, rinsed and tied my hair in a ponytail. It was the fastest I'd ever gotten ready, not a stitch of makeup or even a brush through my tangled locks.

I rushed through my door, tucking my shirt into my belted jeans. I reached Charles, Karina and Dingane and bent to tie my boots.

"She can't," Karina said, wringing her hands.

"She'll be okay," Charles said, soothing his wife. "We'll need you here to prepare."

"What's going on?" I demanded, standing up.

"There's been an attack on a village two and a half hours from here and there are children who need rescuing still. We're afraid the LRA will come back for them," Dingane said.

"Then we go to them," I said without thinking, surprising myself.

"I cannot send you out to that, Sophie," Karina added quickly.

"She needs to stay here, Sophie," Charles explained. "To prepare a small medical ward. We've heard it's many more children than we're handled to equip on a moment's whim. She's the only other one of us trained medically beside myself, but we need at least four in the truck and one of those should be trained. Kate and Ruth are needed here and Mercy cannot be fetched for some time. I'm asking for your help. Can you handle it?" he asked me.

"I can," I said without hesitation.

"It's settled then," Dingane said after examining me for a moment and headed toward the truck after picking up a large container setting at his feet.

Charles rushed off to fetch something and Karina stuck to my side, taking my hands in hers. "The men will not prepare you for this, Sophie, so I feel I must. What you're about to encounter will revolt you. I'm not exaggerating. I want you to steel yourself. Put all emotion toward the back of your mind. Get in there, get them out and come back in one piece. I'm relying on you."

"Of course," I told her, swallowing the knot that had formed so rigidly in my throat.

Karina ran toward the schoolhouse, shouting at everyone who had begun to run around in preparation to receive the children I would be helping bring back. I ran to the truck and Dingane had opened my door for me, allowing me to slide in without a moment to lose. Charles and Solomon jumped in the back, armed to the nines and I almost burst out sobbing. Fear, real fear crept through my body at an alarming rate.

Dingane's engine rumbled into the otherwise quiet night. and I jumped inside my skin, burying my hands in my lap.

"What's happened?" I asked as we tumbled through the large gates. I turned around and saw them close behind me.

"They were attacked in the night, unprepared."

"How many survivors?"

"We're not really sure. We've been told only to hurry and that there may be more than nearby aid may be able to handle."

I swallowed audibly, turning toward Dingane. His eyes met mine briefly and they were alive, full of anxiety and fear. "I will never be able to forget what I am about to see, am I?"

"Never," he said quietly, turning toward me again.

The remaining two-and-a-half-hour drive was met with silence. Thoughts circled my head and I tried so hard to imagine, to prepare myself for what I was about to witness but nothing could have readied me.

I smelled the burnt straw of the village homes before I actually saw them and it enveloped the cab, making me cough violently. Dingane threw a t-shirt at me to cover my face so I did. Finally, after rounding the bush that the little village must have tucked itself into in attempt to camouflage themselves, little piles of remaining flames flickered and twisted throughout the open field before us. I saw no one but heard faint screams and wails tear throughout the night. My gut tightened and my hands gripped the dash in front of me, my knuckles white with strain.

Dingane stopped the truck abruptly and ran into the center of the village. I jumped out and followed suit behind Charles and Solomon but stopped short at the terrifying sight before me.

Groups of small children sporadically spread throughout the camp, bent and weeping, cried into the night over the corpses of their burning parents. I immediately fell to my knees in want to vomit but could only dry heave at the sheer horror. The smell of burning flesh seared into my own and I had to cover my mouth in terror.

"Sophie!" someone screamed harshly beside me. I looked up toward the voice and Dingane stood above me. He grabbed my arms, picking me up and brought me close to his face. "Can you do this?" he asked but his eyes were sympathetic. He brushed a tear away with his thumb but one more fell in its place.

"Y-yes," I sputtered, pushing all emotion away, thinking on Karina's advice.

"Follow me," he yelled over the blazing fires and bawling children.

"But they need help," I hiccupped, pointing to the boys and girls sprawled in panic around us.

"And we will get to them, but we must tend to the hurt now. They're priority."

"Okay," I told him, racing beside him toward what looked like a felled little girl around seven.

We passed Charles pumping a woman's chest up and down to get her to breathe again and I quickly inhaled a sharp breath. Dingane and I both fell to our knees beside the little girl; her tunic was covered in splatters of blood across her chest.

Dingane pulled it back and exposed the wound. Small holes peppered her torso and they appeared to go deeper than anything considered superficial.

"Oh my God," I whispered. "Please, tell me what to do."

"We'll bandage her tightly. Here, press this gauze here," he told me and turned toward the kit I'd seen him carry earlier.

As he rummaged through it, I pressed the gauze tightly against her bleeding wounds and bent over her tiny head.

"It'll be fine," I soothed, knowing damn well it would never be for her again, even if she lived.

My free hand ran across her baby cheeks. Sticky tears mixed with red dirt stained that innocent part of her. Dingane added more gauze to the wound and I sat opposite him, trading the wrap and covering the girl's torso carefully. I know we had hurt her every time we had to lift her small frame to allow the bandage to wrap around completely but not a single whimper was heard from her lips and all I wanted was to gather her in my arms because of it.

Dingane picked her up carefully and brought her to the back of the truck, laying her down across a blanket then covered her up with another. He spoke to her in Bantu and I guessed he'd assured her we'd return because she nodded once.

We ran back toward the village and found two more children in dire need of attention. We wrapped them, transported them to the truck and went back over and over. We'd tended to six wounded children within half an hour.

Dingane pointed toward a cluster of children nearest us and we ran toward them, calling them toward us and encouraging them to get into the truck quickly. Most obeyed save for one who refused to leave his father's side. Dingane pulled the small child off his dead father and wrapped his arms around the young boy, speaking into his ear as tears streamed down his tiny face. I couldn't help the tears that fell quickly on my own as we gathered more and more motherless children. I counted twenty-three orphans in all, not including the ones who had died during the ambush.

I looked around for the woman Charles had attempted to save, but she was nowhere in the truck and I filed that away under "never think about again." Not a single adult had survived, the LRA had made sure of that.

"We have to leave!" Charles yelled over the crying children.

He and Solomon hopped onto the bumper of the truck and held on tightly.

"They won't be able to hold on the entire two hours like that!" I yelled at Dingane.

His tired face found mine over the grouped children. "They will. We've done this before."

And it hit me.

This wasn't an isolated incident. These attacks happened frequently, always targeting innocent families, always leaving children in an already impoverished nation without anyone to care for them.

"Get in, Sophie!" he yelled and I obeyed. He laid a small boy in my lap and I cradled him as best I could, trying to decide which way would be best to hold him that would afford him the least amount of pain.

Dingane shoved two more dazed children between us and got in, starting his truck and tearing away from the scene with decided purpose.

"The LRA is coming back?" I asked.

"They usually do. They use the leftover children as bait. They know we come in search of them."

I turned my head toward the window and let the tears fall freely, the most I'd ever allowed, and the absolutely only time I'd ever cried and had a genuine right to.

Because I wasn't crying for myself. I was crying for the innocents.

CHAPTER TWELVE

The gates opened as if in anticipation of our arrival around four forty-five in the morning, the sun had yet to rise and I found myself begging its return. The night I once found unbelievably peaceful and beautiful now felt unbearably dark, as if a decided lack of hope had enveloped us. As we passed, Kate and Mercy were on the other side, closing us in and running our direction. Dingane tore through and stopped abruptly, close to the schoolhouse, his headlights lighting up the baobab tree as we passed.

He ran to my side and took the little boy from my arms, running him inside. I gathered one of the girls, who'd grown unconscious during the ride back to Masego, and carried her behind him. He passed me again after dropping off the boy and gathered the remaining girl in the front.

Charles and Solomon were carrying those who could not walk on their own and within a minute we were all inside, hovering over children.

"Sophie, grab that bag for me!" Karina ordered, pointing to a bag on the creaky wood floor.

I brought it to her and opened it up. She was working on the first girl Dingane and I had helped, the one riddled with holes in the chest. She was unconscious. Karina stood quickly and ran to a drawer of a metal cabinet she had rolled into the room. Makeshift cots dotted the entire room and each bed was filled with a bleeding child.

She returned, ripping open a paper and plastic envelope carrying an IV.

"I'll need your help removing the shrapnel," Karina said dryly.

I looked behind me to see who she was talking to but there was no one there, everyone else was busy over the beds of one of the children. I looked back and saw her eyes trained on me.

"I can't," I told her.

"Wash your hands with Hibiclens. There's a station set up there," she said, gesturing to a corner of the room.

The room was awash in candlelight since there wasn't any electricity and I could barely see a thing. *They need a generator for these situations!*

"Shouldn't Charles help you with this? He's trained!" I was panicking.

"He's with another child, Sophie. It will be fine. Trust me. She's bleeding out as we speak though."

I ran to the corner and washed my hands, one of the older orphans there stood next to me, ready to rinse for me into the awaiting bowl. She handed me a box of older-looking latex gloves and I took two, putting them on as I walked back to Karina's side.

"What do I do?"

"Spread this wound open for me. I can't seem to reach the metal inside."

Oh my God. Oh my God.

I leaned over the girl and reluctantly pulled the wound as wide as I could. Karina's tweezers were ready and dove in without hesitation, digging back and forth, making me cringe. She pulled out a large piece of sharp metal and it clinked into a porcelain bowl on a small table beside the bed. One by one she removed the metal embedded in the girl's tiny chest.

"There's one more." She pointed to another deep wound near the heart.

"What if it's too deep?"

"Spread the wound."

I obeyed and almost had to avert my eyes at the blood gushing but held my ground. After what seemed like forever, Karina fished out a small but substantial piece of metal and it clinked audibly next to the other shrapnel.

Karina worked steadily, stitching each wound, as I cut strips of clean gauze and readied the iodine solution. She poured the solution over the stitches, covered them all with an antibacterial ointment and we placed the gauze over each one, finally wrapping the girl's frame similarly to how Dingane and I had at the village.

When we were done, Karina gave her a renewed dose of sleeping meds through her IV and I stood, removed my bloody gloves, tossed them in a bin and walked into the night air. The sun wouldn't show its face for at least another hour. I begged for it to rise, to renew the day, to erase the night. The screams would live in my subconscious for the rest of my life.

Sweat poured from my face and neck and drenched my shirt; it clung to my body. The panicked adrenaline was leaving in droves and my hands were shaking with the release.

I heard footsteps on the wood creak behind me. I turned to find Dingane, his white linen shirt had three buttons unbuttoned near his collar instead of his standard two and his usual carefully rolled sleeves were in disarray.

"How is she?" he asked about our little girl.

"She's fine." I paused. "I don't really know. I didn't ask. I don't want to know."

Dingane leaned against one of the wood posts holding up the aluminum awning and nodded.

"How often does this happen?" I asked him, staring at the dark outline of the baobab tree.

"Too often."

"Why can they not be stopped?"

"They are illusive and they get protection from Northern Sudan."

"Why?"

"Who knows. They're evil?"

"Without a doubt." I looked behind me into the schoolhouse. "How are the others?"

"I believe there will be no more death tonight," he said solemnly.

I exhaled the breath I didn't know I'd been holding and quiet tears began to fall. "I'm so sorry for them."

Before the last word had even escaped my lips, the orphans in their beds above the kitchen, the original fifty-nine, began chanting their beautiful traditional songs and this made the tears fall even harder. I had no idea what they were singing, but their innocent voices rang throughout the camp and I couldn't help but take solace in them. I listened for quite some time while the tears streamed.

"I thought they'd be asleep by now. It's close to six in the morning," I said, turning to Dingane.

"They couldn't sleep I've been told."

"Understandable," I said, looking back up at their windows.

After a few minutes of beautiful song backed by a symphony of singing insects and night animals, I turned back to Dingane. "Why do they do it?"

"Because it brings them joy."

"And what is there to be joyful about?" I asked honestly, thinking on the images of dead children curled into themselves at the village. Another burst of silent tears streamed down.

"Life, Sophie. They still live. They breathe, they love each other, they find joy in the world around them for no other reason than because they are children. They are resilient. They will always rise above. Always. It is a curious facet of the innocent young.

"If I hadn't seen it before with my own eyes, I never would have believed it. Cynicism comes with the harshness of the world and only as you get older. I'd give anything to have their inherent happiness."

Dingane turned toward me and I toward him, leaning on the post beside him. We stared at one another for a moment and a sense of understanding passed between us. I didn't believe that he'd ever like me, but after the night we'd experienced, I did believe he would be more tolerant of me.

"You two should get some sleep," Charles said, breaking the trance between Dingane and me.

"You and Karina should sleep. I can stay with them. They'll sleep as well," Dingane told him.

"I can help," I added and Dingane whipped his head toward mine, nodding slightly.

"We'll cancel classes tomorrow," Charles said when Karina met his side. "Sophie and Dingane will watch them for a few hours. We can have Ruth and Solomon relieve them after breakfast."

Karina nodded and both slumped toward their cabin. Dingane sat in the doorway and I followed his example, sitting against the pole opposite him, both our legs spread out before us. I crossed mine at the ankles.

"I'll check them every few minutes," he explained.

"I'm glad Karina had sedatives."

"It's the last of our supply. I'm not sure how we'll be able to replenish."

"You don't have a regular supplier?" I asked.

Dingane smiled softly sending butterflies in my stomach fluttering, the basic attraction I held for him not being able to be denied despite our current situation. "We don't have anything like that, though I wish we did."

I just couldn't imagine that this very desperate place couldn't get aid from western civilization.

"Uganda is a forgotten place, isn't it?"

"Uganda, South Sudan, Kenya, Africa, really."

"Why?" I asked softly.

"Two reasons. People think this, our predicament, is an exaggeration or they're in total denial. Pretending it doesn't exist allows for a light conscience."

I scoffed at that in disbelief but then thought on it. I'd never really heard of these places save for the occasional TV ad asking/imploring people for aid. I never thought twice about it. Ashamed, I turned my head.

"And the other?" I asked him directly after gathering my guilt.

"They assume someone will take care of it, their governments really, but all they need to do is take the problem into their own hands. Governments are unreliable, corrupt entities. It will only be solved by the hands of many. Thousands of small pebbles, giant splash and all that."

It was quiet for a moment and the night air was filled with those singing insects again.

"Once, I took this social studies class," I told him. "In it, we read this story about this woman attacked in an alleyway in New York City." I shook my head. "I can't remember the particulars. Anyway, the gist of it was that many people watched the attack from their windows and assumed someone else called the police and the woman died there, waiting for help."

Dingane lifted his shoulders in acknowledgement, his beautiful, tanned hands lifted as if in explanation.

I remembered the visions of dead children again and turned my head to avoid the humiliation of Dingane seeing the tears fall. I twisted back when he nudged my foot with his.

"It's not a weakness," he stated simply, his arms folded tightly against his torso.

"What's not?" I blubbered, wiping my face with dirty hands.

"Fear, sadness. They're not weaknesses. They are overpowering, defining emotions. They make you human, Sophie."

"They are signs of defect," I told him, reverting back to curt Sophie.

"Says who?"

"Me."

"Why?"

"Because I — because..."

"Let me guess. Because you are not proud of yourself? Because you despise who you are? Because, if you show these emotions, they acknowledge those thoughts?"

I was deadly silent for five minutes at least. "Yes," I stated, breaking the absence of sound.

"Do something about it."

"There's nothing to do. I'm lost."

"Bullshit. You don't really believe that. You want to stick with what's easy for you. You foresee the amount of work it would take to transform yourself and you're too frightened to embrace the challenge. Now, that, Sophie Price, is a real weakness."

Dingane stood and I watched him check each bed, traveling stealthily from one to the other and I hated how right he was.

CHAPTER THIRTEEN

Dingane and I were relieved by Ruth and Solomon around eight in the morning after breakfast, as promised. I was so exhausted, but the idea of sleeping on my sheets after being covered in blood and dirt gave me the chills. I wanted, no *needed*, to wash away the previous night.

"I have to shower," I told Dingane.

His eyes bugged slightly. "Oh, all right. I was going to as well. Would you like to go first?"

"No," I told him, "you go ahead. I'll gather all my things."

"Okay," he said. "I'll knock on your door when it's free.

"Thank you."

Fifteen minutes later, Dingane knocked and I answered.

He popped in his head and his hair was still wet and clung to his neck. I could smell his soap and I inhaled it.

"All yours," he said, moving to leave before stopping short. "Uh, sleep well."

"Thanks," I said, smiling slightly.

I approached the shower with hesitation knowing there would be bugs this time but was surprised again to see it was entirely clear. "That's odd," I said out loud.

"What's odd?" someone asked me. Karina was passing by.

"Oh, there aren't any insects here."

Karina studied the shower. "That is curious." She smiled before scurrying off toward the schoolhouse.

I showered quickly, cleansing the night away as best I could and dressed simply. My feet and eyes were so heavy by the end I wasn't sure if I'd be able to make it to my small hut but somehow I did, tossing my things to the side and practically diving into my bed, burying my net as best I could into the mattress. I was asleep before my eyes could even hit the pillow.

I woke of my own accord which felt strange, but it was still light out and that surprised me knowing how tired I'd been. I shook the insects from my net and emerged, brushing my teeth and fixing my hair into two braids as I'd done that first day. It was to be my standard style, I'd decided. It was easy and stayed out of my way. Two things I would have paid money I never would've associated with the way I wanted to present myself. I wore my standard blue jeans, boots and button-up.

Outside, I could hear the giggling voices of the girls and hearty laughs of the boys, no doubt enjoying their free day of play. When I left my hut, my view was exactly as I'd expected except for one little beautiful hiccup. The girls sat under the baobab tree, dancing and playing, the boys were several hours into a soccer match it seemed.

My eyes spanned across the players, all matching in height except for one. Dingane played alongside the boys, laughing with them, dribbling the ball around them and teasing them for not being able to catch up, which made them laugh all the more. Two boys had fallen down they were laughing so hard. When he spotted me, his smile didn't fade and that bolstered me. He passed the ball to the nearest boy and they continued to play.

Dingane jogged toward me, out of breath when he finally reached me.

"They've put up the food, but Kate saved you a plate."

"Oh, I'll have to thank her."

"Come on. I'll show you where she stored it. I don't think you've ever been in the kitchen before," he said, walking backward.

"I haven't," I admitted when he turned back around. "How are the village children?" I asked.

He dropped to match my pace. "Much better. Many of their wounds were more superficial than we originally thought. The first girl we'd wrapped, Olivia, is the worst off but conscious now and asking questions. We have high hopes."

"How are they handling it? The loss?" I couldn't help but ask.

"As expected. They need time."

"No, they need their parents."

"That is the very definition of stolen, Sophie. Nobody ever asks permission."

When we arrived in the kitchen, we heard the patter of bare feet on the tile floor but saw no one. I went through the swinging door into the eating hall and looked around but saw no one until I turned around and noticed Mandisa, the one who refused to eat, hiding beneath the serving line.

"Mandisa?" I called to her, but she was trembling, too afraid to come out so I went to her instead. "Mandisa, sweetheart," I said, testing out the word. I'd never genuinely called anyone "sweetheart" before, not without condescension. "Come to me."

I held out my arms and could feel Dingane steadily approaching me from behind. I lifted my hand to stay him and felt him stop.

Mandisa shook her head back and forth and squeezed her eyes shut. I took the opportunity to join her underneath the line and Dingane crouched beside us, boxing us in. When Mandisa opened her eyes, they were full of tears, so I did the only thing I could think to do. I grabbed her. I lifted her into my lap and squeezed her to my chest. I rubbed small circles into her back and whispered in her ear. It negated every instinct I owned, but I did it anyway.
"It's not working. What should I do?" I asked Dingane.
"Keep holding her," he whispered.
"It's not working," I told him and tried to push her on him, but Dingane placed her back in my arms so I squeezed her again.

He placed his hand on my shoulder and held fast. "She needs affection."

"I'm not doing it right," I told him, beyond panicked then.

"Yes, you are," he reassured me.

Dingane sat beside me against the aluminum partition and an instant calming sensation washed over me. I knew I could do it. I knew if Dingane was there to help me that I could help Mandisa. So we stayed silent for what seemed like hours and all I could wonder was if I had it in me to calm a toddler who'd just lost her mother, who refused to eat and was a complete stranger. I wondered if her life would always be teeming with the strife she so obviously struggled with. I wondered if she would continue to starve herself with grief, or if we'd be able to feed her through a tube. I wondered if she would ever be a normal child again. I wondered if she would even make it to adulthood, or if she would forever be lost to the cruel world she had already been subjected to at such a young age. I wondered about the practical and impractical and while I pondered her young life, she calmed down. She stopped crying and held on to me tightly.

I turned toward Dingane and felt his relief as well. We were a silly lot, the three of us, burrowed underneath that aluminum serving line, but despite what it appeared to the outside world, we had just conquered a mountain.

Dingane shimmied out of our cozy spot, but I was hindered by toddler so he dragged me out by my hips and practically lifted the two of us off the ground in one fell swoop, sending shivers down my spine.

"That was impressive," I deadpanned.

"Thank you," was all he replied, making me smile.

I followed Dingane into the kitchen and he removed my food, dumping it into a pot to reheat it for me. I tried to hop onto the counter with Mandisa in my arms but failed miserably.

Dingane rolled his eyes and easily lifted Mandisa and me onto the counter. My cheeks flamed when he touched my waist, but he didn't seem to notice, too engrossed in stirring it seemed. I watched him in that moment and was overcome with attraction. It felt so wrong to focus on the boy before me when I held a very needy girl in my arms, but I couldn't help it. I turned my face away from him and brought Mandisa closer to me, laying my cheek on her head the way I'd seen Sav's mom do it a thousand times before.

CHAPTER FOURTEEN

"Mercy's back today," Dingane told Karina at lunch.

"I was wondering when she'd be back," I stated.

It'd been over a week since we'd seen Mercy, and Dingane and I'd taken over the laundry duties while she'd been gone. I wasn't wondering, really, I was dying for her to come home. Teaching all day and doing laundry all night was becoming unbearable, even Dingane was complaining and he never complained, ever.

"Where'd she go?" I asked.

"South Sudan. She's family there. She was checking on them."

"Isn't that rather dangerous?"
"Yes," Dingane answered shortly.
"Okay," I sang.
"He tried to convince her not to leave, but she wouldn't listen. Her aunt's been sick for months," Karina explained.
"Oh, I see."

Mercy chose that moment to walk through the eating hall and waved at me. I waved enthusiastically, unsure if I was happy to see her because I wouldn't have any more laundry to do, or if it was because she was back safe and sound. I frowned into my plate. When she approached I found myself jumping up and hugging her. *Huh, guess I sincerely missed her.*

Over the last few weeks, Dingane and I had intermittently examined those parts where we suspected the soldiers had stalked us from. We hadn't seen any sign of boot prints since that first day, but Dingane refused to relax.

"Can you not calm down for a few moments?" I'd asked him at the time.

"Do you not remember the village?" he asked me in answer.

That was the end of that.

Dingane and I had come to an understanding of sorts. I kept as quiet as possible, did my work and he would tolerate me. But after those first few weeks, I'd grown tired of submission so I showed him what I was capable of. I showed him I had enough initiative, enough industry, to strike out. I was also, simultaneously, recognizing something in myself I didn't know could exist.

I was worth more than the sex I'd defined myself with.

Yet Dingane still treated me with latent disdain.

The child survivors of the village were adjusting swimmingly apart from a few minor hiccups here and there, but nothing we couldn't handle. Charles, Karina, the rest of the staff and I were becoming great friends. I was truly falling in love with them and my purpose for being there, which I discovered was more than just serving a sentence.

I was learning Bantu, not enough to hold a conversation but enough to ask the younger ones if they needed to use the restroom, if they were hungry, etc.

Mandisa had started eating again thanks to Dingane and me. After our powerful breakthrough in the kitchen, she'd warmed up to me though I hadn't any idea why at the time, but Karina helped me see that Mandisa chose who she thought could help her the best and she felt that was me. Who was I to argue? If I could help, I was going to. She'd gained almost seven pounds in two weeks. Mandisa had even taken to occasionally sneaking into my hut late at night and sleeping with me. I wouldn't have admitted this to anyone but she was my favorite.

A week after Mercy came back, Dingane and I had to make another patrol near the watering hole. After classes, we got into his truck and headed that way.

"Oliver's driving me nuts," I told the window.

"He drives us all nuts."

I laughed. "He's too smart for our lessons."

"I know this."

"So why don't we alter his curriculum accordingly?" I asked.

"That's a fine idea," he conceded too easily.

I sat up a bit and stared at him in shock. "What? No argument?"

He only rolled his eyes.

"No, seriously. No argument? No telling me 'you've got this' or dismissing me? I must confess, I suspect I'm living in an alternate universe." I pretended to check out the window. "Nope, pigs aren't flying."

"Har, har." He sighed, parking the truck. He leaned over and removed his pistol from the glove compartment. I got out, not wanting to be anywhere near it. I had a healthy respect for guns. Very healthy.

"You're scared of it," he proclaimed to the wind.

"I'm not," I said, moving to the other side of him, the side without the gun.

"After we check things out, you're going to shoot it."

My mouth dropped open to my chest. "Absolutely not!"

He stopped short and grinned at me. "You absolutely are. I can't have you frightened of it. What if there's occasion to use it?"

"I'll never have need to hold it, much less use it."

"Don't be naive, Sophie."

"I won't need to know."

"This is a 'just in case' kind of situation. Once I teach you how to aim and shoot it, I won't ever ask you to use it again."

"Fine," I gritted, continuing on without him.

I could hear him snicker below his breath behind me. "It's not funny," I sang.

"I beg to differ. This is going to be delightful for me."

I deliberately walked faster.

"Stop," he said, catching up. "I'll stop teasing. Just stay near me."

I obeyed but didn't acknowledge him. We searched the entire watering hole and found no evidence that anyone was there. We rounded the entire bit of land and were nearing the truck. I made a mad dash toward it, hoping he'd have somehow miraculously forgotten our lesson, but there was no such luck.

"Wrong way, Sophie," I heard him say. I stopped, disrupting the dirt beneath my feet and turned around, slightly winded.

"You can't be serious."

"I'm deadly serious. Now, follow me."

He led me toward a covered area and found a thick rotting stump, picking it up as if it weighed nothing and setting it against a still-standing tree.

"This is your target," he said, checking the barrel and unloading the gun of all bullets.

"Why are you removing the bullets if this is a shooting lesson?"

"Because there are a few rules you need to recognize first, and I think you'd be more comfortable holding an unloaded gun."

He was right.

"Okay," he continued, "first rule's you always handle a gun as if it's loaded, even if you know it's not."

He handed me the gun and I reached for it with a shaking fist. I took it and held it in my palm.

"It's heavy."

"In more ways than one."

"What next?" I asked, staring at the cold piece of metal laying flat in my hand.

He fixed my grip and pointed the gun down. His hands were warm and my breath caught a little. "Next rule," he said, "always keep a firearm pointed in a safe direction," he explained softly. "If you accidentally fired it, we'd want the bullet to avoid others."

"Okay," I wheezed.

He removed his hand from mine and I found I could breathe more easily.

"Next. Always keep your finger off the trigger and outside the trigger guard," he said, pointing to the section of metal that protected the trigger. "Until you've made a conscious decision to shoot, keep that finger off the trigger."

I nodded and gulped. His finger barely touched mine, but the world seemed to have disappeared around us. His breaths matched mine, but I was positive he was only nervous about teaching me how to shoot.

"Anything else?" I asked, breaking the trance.

Dingane shook his head and stuck his hands in his pocket. "Yeah, uh, where was I?"

"Trigger."

"Yeah, uh, next rule is to always be aware of your target, backstop and beyond. Make sure with one hundred percent certainty that your line of fire is clear of people and property. Don't take anyone's word for it. You're the only one responsible if something should happen, so make sure it doesn't."

"Sounds good."

"Okay."

"Okay, what?"

"Check, Sophie."

"Oh!" I exclaimed, realizing what he meant.

I handed him the gun and circled my target, recognizing that nothing laid beyond my line of fire for miles besides grass and the occasional tree. I returned to Dingane's side. He handed me the weapon once more and I pointed it toward the ground carefully and made sure my fingers were nowhere near the trigger.

"It's clear," I told him.

Dingane physically twisted my body toward my target stump then stood beside me.

"Since this is your first time shooting, I'd recommend you hold the gun with both hands."

I positioned my hands the way I thought I'd seen guys on TV held it. "Like this?"

He laughed. "No, uh, like this," he said, grabbing both my hands and positioning them properly. "You should always grip high on the backstrap. This'll allow you leverage when the gun fires and it'll prevent it from recoiling into your body." My hands started to shake a little and he steadied them with his. "Your other hand should rest on top of this hand, right under the trigger guard and cup the back of your trigger hand.

"You'll need to stand with your feet and hips at shoulder width," he explained, moving close behind me, flush with the back of my body, sending electric shocks careening through to my toes.

I spread my feet apart and stood still, staring at my target. Dingane didn't say a word but slowly used his feet to spread my own a little farther apart. My breath hitched in my throat.

"Comfortable?" he whispered in my ear.

I swallowed. *No.* "Um, yes."

Dingane stepped from behind me and the breath I'd been holding whooshed from my lips.

"Let me have the gun," he said and I handed it to him.
He started loading it and my already rapid pulse beat with unknown intensity.

"Make a circle with your thumb and forefinger, pick an object around you, hold it out at arm's length and find that object within the circle." He paused. "Got it?" he asked, still loading.

"Yes."
I chose his face.

"Keeping that object within sight, bring the circle toward your face. The circle should naturally gravitate to one eye."

"My left," I told him and he looked up.

"Mine too," he whispered. I dropped my hands to my side. "That's your dominant eye. You'll use that one to align your sights." He handed me the gun and stood behind me closely, gripping the gun with me. "This is very loaded."
You can say that again, I thought.

"Acknowledge me."

"It's loaded," I repeated.

Dingane fixed himself hard against my back and my eyes slid closed at his warmth and the feel of his solid muscles. He fixed my stance once more with his feet and I could feel the blood rush to my belly. His mouth rested against my ear and I could hear every breath he took, slow and steady.

"Align your sights," he spoke against my ear.
I nodded, my target within sight.

"Don't press yet," he teased.

"Why?" I barely rushed out.

"Don't pull. Never pull. Whenever you're ready, squeeze the trigger until you feel resistance, but let it surprise you. Don't prepare yourself for the bullet, concentrate on applying pressure directly and let it show you exactly what it feels like the second it releases from the gun."

I nodded and took several steadying breaths, keeping my target within sight. Time seemed to slow to a turtle's pace. The world swirled quietly around me; the only significant sound was the deep rise and fall of Dingane's chest.

My finger left its reclined position and rested on top of the trigger. My body tensed and I could feel his body cull itself tightly around mine in preparation. Two deep breaths and my lungs held still as my finger squeezed the trigger.

The world held still as the bullet rushed from the barrel toward the awaiting stump. The seconds to follow will forever brand themselves in my mind. The bullet struck home, shredding small parts of the stump outward in a halo of splinters, falling and settling onto the bed of dead undergrowth below. The bullet leaving the gun thrust my body against Dingane's, but he seemed prepared for it, holding me still against him.

When it was all done, the world rushed back to reality around me, the sights and sounds loud against my eyes and ears. I began to breathe deeply and Dingane slowly turned me toward him. I pointed the gun at the earth and faced him, staring directly in his eyes.

"You did well, Soph," he began softly. He'd never called me Soph before. "Feel all right?"

I nodded, unable to speak.

He kept eye contact but removed the gun from my hand, holstering it and returning that hand to my shoulder. He watched me intently and a deluge of emotions washed over his face. His eyebrows pinched together as if he was trying to fight something. Finally, his face relaxed then both his palms rounded my back and up my shoulders, fisting both my braids.

"They're falling out," I finally spoke.

"They always do at the end of the day," he added, never breaking his stare, inches from my face.

My eyes closed when he pulled the bands holding both braids and they slipped off into his hands. His fingers deftly freed both plaits painfully slowly all the way to the top of my head. Finally, I felt his fingers sift through the length to the ends.

"It's the favorite part of my day."

My eyes opened lazily. "What do you mean?" I whispered.

"When you undo them and run your hands throughout the waves. That's my favorite part of the day."

I inhaled slowly through my nose to keep from falling over at that revelation.

"I thought you hated me," I confessed.

He opened his mouth to answer, but we were startled from our proximity when the hand radio in the truck starting blaring incessantly.
"Dingane! Dingane!" we heard over and over.
"Shit," he said, squeezing his eyes closed. "I forgot to tell them we'd be shooting off the gun."

He ran toward the truck, leaving me there astounded by what just transpired between us.

The ride back to Masego was unbearably quiet, both content, it seemed, to revel in our own thoughts. My own were inundated with sifting through what had just happened. My eyes kept flitting between us and I found myself wishing we could finish what had barely gotten started.

"Karina's pissed," he said, startling me.

"Why?" I asked.

"I should have told her we'd be shooting off the gun. We scared her half to death."

Guilt overwhelmed me. "I'll have to apologize to her."

"Why should you apologize?"

"Because I shot off the gun."

"No, I'll do all the apologizing. It was my fault."

"I don't think..." I began but was cut short by the sight of Karina standing just outside the fence, two fists settled stiffly against her hips. "Uh-oh." Dingane sighed loudly.

"I know, I know," he said, exiting the truck and slamming the door. I followed suit.

"You two!" she said, storming over. I almost laughed out loud but stopped myself when I saw the expression on her face. Fear and sadness bathed it completely, sobering me. She grasped at her chest before reaching him and embraced Dingane with the fiercest hug imaginable. She waved me over and wrapped her arm around my neck. Both Dingane and I laid our hands on her back and stared at one another. We both felt so guilty.

"I'm sorry," we said in unison then broke into laughter.

"We're so sorry," I told Karina.

She distanced herself a little and wiped at her eyes.

"I was preparing myself for the worst." She audibly sighed. "I think Charles lost five years off his life. The whole family's in an uproar."

Guilt washed over us again. There was nothing to say.

"Come on," she said, wrapping an arm around each of us. "Let's go reassure everyone."

When we opened the gate we were engulfed by children, all worried.

"How do you say 'I'm sorry' in Bantu?" I screamed over their chatter.

"Most understand English, Soph." Dingane laughed and started touching their heads. After a few minutes of reassuring them, tiny heads bounced off to play before the sun set all except for one. Mandisa. I picked her up and rested her bony little behind on my hip. I didn't say anything, just hugged her and walked with Dingane toward the baobab tree. We three stood there watching the boys play soccer and the girls congregating or singing or jumping rope.

When the sun disappeared over the horizon, leaving the sky pink and orange, Kate, Ruth and Karina called them in for baths and to brush their teeth. It all felt so normal, so gloriously wonderful. It was too bad their lives were tainted with bouts of inexplicable violence. It made me that much more aware of why I was grateful Dingane taught me how to shoot.

I set Mandisa down to join the other children. She kissed my cheek and I almost cried.

I stood. "Thank you," I told Dingane, staring at the colorful sky.

"For what?" he whispered toward the same sky.

"For teaching me. Seeing them reminded me why I wanted to be able to defend them. They're defenseless. If it's ever up to me to guard their lives, I'd do it in a heartbeat. I couldn't possibly hesitate."

Dingane turned toward me and I faced him almost afraid of what he'd say, or more truthfully, what he wouldn't.

"You're welcome," he stated simply, disappointing me.

But then his gaze raked my face with such powerful intensity, I could feel it melt into my throat and shoulders, sending chills through me.

He closed the distance between us. "Will you be showering tonight?" he asked, surprising me.

"What? Why do you keep asking when I'm about to shower? Do you watch me or something?" I teased.

His face turned bright red. "Of course not!" he exclaimed loudly, which made me laugh.

"Then why?" I asked again.

"Goodnight, Soph," he said grinning, using that nickname again and heading toward his hut, which just so happened to be happily situated right next to mine.

"Goodnight, Ian," I told him.

He turned around and fought a smile, biting it away with his teeth.

I wasn't tired so I thought I'd help the women bathe all the girls. The chattering females made me smile as I approached the communal bathrooms. Seven stalls lined the walls as well as seven showerheads with poor plastic coverage. They always bathed the babies first and any girl who could properly wash herself was told to do so. The women just supervised. I joined Karina's and Kate's side. They were laughing about something when I approached them.

"What's so funny?" I asked.

"Oh, nothing," Karina explained. "So you learned how to shoot a gun, did you?" she asked wryly.

I bent my face toward the tile floor. "Yes."

"I'm glad."

My head whipped up. "Yes, I am glad. Every adult here should be able to. Though I wished I'd been informed," she chastised.

"I'm so sorry, Karina," I began, but she cut me off, wrapping her arm around my shoulders.

"Stop. I know you're sorry. That's the last you'll hear of it from me." She kissed my temple and I felt so incredibly loved.

"Karina?" I asked after a few minutes of silence.

"Hmm? Just a moment. Christine! No, dear," she said, stopping Christine from splashing Kate, whose back was to her. Christine frowned. "I'm sorry. What, my love?"

"Oh, I was just curious about something."

"What about?" she asked, distracted by Christine again.

"Why is Dingane so interested when I shower? I thought maybe you might know."

Her answer shocked me speechless. "He sweeps all the bugs out for you. He heard you say how you hated them," she absently remarked. "Excuse me, dear," she continued, heading for Christine.

I walked away in a daze, not believing it. *But he hates me. He may be attracted to me, that's obvious, but he doesn't care for me.*

I hit the dirt outside and made a beeline for the showers, the small outside light illuminating it in the middle of our makeshift village. When I rounded the corner, I shone the flashlight I carried with me into one of the rudimentary stalls. Insects. Everywhere. The wood walls were covered with them. I almost couldn't believe my eyes. Every inch seemed infested. I accidentally dropped my light and bent to pick it up. *That means he's been waking up extra early every morning and sweeping them out. Why would he do this?*

"He likes you, dumbass," I said out loud.

My lips twitched at the corners and I stood. I practically sprinted to our huts but just stopped myself from banging my fist on Ian's barely-there door. My hand fell to my side. I couldn't bring myself to confront him with the evidence. If he'd wanted me to know he was doing it, he'd have let me know. My teeth couldn't fight the smile plastered on my face. It was time for bed.

CHAPTER FIFTEEN

It was the best night's sleep I'd had since I arrived. I awoke early, grabbed my shower bucket and I ran across the cool morning air to the wood stalls and stared inside.

Clear.

I searched the grounds and spotted Ian's back on the other side of the baobab tree. His head raised as if he felt my stare and turned around, scouring the landscape around him. His eyes caught mine and the morning sun glinted off his bright blue eyes, making them even more vibrant. I inclined my head toward him and he nodded subtly in return. Butterflies drowned my empty stomach in flutters.

I showered, not even recognizing how cold the water was that morning like I did every other morning. When I dressed in my room and began plaiting my hair, my hands felt clumsy and nervous. I was so flabbergasted at myself. I couldn't believe I was acting the way I was. Me, the queen of control. The queen of attraction. *La Fée Verte*. The old name crept into my conscious and I dropped my hands, studying myself in the mirror. The prior giddy feeling I was so happy to enjoy a moment before felt terrible now. I realized I didn't deserve Ian. Recollecting all the terrible things I did back home made the wonderful butterflies die and nausea take their place. I steeled my hands, fighting back the feeling I was being swallowed by a black hole and finished my hair.

Karina's knocking at my door reminded me I was there to do a job.

"Sophie, my love, are you dressed?"

"Yes," I said, opening the door for her. Her face was white as a sheet. "What's wrong?" I asked, my stomach dropping to the floor.

"Mercy has measles."

"Measles? How? I don't understand."

"A nurse confirmed it late last night. She will live, I'm certain, but the young ones, none of them are vaccinated and two of the children have fevers," Karina explained, wringing her hands.

"Why couldn't you vaccinate?"

"We lack the resources."

"Okay, well, what does this mean? What do we do?"

"We call Pembrook."

This surprised me.

"What can he do?"

"There are a few options, but we have little time. He'd have to work with short notice."

I grabbed my satellite phone and checked the battery. It was nearly nonexistent. I dialed anyway and sat at the edge of my bed while Karina paced back and forth on my creaky floor.

"Hello," a shaky Pembrook's voice sounded.

I took a deep breath. It was so good to hear a familiar voice. "Pembrook!" I screamed into the bad connection.

"Sophie? Is that you?" The connection broke. "...are you?"

"I missed that last bit, Pemmy. I'm fine, if you asked. Listen, I need a favor. I'm running on low battery here and I need you to arrange for a shipment."

"What...for?"

"Measles has broken out here at Masego and none of the children are vaccinated. Karina says there are several options available to us. Can you get in touch with Ford and arrange something?"

Several seconds of silence followed and I feared we lost him. "...I'll contact you tonight. Charge....if you can."

"Thank you, Pemmy!" I yelled before the connection broke.

Karina sat next to me. We were silent for a few minutes letting everything sink in.

"What if he can't get anything?" I asked her.

Karina wrung her hands continuously. "We quarantine. We treat fevers. We hydrate."

I sighed loudly. "Jesus, Karina. When does it stop?" I turned toward her.

"It doesn't stop, love," she said, stopping and resting a hand on my shoulder, a wan smile gracing her beautiful face. "We do the best we can when we can and have faith it will all work out." I nodded. "Let's get something to eat and discuss what we need to do with Charles and Din."

We sat at the tables, my satellite phone resting in the center of our group.

"It's dying," I admitted, pointing to the phone.

"We really need a generator," Ian said quietly.

"We can't afford it, Din," Charles added.

"No one will have electricity nearby," Karina put in.

"And the closest city?" I asked.

"The closest city with guaranteed electricity?" Ian said.

"Yes."

"Jinja?" he asked Charles.

"Probably."

"How far is that?" I asked.

"Two and a half hours. Approximately."

"Pemmy could have called by then," I told them.

"True, but it's our only other option," Charles said.

Mandisa came to my side and I slid her onto my lap without thinking, resting my cheek on her head. "What if I turned it off, waited a few hours then rang Pemmy myself later. That way we could guarantee ourselves the information?"

"I don't think there's enough juice to boot it back up," Ian observed, "but nice."

"Nice what?"

"Thought. It was brilliant."

I rolled my eyes.

"I was being sincere," he said, offended

"Oh," I said sheepishly.

I turned toward the table once more and spotted Karina eyeing me with interest. I shrugged my shoulders in question, but she just grinned and shook her head.

"Then we go to Jinja," I conceded, slumping a little in my chair.

"I'll take over your classes," Karina said.

One of Mandisa's friends passed by and Mandisa scurried from my lap toward them.

"Silly girl," I muttered.

"She's fond of you," Ian said, when the others got up to get plates for themselves.

"I hope so."

"She loves you."

I whipped my eyes toward him. "You think so?" I asked softly.

"I know so."
This bolstered me like nothing ever could. If a child chose to love me even though I was so undeserving, did that mean I could earn Ian's love? Could I become worthy? I studied his beautiful pale face, framed with messy black hair and piercing blue eyes. God, he was so fascinating to look upon.

"What?" he asked, running his hands through his hair. "Do I have something on my face?" He smoothed his hands down his expression.

"No, nothing," I answered, standing up to grab a plate.
Ian got up and stood close behind me a few seconds later and I could feel the smile on my face grow to impossible lengths.

"Will Pembrook come through?" he asked the back of my head.
Now, I knew boys. Well. He knew Pemmy would try his best. He just wanted to talk to me and that brought the butterflies back.

"He will try his damnedest." I cleared my throat. "Have-have you been vaccinated?" I asked reticently, afraid of his answer.

"I was the last time I visited home."

"That's good," I said, relieved, lining the linoleum with the toe of my boot.

"Jinja's a dangerous drive," he stated.

"Why doesn't this surprise me?" I added sarcastically. "What is it about this bloody place? It's the land of every extreme possible."

Ian grabbed my arm unexpectedly, the heat from his hand warming me to an impossible temperature, and turned me toward him. "You're right but with extreme suffering, there is extreme happiness. With extreme earth there is extreme beauty."

I thought on what he'd said and remembered the view from my plane when I arrived. "You're right. Lake Victoria was one of the most beautiful sights I've ever seen."

"It's incredible."

"The children here are *extremely* loveable," I declared.

"Good one," he said, smiling. "That they are."

Four giggling girls walked by us arm in arm singing a traditional song, making my heart swell.

After breakfast, we grabbed the satellite phone and hopped in Ian's truck. I took note of the rifle strapped behind the seats and my blood began to pump, adrenaline flooding my body.

"It'll be all right," Ian assured me.

"How do you know?" I asked when he revved the engine.

"I don't," he said, "but I'll protect you."

My heart began to slow and my breathing steadied...because I believed him.

The truck was too loud to hold any kind of conversation and that disappointed me. I was dying to talk about whatever that thing was that happened between us at the watering hole. I was determined to get to the bottom of it as the sat phone charged.

The two-and-a-half-hour drive was ridiculous to me considering all we really wanted it for was electricity. Jinja was surprisingly well developed since all I'd ever seen from Kampala to Masego was undeveloped land excluding a random petrol station here and there. Ian told me it was the second largest city in Uganda. I had to keep myself from laughing while looking on it knowing those statistics. The main roads were paved, which was a rare sight, but they were poorly maintained and buckled in many spots. The establishments were plentiful but mostly one story. The roads were filled to the brim with bicyclists. Our truck seemed to be the only one among a handful in the entire city.

"The source of the Nile is here," Ian explained after parking in front of a promising-looking restaurant.

"Get out!" I exclaimed, genuinely surprised.
He opened the door for me and I stepped inside. We were the only ones. An Indian woman called us over.

"Excuse me," Ian said, "I wonder if you wouldn't mind if we trespassed on your kindness for a little while. My friend's phone is almost out of battery and we need to charge it. What would it cost us to use your electricity for, say, eight hours?"
She held up her hands to stay us and went behind a door, emerging with a pen and piece of scrap paper. She wrote down a number and I bent over to examine what she'd written. It read "2 American

dollar." I nodded at the figure and handed her two dollars from the small stash I'd brought. We set the phone up to charge and sat at a nearby table.

Suddenly things became uncomfortable between us. We both knew it was the only privacy we'd be afforded for some time and neither of us was bold enough to speak our minds. *This is so unlike me.* I stared out the dirty window before me, watching the men in dress pants and button-ups cycle along the streets. The woman interrupted the awkward quiet by setting a pot of tea and two cups at our table.

Ian thanked her and poured the tea over a sifter to catch the leaves, handing me a cup. Our hands touched and a spark of literal electricity shocked our hands apart.

"Static," I whispered. We stared at one another, our hands inches apart on the table. I brought my gaze down and inspected them. "Talk," I ordered finally, taking in his eyes again.

"The lesson." A breath whistled through his nose.

"I thought you hated me."

He shook his head, his hair falling a little into his eyes. "I don't hate you, Soph. I never did."

"Then why treat me like a pariah?"

He sat back but kept his hands flat on the table, his eyes searched me deeply.

"You're leaving." I nodded in acknowledgement. "In a few short months, you'll be gone, back to your life in America. I didn't *want* to be your friend."

I sighed loudly. "So that whole bit about knowing who I was, what kind of person I was. Was that bull?"

His eyes cast down. "No, I, uh, it wasn't." His eyes met mine again. "I'm just-I was quick to judge. I was wrong when I thought you couldn't change. So few can do it."

I brought my hands down and wedged them between my crossed legs.

"You think I've changed?"

"Sophie," he offered as if in explanation, his brows pulled tightly across his forehead.

Tears sprang silently and cascaded down my face.

"Soph," he said quietly, reaching for me, but I refused to budge. "You've been transformed for a while."

I choked back a sob. It meant so much to me to hear those words.

"Then why?"

"I told you. You're leaving. I feel like an idiot admitting to this but I confess, I don't do well when people leave. I promise myself I won't get attached. It's a defense mechanism in my line of work," he admitted with a slight smile.

"And now?"

"I-I would be honored to call you friend," he said succinctly, with an odd finality, as if he meant this as more a fact than an opinion.

I hadn't realized how much I'd wanted to be his friend. I'd never been respected by a man before, not truly.

Click.

And this was my new epiphany. Men wanted me. They all did, however briefly, but none of them wanted *to keep me*. That's what I needed. I needed to be owned, loved. But not by a man. I knew then that I never *needed* to be kept by a man. What I *needed* was to love myself, to want to keep myself around. And in that revelation, I knew that if I *wanted* to keep myself, that a man wanting to keep me would just be a by-product. Who wouldn't want to keep someone who respected himself or herself?

"And I would be honored for you to *call* me friend," I finally told him once I'd collected myself. His expression softened and he grinned at me.

"Your heart is startlingly beautiful, Sophie," he stated after a brief moment of fixed gazes.

My breath sucked into my chest at an alarming rate. There was no mention of my face, my legs, my ass, my breasts, my hair, my clothing, the way I carried myself, what I wore or how I wore it. There was no mention of me other than the part no one could even see. I'd been called beautiful so many times. It gratified me, validated me, but it was all empty, a facade. This was the first time someone had called me beautiful and it actually meant something to me. The praise slammed into my skin and permeated my body, leaving me flushed and overwhelmed.

My hands clenched on the table. I wanted so badly to rush him in that moment, to run my hands through his straight, silky, black hair and memorize his mouth with mine but something stopped me. I ignored the instinct, told myself that Ian was different. I decided I'd let him take the reins because I had never let anyone do that before. I was going to let him set the pace, let him discover me on his own. Giving him control gave me more power than I imagined I could own. Letting him worry about the next move was incredibly liberating and I knew with absolute certainty that the ride was going to be the best of my entire life.

Sophie Price had just learned self-control.

"Thank you," I told him softly, "very much. That has to be the best compliment I've ever gotten."

"Surely not," he said, puzzling over my quietude.

"It is."

"Curious," he said simply.

He leaned forward and rested his forearms farther up on the table, closer to my hands, gripping the edge. I removed one hand and picked up my cup, taking a small sip. The tea was surprisingly good.

"Tell me what your life back home is like," he asked.

I sighed loudly. Adrenaline shot through me. *Be honest,* I told myself. "I lied to the children," I began.

His brows pinched. "What do you mean?"

"That day, when Oliver asked me about my parents, I said they were nice." I gave him a small smile. "They most definitely are not."

Ian studied me carefully. "How?"

I braced myself. I knew I was about to unload on this guy. This perfect, unselfish boy who would probably want nothing to do with me after what I was about to reveal to him, but it didn't matter. It was my past. I couldn't just brush it under the table. "My parents are the epitome of self-involved. They are beyond wealthy, uninhibited, unwise, shallow, every combination of terrible you can think of.

"Since I was an infant, I was raised by a nanny. I was indulged to impossible levels and to my own detriment, I can admit now. At fourteen, I fired the nanny and my parents decided I could raise myself, so I did." I hesitated and Ian squeezed my hand. I was mesmerized for a moment as his fingers rubbed the tops of mine. Butterflies took over and my breathing became labored. I looked up at him and lost control of my thoughts.

"And?"

I was startled back to the present. "And I gave myself no boundaries. If I wanted to sleep with a boy, I did. If I wanted to try a drug, I did. If I wanted to drink to the point of excess," I began and trailed off.

"Go on," he said.

"My goal in life was to rule my tiny, elite world, so I did. I manipulated, used, disrespected and took advantage of every person I called friend. Don't get me wrong, none of us were saints by any means, but I led them all. I influenced them all. I pulled and played with their puppet strings. I was the ultimate puppeteer. I was cruel and unrelenting. I was no better than my parents."

I continued on with details of past indiscretions, ending with the day Jerrick died, the day I was caught with cocaine, my interaction with Officer Casey and even Spencer and his father. I confessed it all, spilled it at his feet and the sum of all my actions surprised even me. Humiliation filled my cheeks and I tucked my chin into my chest when I was done.

Ian sat back against his chair and his hands released mine, leaving them bereft of the boiling heat I was becoming so addicted to. The air left his chest in one whoosh and shame inundated me. My eyes burned. I steeled myself for rejection, for a reaction of disgust, pinching my eyes closed and turning my face toward the window of passersby, but it never came.

Eventually my gaze returned to him and he was staring at me, hard. "My parents are high-ranking political officials in Cape Town," he began, astonishing me. "I was raised by boarding schools during the school year and nannies in the summers. My parents only had time for their professions, so my brother and I found solace in many vices."

I was taken aback at this admission.

"What's his name?" I asked, suddenly and outrageously curious to know everything about Ian's life.

He half-smiled. "Simon."

"Go on," I said, borrowing his phrase.

"When I was seventeen, at a party, we were all drunk and I was caught in a *compromising* situation with another official's daughter. Smartphones were involved. Needless to say, lots of pictures were also involved. And the media had a field day with it. The girl was labeled a whore, I was labeled Cape Town's bad boy. My parents were not amused.

"I lived an utterly selfish existence up until that point, but when I saw Mel, the girl involved, when I saw her name in the headlines and the stigma it ended up attaching to her, I was thoroughly ashamed of myself. It had been my fault. I should have been looking after her.

"Poor Mel had to transfer to America to finish university. She's still there, from what I've heard."

I was shocked silent by his confession. I never, in my wildest dreams, thought Ian could have been defined as anything else but perfection, anything other than infallible. He was human after all.

"So how did you end up at Masego?" I asked him when he seemed to have trailed off into his own thoughts.

He took a deep breath. "My parents kicked me out. I was done with school. They'd done their part, or so they said they did. They cut me off after too many follies and I was shoved out. I had a friend named Kelly who worked with a gorilla rescue in the Congo. I joined her and one day we were called to Uganda, near Lake Victoria. Turned out, the police had confiscated three baby gorillas from poachers and they needed rescuing.

"I'd been with Kelly for six months and really enjoyed what I was doing. I felt like I was accomplishing some good, and I was, but while I was in Uganda, on our way to get the babies, the strangest thing happened." I was riveted and found myself leaning toward him. "We stumbled upon a little girl, no more than seven years old, walking by herself on the side of the road around two in the morning. We stopped to inquire if she needed help but she waved us off."

"Kelly was ready to keep going, but I insisted we help the little girl. I got out of the truck and approached her. She was obviously dehydrated and starving. I could see her ribs through her skin and my stomach wretched for her. I picked her up and put her in the cab with us. I asked her questions, but she was despondent, too distraught, too hungry, too *unable* to speak.

"We took her to Kampala with us, about an hour from where we'd found her, and where we were expected to retrieve the gorillas. While Kelly readied the truck to transport the animals, I took the little girl to get something to eat, to get her to drink and even paid some women at a nearby restaurant to bathe her while I fetched her something decent to wear. Her clothes were threadbare.

"When everything was done, the little girl looked brand new, happier. She finally spoke to me and told me her name was Esther. She told me her parents had died and her grandmother was only able to take care of one of one child, so the girl chose to have her grandmother look after her three-year-old brother."

Tears I'd been collecting fell in unison at the proclamation and Ian took my hand. "It has a happy ending," he said, smiling and I smiled back.

"We had stumbled upon her trying to *walk* to Kampala for help. I took the little girl and found out through the locals Charles' and Karina's names and number. I called them and they came to pick her up without hesitation. I never went back to the Congo with Kelly."

"Amazing," I whispered.

"They are," he answered.

"No," I balked. "I mean, yeah, they're amazing, but I was talking about you, Ian."

"Sophie, anyone would have done what I did."

"No, they wouldn't have, Ian."

He playfully rolled his eyes and shrugged off my compliment.

"Why Ian?" he asked after a few minutes of silence.

"Because," I offered without further explanation.

"I like it," he said, staring out the window.

"Why?"

"'Dingane' makes my heart ache to hear it."

I sat up a bit at that. "Why let them call you that then?"

"It means something to me every time they say it. It reminds me of who I am and who I never want to become again."

"What does it translate to?"

He sat up with me and peered hard into my eyes. “Exile,” he said succinctly.
I fell back then turned to realize that the sat phone was fully charged.

We’re not done, Ian Aberdeen, I told him silently.

And he knew it. I could feel it in the intoxicating charge in the air. He knew it.

CHAPTER SIXTEEN

I tossed an extra two dollars on the counter as we left the restaurant and the woman waved at us emphatically in appreciation. Ian and I walked silently toward his jeep, both pondering, I guessed, about the bombshells we'd just laid on one another. It was the first time we had ever been vulnerable to one another and it felt overwhelmingly powerful.

As we walked, I suddenly felt a whoosh of air as Ian pulled me toward him violently just in time for me to avoid the bicyclist who'd lost control and was barreling toward us. Ian grabbed me by the waist, swinging me away and rushing me back onto the sidewalk and against the outer facade of the restaurant we'd just been inside of. As he pressed me against him, that same flush-inducing heat creeped up my neck and face and one of his hands traveled to the back of my neck while the other rested on my hip. My heart beat into my throat but not from the narrowly missed collision. I was losing control of my reaction and that had never happened to me. I was always methodically in command of the way I let a boy affect me and had their reactions to me checked as well. Always in control. Proximity to Ian Aberdeen was my kryptonite.

"Are you okay?" he whispered.

Far from it, I wanted to say, gazing into his breathtaking face. "I'm fine, thank you," I said quietly instead, afraid of blemishing the moment.

We were walking a razor's edge and my blood pulsed dangerously in my veins, pooling at the skin where his hands rested, heating me up from the inside. He backed away slowly, but the muscles in his arms bunched as he forced his hands to leave my body. I felt alone too quickly, but there was nothing I could do. In my past life, I would have dragged him back to me, but I was no longer that Sophie so I followed his very delicate lead.

We hurried to the jeep and he opened the door for me before rounding the front and settling in himself. He started the engine, but I grabbed his arm before he could put it in gear.

"Wait," I told him.

"Yes?" he asked, breathing unusually hard and whipping his head my direction.

"I should call Pemmy for an update."

"Oh," he began before clearing his throat and facing the windshield, "of course."

My heart beat rapidly at his obvious disappointment. I watched him for a second as I pretended to dial Pemmy's number. *Kiss me then*, I kept ordering him silently, but he never obeyed. Instead, he gripped the steering wheel with such ferocity I believed he might bend it. I dialed Pembrook in earnest and got him on the second ring.

"Sophie!?" I heard on the other line.

"Pemmy! Yes, it's Sophie! We charged the phone, so it's got a full battery. If I use it sparingly, I think it could last a few days. Do you have any news?"

"Good...hear...the doctor...I've arranged a plane," he said, breaking in clearly. "They should be in Kampala in forty-eight hours with everything you need. I could only get clearance for medical supplies, Sophie, so let Karina know I couldn't include food or clothing this drop. I've arranged for armed escorts...delivery to Masego."

He broke out at this point and we lost connection. I tried again with no luck. I turned the sat phone off and tucked it into its canvas carrying bag before looking Dingane's direction.

"Did you hear him?" I asked.

He nodded. "Forty-eight hours," he spoke solemnly. "We'll have to quarantine in three sections. Confirmed cases, suspected cases and children showing no signs of illness."

"What are the odds we can keep most of them clean?" I asked.

"I've no idea." Ian turned to me. "It'll be you and me with the sickest children."

"We don't even know if any of them will be ill, Ian."

His face softened. "Sophie, that's an inevitability."

Ian put the jeep in gear and we sped off in the direction of Masego and into a pinkening sky. The sun would be leaving us soon, making me nervous for some reason I didn't know.

An hour after we'd left Jinja, the tension in the truck was palpable. So many emotions swirled around us and I wanted so badly for Ian to pull over and cut that tension with his mouth. I stared out my window, my elbow resting outside the window. I felt strands of hair whipping against my face. My braids had started to fall out. I checked the mirror to see if it needed to be let down or if I could just tuck in the strays. It was a mess.

I swallowed knowing the simple act of releasing my braids was more intimate a moment than I'd experienced in even my most vulnerable moments with other men. I looked over at him and brought my hand slowly to my left braid sliding the tie off painfully slowly. I wanted him to notice.

Ian's eyes flitted my direction, his breathing grew deeper and deeper, and I could feel the heat of his gaze pool in the pit of my stomach. I dropped the band in the seat next to me before lifting my hand to release the braid but Ian's warm, callused hand stopped mine. He slowed the truck a bit before threading his fingers over the top of my belt and sliding me closer to him. My eyes lidded and my breath rushed out of me. He turned me to face him and with his free hand, he undid each plait much like he'd done during the lesson. When he was done, he slowly lifted his fingers and cupped the side of my face, before turning his head toward me. I couldn't stop myself from placing my hand on his forearm and closing my eyes, reveling in his scorching touch. I took three steadying breaths and tried desperately not to melt into him.

I opened my eyes to look on him, but he glanced back to the road, narrowing his eyes slightly.

"No," he whispered as a body of light unexpectedly shone brightly into the cab. He whipped my body down and covered my head with his chest.

I was beyond shaken as he veered the jeep into a sharp turn, coming to an abrupt stop perpendicular to the road we were traveling.

Before I had a chance to react, he was shoving me out the passenger side door ordering me to keep my head down. Adrenaline leaked into my limbs and I obeyed without hesitation. With stealth-like speed I didn't think human, Ian slid out, tossing open the glove box and removing his revolver, cocking it and handing it to me without so much as a word before settling next to me. He sidled over to the back seat door and threw it open, leaning in to retrieve his AK just as the first bullet came whizzing over the top of the jeep. My heart froze in my throat and I ducked farther down, tucking myself against the side of my door. Ian shimmied out and slammed the door shut.

"Shit," I heard him say as he steadily unfolded the stock and clicked the magazine in place. "Keep your head down, Soph," he said, sliding to my other side and bracing his gun on the hood of the jeep.

Immediately, gunfire rang throughout the quiet night and my own revolver shook in my hands. Ian returned fire. After a minute, but what felt like an hour, I calmed myself down enough to grip my gun without trembling. I adjusted my body to set next to Ian's.

"Don't even think about it," Ian said coolly to the night in front of him before sending a spray of bullets our assailer's direction.

"I have to help you."

"No, you only fire their direction if they're upon us, Soph."

Another round of bullets screamed our direction, shattering the only closed back passenger window and hurtling above our heads. Ian crouched down long enough to meet my eyes and a million promises transferred in that brief moment. He tore his gaze from mine and raised himself abruptly, repositioning his gun before firing their direction.

"Hand me one of those magazines?"

It was dark but the headlights of our attackers' vehicle lit through the underbelly of our jeep and I spotted one of the magazines he asked for. I picked it up and handed it to him. He dropped the hot, used magazine to the ground and replaced it so quickly I barely registered it. He fired back within seconds.

"Who are they?" I asked.

"Thieves."

"With automatic weapons?" I asked in disbelief.

"Yes."

Ian unleashed an ungodly amount of bullets their way and they answered in kind. I covered my ears as best I could and tried so very hard to keep the tea down. Despite every attempt, I could not stop my body from trembling.

And just as quickly as it had started, it seemed to end. I heard doors slamming and their engine roaring to life, then their headlights disappeared. Ian hesitantly stood and I followed suit, sidling next to him and gripping his shirt in one of my hands. He tucked me behind him as we watched the attackers turn away from our jeep and go the other direction.

I could feel my blood returning to my extremities and they felt heavy, but it was short-lived when the men turned suddenly and came barreling our direction, firing bullets all the way.

Ian turned us into the side of the jeep and pushed us to the back before landing on top of me and burying my head into his chest. I could hear the attackers shattering the windshield with bullets before speeding off into the night. We laid like that for several minutes before he would let me raise my head. As soon as I raised it, he hugged me like we were dying. I gripped his back, desperate to be as close to him as possible, burying my face in his neck. It took a good fifteen minutes for our breathing to steady, but he still held me more tightly than I'd ever been held in my life.

He suddenly remembered himself and jumped up into a sitting position, searching my face and body, running his hands where his eyes roamed, checking for injuries and warming me up from the inside.

"Are you okay?" he finally asked.

I sat up and took in his own body. "I'm fine. And you?"

"Not a scratch," he said with a slightly shaky smirk, making my eyes burn in relief.

He grabbed me and hugged me to him again. "God, Soph," he breathed into my hair. "I was so worried."

That's when I noticed his body had finally accepted it was over and he began to shiver against mine as the adrenaline left him. He pulled me away and ran his hands across my face and through my hair, down my neck and rested them on my shoulders a moment before bringing my face back into his neck. We sat there in the dirt, holding each other, molding our bodies together as closely as we could get them, fear draining from every pore.

I couldn't believe how incredible he had been during the attack. I had never seen a man move like Ian, nor had I seen one so quick on his feet and easy to protect. It was the sexiest thing I'd ever seen in my entire life. It all came so naturally to him, I doubt

he even thought twice about each action. He was calculated and aware and amazingly hot.
My hands laid flat against the hard muscles in his back, still strained and warm from the danger we'd just endured. His t-shirt clung to him and I found myself running my hands up the ridges of muscles to his shoulders just to feel them before wrapping my arms around his neck.

He held me tighter when I encircled my arms. "The windshield is done," he breathed into my throat, bringing me back to reality.

I pulled my face back and ran my hands across his face. "Will we be able to drive?"

He followed my lead and ran his hands through my hair. "We'll have to cover our faces the best we can, the dirt will be overwhelming, but, yeah, we're only about an hour away from Masego."

A small tear fell down my face. "We almost died, Ian."

He wrapped his arms around my frame and brought my head to his chest. "We're alive."

"But..."

"Shhhh," he spoke into my hair, "I told you I'd protect you, didn't I?"

"You did," I confirmed into his shirt.

"I would *never* let anything happen to you, Soph."

Clarity came to me in that second because I believed him.
"Thank you," I whispered, bringing my face near his. "It's not enough, but I have to say it. Thank you for

saving my life."
"It was my absolute pleasure."

I giggled despite myself. "So polite."

"Trust me, Soph, I am trying really hard to be polite right now."

My brows furrowed. "Why?"

"Well," he cleared his throat. "You're, uh, you're sitting on my lap."

"Oh." I blushed. Actually blushed! Sophie Price, who hadn't blushed since she was a schoolgirl, felt embarrassed!

I scurried off his lap and he stood, offering his hand to help me up. He reached into his glove compartment again and pulled out a flashlight, lighting up our small area with a click. We examined the damage. Since most of the windows were down except one of the back passenger windows, none shattered but that one and the windshield. There were bullet holes riddling the sides of the jeep but when Ian lifted the hood, the engine appeared to be unscathed.
"Thank God," he breathed.
"Agreed."
Ian rounded the side of the jeep and picked up his guns, placing them back in the glove box and the back of the vehicle. He grabbed an old t-shirt in the backseat and effortlessly ripped it in two.

"Here," he said, handing me one half of the shirt, "tie this 'round your mouth and nose."

I grabbed it and nodded. Following his lead, I wrapped it around my face and cinched it as tightly as I could behind my head.

"We look like we're about to rob a bank," I told him.

He chuckled and the corners of his eyes creased with the smile I so rarely earned. It was a shame I couldn't see it for myself. He sighed loudly and opened my door for me. I hopped up and buckled myself in.

The drive to Masego was terrible, dirt flew in so badly it created a thick coating on our skin and clothing but we could breathe at least, despite how difficult it made it to see. It took twice the amount of time to get home because Ian had to drive slowly enough that rocks and debris couldn't harm us too badly.

It was after eleven when we got home, so no one was there to let us in. I got out with Ian this time and helped him open and close the gates.

"I don't want to scare Karina with the sight of this truck, so I'm going to park it where it's semi-hidden."

"She's going to see it anyway," I mused.

"Yeah, but hopefully she'll see me first and it'll give me a chance to explain."

"Ah, I see. Should we go ahead and wake them up?"

"I don't see the point. The plane won't be here for another two days. Let them sleep."

The grounds seemed peaceful and that made my heart and soul quiet down a bit from the night's near catastrophe. Ian brought the truck behind our hut, out of view from Karina and Charles' cabin and we got out. He removed his half of the now filthy t-shirt. I struggled with mine so he came around and helped work through the knots.

"Good Lord, Soph, how did you do this? Your hair is caught in it." He laughed again.

"Note to self," I said out loud, "Ian is happiest when in dangerous situations."

He whipped my body around and his mouth gaped open, but it still couldn't hide his grin. "What does that mean?"

"You've laughed twice tonight. That's the most I've seen you laugh, especially if none of the kids are involved with their daily shenanigans."

"So you watch me then?" he flirted, edging closer.

"About as much as you watch me," I flirted back.

"I-I, uh-," he stuttered.

"That's what I thought," I teased.

"Are you to grab a shower?" he asked.

"No, I am not *to grab a shower*. I was hoping to swim in this filth all night."

"Sarcasm noted."

He smiled and it was the most glorious thing I'd ever seen. I fought the urge to grab him and run my tongue along his teeth.

"Grab your stuff," he continued. "I'll meet you there."

He startled me, but I didn't let it show. I hurried to my half of the hut and tossed my shampoo, body scrub, etc. into my bucket before grabbing my robe. I practically ran to the showers and caught Ian mid-sweep.

"I knew you did this, by the way," I told his back, stunning him still.

His shoulders sagged and he turned around and smirked. "How?"

I wasn't about to rat Karina out. "It's shockingly free of creepy crawlies every day, Ian?"

"I suppose that seems a bit lucky."

"Thank you," I told him quietly.

"At first I did it because I didn't want to hear you complain."

I approached him and blocked him into the stall. "And now?"

He swallowed but looked me dead in the eye. "Because I want to." The intimacy of his stare shocked me silent, my mouth gaped. "I'll be right back," he told me.

I stepped aside, against the edge of the wood stall, to make room for him but his massive body still slowly grazed mine, stealing my breath away. I locked myself in and undressed, tossing my clothing over the side and setting my bucket on the stone beneath my feet.

I turned on the water and immediately began rinsing off my face. The water was cool but not cold. I welcomed it as I could feel the dirt leaving my body. It trailed down my legs and pooled near the drain in an orange haze. I closed my eyes and let the water rinse away the night. I turned my face from the stream and began to wet my hair. When I opened my eyes, Ian was in the stall across from mine astonishing me yet again for the umpteenth time that evening.

He was staring at me, the water slicing down his head and down his shoulders. The stalls were too high to expose anything more. He could only see my face and top of my head but just knowing we were both naked and within ten feet of one another was enough to make me flush from head to toe. He was breathtaking. Breathtakingly sexy. Breathtakingly beautiful. Breathtakingly real. Just breathtaking.

"Hi," I choked out.

"Hi," he said, flirtatiously smiling.

I couldn't look at him anymore, so I bent to grab my shampoo. After pouring a handful, I stood and purposely avoided his eyes, though the heat of his gaze was enough to make the water boil. I worked the soap through my hair from root to tip twice before almost losing it or worse, giggling uncontrollably. I ducked under the running water to rinse and caught his stare again.

I smiled the largest smile I owned because I just couldn't help it anymore.

"I'd give anything to wash your hair for you," he said suddenly, rocking me to my core and wiping that silly grin right off my face.

"I'd give anything for you to do just that," I told him candidly. This time he smiled and grabbed his own shampoo bottle.

He shampooed his hair and I bit my bottom lip to keep from saying something stupid like, "Let me help you" or "Let's conserve some of this water we're wasting." I blushed once more and he noticed.

"What?" he asked.

"Nothing," I said, turning to my bucket and grabbing my face soap.

I scrubbed my face much more thoroughly than I suppose was necessary, but I just couldn't look at him anymore. He was torturing me just by existing. I rinsed the soap from my face and grabbed my conditioner, applying a generous amount and letting it set in my hair while I used the loofah on the rest of my body. My smile just kept getting bigger and bigger and embarrassingly bigger. I tried to avoid looking at him but his laughing did nothing to help matters much.

Finally, when I'd rinsed every last drop of soap from my body, I stood underneath the shower and began to rinse the conditioner. I looked his direction and it was obvious he was done but he was sticking around for the free show.

"Still here?" I asked.

"If the situation were reversed?" he countered.

I closed my eyes. "I'd still be here," I told him, smiling again.

When I opened my eyes again, he'd rested his forearms on the top of the edge of the stall, the water still cascading down his incredible skin. We kept up eye contact until the conditioner was long gone, no trace of it whatsoever anymore, but I continued longer than I should because it was Ian Aberdeen and his royal hotness was just as enthralled with me as I was with him. Eventually, I turned the water off and he followed my lead. I began to towel dry my hair and he wrapped his around his waist. I slipped on my robe and flip-flops.

We both stood there waiting for the other to get out. Neither of us wanting the incredibly frustrating but totally exhilarating past few minutes to end. Finally, Ian made a move, unlocking his stall door. I followed his lead and met him in the center of the stone walkway between our stalls.

"Hi," he said, peering down at me.

"We've done that."

"We have?" he asked, distracted.

"Yes," I said, my eyes riveted by his lips.

He breathed heavily out his nose. "I'll walk you to your side of the hut now."

"'Kay."

"I'm going to escort you." He paused, staring at my face. "Any second now." Another pregnant pause as his eyes guided down my neck. "Just as soon as I can uproot my feet from this stone, I'm going to walk with you." He smiled taking in my face again.

I fought a smile of my own when he grabbed the lantern hanging on the hook above us, his broad chest expanding right in front of my face. We stood still for a minute.

"Come on," I told him, walking away first.

He quickly caught up with me and held the lantern ahead of us. We didn't say a word on the short hike to our hut. We didn't even glance each other's direction. I walked right to my side and went inside, turning to say goodnight but he'd already gone into his side, leaving me disappointed and just a teeny bit pissed.

I lit the small candle on my washstand and dressed in yoga pants with a long-sleeve fitted tee. I draped my wet towel at the foot of my bed and tossed my robe on its hook. I kept my flip-flops on because it was Uganda and you never took your shoes off ever. I'd just finished brushing my teeth and hair when I heard a faint knock on my door.

My heart leapt into my throat. "Yes?" I barely choked out.

"It's me," Ian said quietly. "Can I come in?"

I glanced around my room a little bit frantic. I backed up a bit and stood beside my bed. "Come in."

Ian tore through the door, the rush of wind snuffing out the candle, and stood looming over me in my small side of the hut. The door swung behind him and shut with a crack, startling me.

And just like that, Ian Aberdeen rushed me.

He grabbed my face and neck with his rough hands and brought me to him, practically lifting me to his lips. He devoured my mouth with his and I moaned into his mouth, spurring him on. His tongue found mine and it was warm and tasted of cinnamon.

A rush of adrenaline spiked through my body and pooled in my belly. I wrapped my arms around his neck and he brought me closer to him, threading his fingers through my hair, rooting his fists at the back of my head, pulling lightly as if it was taking all his control not to throw me down on the bed. This made my eyes roll into the back of my head and I tightened my already closed lids.

He tore his lips from mine and we stood panting, the stars barely shining through the cracks in the door but enough to light up his face. I recognized his painfully strained expression. He didn't know if what he'd done was okay with me, and I found myself so attracted to him for being so considerate. To reassure him, I ran my hands across his forehead to smooth out the lines.

"Ian," I whispered before he attacked me again, hushing me on the "n."

I gripped his shoulders as he harshly kissed my lips then followed my jaw line down my neck, making my head fell back. "Sophie," he sighed between each kiss, making my toes tingle. His mouth found mine again and I kissed him back hard, breathing him in as best I could. My hands found his hair and I pushed them through the length until they met his neck then climbed back up, entangling my fingers in the damp mass. It felt like I couldn't get close enough to him. I wrapped one leg around his calf and he groaned into my tongue, vibrating the back of my throat. I shivered.

"Oh, God," I breathed into his mouth.

He smiled against my teeth and it was the sexiest thing I'd ever felt. "You taste like cherries," he told me. His voice shivered against my skin, making me smile back.

He rested his forehead against mine. "You taste like cinnamon," I countered.

He pulled himself away and immediately I hated it. "Goodnight, Sophie Price."

He backed away from me slowly, never breaking his stare or his smile. He opened the door and let it fall shut again. "Sleep well," I heard through the cracks.

I brought my fingers to my smiling lips and ran them across the swollen skin. "You too," I answered so softly I barely heard it myself.

I'd been kissed before, many times, but *never* like that.

CHAPTER SEVENTEEN

I woke up in the middle of the night and felt like I'd fallen asleep next to a blasting heater. In a sleep-induced haze, I figured it was just the warming temperatures outside. As strange as it seemed for Uganda's summer to be during America's winter, I was expecting it but I realized with a start that the unusual warmth was just a bit too hot.
I lazily opened my eyes and they were met with a dull pair of brown ones. I shot up.

"Mandisa!" She wasn't responding to me and my heart leapt in my throat. "Mandisa, baby." I pushed her growing hair out of her eyes and tried to get her to look at me, but it did no good. I jumped to my feet

and pushed my door open. It was still dark out.
"Ian!" I yelled, panicked.

Immediately, a disheveled Ian appeared next to me. "What's happened?" he asked.

Tears began to spill. "It's Mandisa," I explained, pointing to my bed.
He ran to her side and felt her head and neck. "She's burning up."

"The kitchen!" I said, thinking of the nearest running water source.
Ian scooped tiny Mandisa in his arms and he practically swallowed her small frame.
We ran around the baobab tree to the kitchen and I started running the cool water, plugging the drain. The stainless steel tub was large enough to submerge her.

I tossed a bunch of kitchen towels in the sink to cushion her and Ian rested her in the water. The cool water was shocking enough she should have protested but not a peep came from her tiny lips and I found myself taking my panic to the next level.

We frantically doused her to get her temperature down.

"Sweetheart?" I asked her after a few minutes but she didn't respond. "God, Ian," I breathed out.

"I'll get Karina," he said and ran off toward hers and Charles' cabin.

I continuously covered her in the cool running water and prayed like I'd never prayed before. I begged her under my breath to respond to me, but she just stared blankly ahead and my heart sank into

my stomach.
"Where is she?" a sleepy Karina said.
"In here," I heard Ian explain.
Karina came to my side quickly and brushed the hair from my shoulder with her hand, assuring me the way a mother would. "Ian," she said, looking down on Mandisa. "Grab my kit, please?"
Ian ran from the room and returned with Karina's big bag of remedies she kept handy at all times.

She pulled out a needle and looked over at me. "It's just an acetaminophen injection because she won't chew medicine."

I nodded as if my approval was even needed, but Karina gave me that respect anyway. She filled the needle and Ian helped me lift her shoulders. Karina dried and swabbed the little fleshy part of Mandisa's arm with alcohol then injected the medicine. I felt an almost immediate sense of relief knowing we were tending to the outside and Karina was tending to the inside.

Karina felt the water in the basin and asked Ian to drain it as Mandisa's body temperature was making it warm. He did as she asked then plugged the drain once more. "Keep pouring that water over her head, Sophie."

Ian and I worked methodically, pouring and draining, draining and pouring. Twenty minutes passed and Mandisa was noticeably cooler but still unresponsive.

"Why isn't she getting better?" I asked.

"The medicine will make her sleepy," Karina explained before grabbing my shoulder and turning me toward her. "She's also very sick, Sophie."

Karina took her temperature and it was within a safer range so Ian grabbed a large towel and wrapped her little body up. I grabbed a clean smock from the laundry that looked like it would fit her and helped Karina change Mandisa into it. When she was all dry, I made Ian take her to my hut to sleep while we figured out where we were going to put everyone.

Karina left to check on all the children in their dorms to make sure no one else had fevers.

"My heart is in my throat," I said quietly after Ian tucked Mandisa in my bed.

He covered her loosely in my sheet and we silently watched her. He wrapped his arm around my shoulder and the flood of memories from the night before surfaced, reminding me that I was allowed to hug him. I grabbed him and buried my face in his chest, so grateful for his comfort. He ran his hands down my hair and kissed the top of my head, making me sigh.

A low knock sounded at the door and we pulled apart abruptly. It was apparent when our eyes caught that we didn't want to reveal ourselves to Karina, or anyone for that matter, until we had actually figured out what we were to each other.

"Come in," I said, and Karina entered.

"Three more," she explained, all life drained from her eyes.

"Sophie and I will take care of the ill, Karina. We've been vaccinated. We talked to Pembrook yesterday and he's arranged for a plane that should be here in within thirty-six hours."

"Thank God," she whispered, grasping her heart. "We'll set all the ill in our cabin then."

"Those unaffected should stay in the dorm, but those we suspect may be getting ill need to be sectioned off as well," Ian said.

"Solomon and Ruth's, maybe?" I offered.

"Where will they stay?" he asked.

"They've left with their children to Ruth's sister's house," Karina told us.

"I can understand that," Ian offered in disappointment.

"When she wakes," Karina said, pointing to Mandisa, "move her to our house."

Ian nodded and Karina was gone.

We looked at each other and so many emotions flitted between us. In Ian's eyes I read the gravity of the storm that was brewing on our doorstep, selfish disappointment that we couldn't explore what was going on between us and obvious shame in that he thought of himself when he shouldn't have been.

I couldn't blame him because I was thinking the same thing. I grabbed his hand to reassure him that it would happen, that we'd get our day. He smiled softly and that was all the time we allowed to acknowledge that disappointment. We had bigger fish to fry.

The next day and a half was pure chaos. Mercy was the only adult who seemed to be affected unless the virus was still incubating, but that was okay with us just as long as the vaccines came soon. Ian and I spent the next night repeatedly up and down, caring for very ill children, reducing fevers, treating symptoms and working our fingers to the bone in a futile attempt to disinfect.

Every few hours we'd get a new kid. We were running out of fever reducers and saline bags. Our only hope was the shipment and that was arriving later that second evening. We got hold of Pemmy once more and he informed us that I, personally, would have to sign for the shipment at seven.

Karina agreed to help us get the infected children in the best possible place before we left and she would sit with them until Ian and I could get back. In total, we had seven ill children, and four we suspected would eventually become ill. The remaining, we kept as far away as possible.

When we were as prepared as we could possibly get, we made our way to Charles' truck. Karina had yet to see Ian's jeep and we wanted to keep it that way. Charles was nervous the news of our attack would send his wife over the edge, so we repaired it as much as we could with what little we had and kept it hidden.

When he started the engine, it was quieter than Ian's rumbling jeep. I rested the back of my head against the seat and closed my eyes, yawning. When I opened them and peered back at Ian, he laughed.

"You're exhausted."

"No shit, Sherlock."

He laughed louder, making my heart sputter. "Irritable when you're tired, are we?"

I smiled across the seat at him. "Irritable, are we?" I mocked, pathetically attempting his *Sith Ifrican* accent, which made him laugh even harder.

"Just a bundle of laughs today," I teased, drawing out my words from sleepiness.

"Well, I'm a bit delirious with the only," he pitched his brows toward the roof of the jeep, "seven hours of sleep I got in the past two days."

I yawned loudly at the mere mention of sleep. I leaned my head against the window. "Classes are cancelled for two days after the kids recover. I'm making an executive decision and I'm going to sleep for both of them."

"As long as I get to sleep with you."

My eyes bugged from my head. "Pardon?" I asked in disbelief.

Ian stared at me, eyes wide. "I-I just meant...I meant that, uh, that I also wanted to sleep with you."

I laughed out loud.

"I mean, not *with* you but sleep in my own bed during the time in which you also sleep...in your bed. We'd be asleep in two separate beds. You in yours and me in mine." One of his hands left the steering wheel and ran the length of his face. "God, I'm deprived." A quick glance my way. "Of sleep! Deprived of sleep!" His hand slapped the wheel. "God, shut up, Din."

I smiled at him softly. "I got you, Ian." *Boy, do I ever.*

It's not surprising I slept most of the way to Kampala. We arrived shortly before the plane was scheduled to land and rushed into the airport.

"Does this bring back memories?" I asked Ian.

He smiled. "It certainly does."

"You hated me."

"I definitely did not hate you."

"Oh, just admit it. You kind of did."

"I didn't think you were worth Masego's time."

"Ouch. I guess I kind of deserved that."

"Don't get me wrong. I made a rash judgment. It also didn't help you were so goddamn beautiful."

My breath sucked into my lungs and I couldn't think to respond, so I let him grab my hand and lead me through to the tarmac just as our plane descended. I felt a weight lift from my shoulders when the tires touched down. Our hands broke and we rushed the cargo plane. I didn't want to think what it cost to arrange for that. When the hatch lowered and the deck collapsed, tears spilled down my face.

Pembrook, dressed in the most ridiculously hilarious outfit I'd ever seen him in, jeans and a flipping t-shirt, struck ground. The same ground I stood on, Pembrook stood upon and I felt like a little piece of home had followed him. I may not have had the best home life, but it was all I had ever known before Uganda. I was well-traveled, yes, but they aren't lying when they say home is where the heart is.

My cheeks flushed as I turned toward Ian who approached Pembrook as I stood mute a few feet behind. He was my new home. Ian was home. Butterflies rushed throughout my entire body and my hands clenched the shirt that lay at my stomach. *Oh my God.*

Pembrook waved my direction and approached me. I met him halfway and yelled over the deafening engines. "Pemmy! I didn't know you'd be here."

"Neither did I, but I thought I'd take a few days off and check on you. Report back to your father that you're still alive."

"Thank you, Pemmy, but we both know my father doesn't care how I am."

"That's not...." he began, but I cut him off.

"I'm still glad you came."

He smiled warmly and hugged me hello. I realized then that Pembrook was my family. "It's good to see you too, Sophie," he said, patting my back. He pulled me from his arms and examined me. "You look...well, not dead."

Ian and I both laughed. "We've been up caring for ill children, Pembrook, cut me some slack, will ya?" I teased. He watched me for a moment as if he wasn't sure if it was me or not and that made me laugh harder.

He cleared his throat. "Yes, yes. It's why I'm here. Follow me," he ordered and marched up the hatch into the hull of the plane. "I took the liberty of getting as much as I could think to replenish what supplies you've already used as well as for future use."

My eyes took in the boxes and boxes of saline, different meds, needles, sterile gloves, etc. and I almost cried. I lovingly ran my hand across the top of the saline boxes. "I'm so grateful."

"For what? You asked. You're my, ahem, employer and I complied."

I turned and rolled my eyes at him. "Thank you anyway, employee Pembrook. You went above and beyond the job requirement."

He smiled in answer.

"I'm going to see if I can get permission to bring Charles' truck around. Be right back," Ian said.

I watched Ian walk away and continued to watch him until I could no longer see him.

Pemmy cleared his throat, snapping me away from my stare. I turned to him.

"Are you happy?" he asked simply.

"I am," I answered without hesitation, startling even myself with how easy it was to admit it.

Suddenly an idea took hold. Christmas. It was only six weeks away. It was going to be my first warm Christmas. My family had always flown to Switzerland for the holiday for no other reason other than my mother's friends vacationed there together.

"Listen, before Ian returns."

"Ian?" he asked, amused.

I waved him off. "Dingane, whatever." But paused, an overwhelming need to defend him bubbled forth. "His name is Ian, you know."

"Is it?" he asked, stupefied.

I felt my face warm. "Yes, anyway, before he comes back, I need to arrange to have a plane return here in a few weeks time. Can we make that happen? You're a signer on my account. You can use my private funds if my dad won't let you otherwise."

"I don't think that's necessary," he said, bemused. "Your father has given me carte blanche to give you whatever you need."

"Honestly?"

"Yes, Sophie. What do you need?"

I breathed a sigh of relief. "A generator, first and foremost. For God's sake, a flipping generator big enough to run an orphanage for weeks at a time. Something substantial as well as the necessary hands to install it." I ticked hundreds of things off my mental list, a list I didn't even know I'd been keeping mindful of. *Huh*. I snapped my fingers. "You know what? I'd also like you to arrange for a construction company to rebuild the main house with an up-to-date kitchen, big enough to prepare meals for at least a hundred children, bring the supplies as well as the hands from America."

My imagination was running wild. Pembrook had filled pages of the little pad he'd been writing my demands in. He occasionally shook his hand out, but I kept going, afraid I'd forget it once it slipped from my tongue. I imagined a much better Masego by the time I would have to leave.

Have to leave.

I'd forgotten. I was going to be leaving Masego in a few short weeks. I had two months left. That was all. A feeling of dread filled me.

"And I'd like boxes of shoes," I mentioned frantically, "more than they'll need, enough to fill a room with, including clothing, smocks for the girls, uniforms for the boys, varying sizes. Call TOMS Shoes in Dallas, let him know what you're doing, they'll help."

I chewed my thumbnail, something I never did. I would tell Pembrook all the time how it ruined a girl's nails and only trash did it. I noticed him regard me and I pulled it from my mouth.

"Is-is that all?" he asked, obviously stunned.

"Toys. Wrapped. For some reason, the only thing the girls here like to play is house. So lots of that crap. The boys can think of nothing but soccer. Make sure we get them before Christmas. Is two weeks prior sufficient?"

"Yes."

It got silent as I continued to pace the width of the plane. I looked up and noticed Pembrook's mouth gaping.

"What?" I asked.

"Nothing," he said, examining his lengthy list, but I knew him well enough to recognize I'd astonished him. I felt a slight pang in my chest that I could have possibly made him proud.

I heard Charles' truck rumble near the hatch of the plane and I turned to Pembrook. "Not a word, cool?"

He nodded in acknowledgement.

Ian and I helped the crew load everything Pembrook had brought and when it was as full I'd ever seen it, Pembrook hugged me tightly. "Give Charles and Karina my love?"

I nodded, afraid if I said anything I'd cry. Pembrook shook Ian's hand and we watched him disappear behind the rising hatch. "He loves you," Ian said.

A tear slipped free. "I know."

CHAPTER EIGHTEEN

Apparently, four more children had gotten ill during the nine hours we'd been away when we arrived around five in the morning. When all I had been thinking about was sleep, Karina approached us both with two giant cups of coffee. I selfishly cringed but quickly scolded myself. We all unloaded the supplies and readied to inoculate all the children.

We administered vaccines to all the adults then sent them on their way to set up stations at all three quarantines. I secreted one off to Mandisa and stuck her as soon as I possibly could. I wanted her to get better immediately. Selfish, I know, to put her before any of the other children, but I felt like Mandisa was mine. I can honestly say I didn't regret it.

After each child received their shot, we replaced empty saline bags and treated fevers just as the sun was rising.

"That's almost twenty-four hours straight without sleep," Ian sleepily said, stumbling toward me in Charles and Karina's cabin. He fumbled across the sofa I was strewn across and laid next to me, his eyes closing quickly.

"Careful, Aberdeen," I lazily drawled, a secret smile gracing my lips.

He grinned, his lids still seemingly fused. He knew exactly what I'd meant. "I will," he promised around gleamingly white teeth, throwing an arm over my shoulders. The smile slowly slipped from his lips and his breathing deepened and steadied. Then it was my turn, though I'm sure my smiled stayed.

Around two in the afternoon, I woke to children's laughter and a heavy arm laid across my back. I peeled open one lid and faced the back of the couch. I quickly shut them, my nose scrunched together in an effort to keep them closed, and listened for a moment.

"What are they doing?" I heard Mandisa ask someone.

"They're sleeping, Mandisa, leave them be," Karina answered. Her voice was lighter and I breathed a sigh of relief. I could tell the vaccines were working because Mandisa was lucid. My heart soared.

"He will bury her," she offered.

"He will not," Karina said, giggling. She was in the kitchen, stirring something in a metal pot. I could hear the gentle rhythm of the spoon scrape the bottom back and forth.

"He will. He is too big. He is going to kill her."

"*Mandisa*," Karina playfully admonished.

"We get him off her."

"Mandisa, come over here and sit on this chair," Karina ordered.

"I can't leave. I have to watch he does not cut off her air."

"I have crayons," Karina tempted.

I heard hesitant little feet walk to the table. She began coloring and I could hear each individual stroke against the wood tabletop.

"They are married?" Mandisa asked after a few minutes. I was forced to bite my lip to keep from bursting out in laughter.

"No," Karina answered.

"But his hand is on her back."

"I'm sure it was an accident, Mandisa. He wasn't trying to be disrespectful to her. They were probably very, very tired from caring for you and your brothers and sisters last night."

"It is okay this time then," Mandisa concluded.

"Yes, because it was an accident," Karina said, though a bit too loudly.

My shoulders shook with silent giggles until Ian's fingers bit down slightly on the skin of my shoulder, sending tingles down my arms and sobering me quickly from the flush the touch his hand gave me. His face was buried in my left side and I felt the slightest brushed kiss against my shirt there. It was warm and sweet and sent my eyes rolling into the back of my head. I stifled a shudder and awaited his next move. His thumb stroked small circles against the shoulder bone there, so softly the movement didn't even register with my eagle-eyed babysitter. It sent me into an internal frenzy. I wanted so badly for him to tuck me into his side tightly and kiss my neck until I fell to pieces.

I sighed softly, inaudibly, and felt Ian grin into my shoulder. He was so unbelievably sexy and I didn't think he was even trying. I stilled my body in preparation for whatever he had planned and I thought I was ready for anything. Anything *except* what he did next.

I felt his warm breath, concentrated on it, reveled in it even, right before he softly bit through my shirt and caught a bit of skin gently. My breath caught in my throat and I swallowed hard. He caught the movement and I felt his chest inhale quickly against my back.

"Don't move," he whispered so softly I barely heard him.

My body felt cemented in place next to his, as if his mere suggestion dictated law and I was powerless but to obey. It sent a thrilling buzz permeating throughout my abdomen and chest, tingling right through to my toes.
"Feel this," he told me before letting his fingertips flow like water over the curves of my hand laying flat on the sofa, out of sight.

I closed my eyes and let the drugging, lazy sensations of his touch drag through my limb, sedating it to the point of numbness. It was such a heady, provocative feeling. I felt my cheeks blush bright pink. My body flushed with warmth every single time the tip of his finger found the curve of my thumb and again when he reached the pad of my ring finger. He chased that warmth so slowly, seemingly stretching time, and traced it like he didn't have a care in the world...except for me.

My chest swelled with something I couldn't quite peg but I let it saturate my soul and heart anyway because it was the best feeling I'd ever felt and I would have paid any amount of money for it to continue.

We were suddenly startled when we heard the cough of one of the kids in Karina's bedroom and we both bolted upright, ready to aid them.

Karina looked on us softly and smiled. "I've got it. Lay back down," she said kindly.

When she left the room, Mandisa followed. Ian sat in front of me but moved to face me and I looked on him differently than I had the night before. My hand moved to his face and my fingers sketched his solid chin around to his high cheekbone and up to his temple. I dragged my thumb down the bridge of his nose and over the tops of his lips. His bottom lip caught a bit and it briefly exposed his perfect teeth. I pressed both hands to his cheeks and stared into his eyes when he lifted his own arms and dragged his fingers through the hair at my temple, fisting it into the length at the sides of my head. He held them there, staring back.

We heard Karina move toward the door and I could tell we were both loath to stop touching one another. Skin to skin felt so right, so, so, right. Our hands gently fell away and the pull to put them back was overwhelming. We both stood for a moment, intensely staring, then Ian walked past me without a word toward Karina's room, greeting her at her bedroom door.

"Good morning, Din," she told him.

He kissed her cheek. "Good morning, Karina." He walked past her into her bedroom, probably to check on whoever was coughing and Karina approached me.

"Good morning, my love," she said, embracing me tightly.

"Good morning."

"I know about Din's jeep," she spoke into my hair.

My stomach fell to the floor. "Oh, uh, about that..."

"It's okay," she said, brushing my hair back. "I'm grateful you decided to wait to tell me. I don't think I could have handled it all at once." She smiled sweetly and I kissed her cheek.

"How are the children?" I asked.

"Miraculously improved," she stated with a wink.

I couldn't stop the smile blasting across my face, not that I wanted to. "What a relief," I sighed, sagging back onto the sofa.

"I'm so grateful," she said, her eyes glassing over.

"Me too," I told her, patting her weathered hand relaxed on the armrest. "I'm incredibly grateful," I said quietly, but the phrase meant so much more than it implied.

Over the next few days, life returned to normal at Masego, our inventory was restocked, children gained energy and classes resumed. Ian and I didn't get to sleep for two days, but we did get back into some sort of routine and that made it easier to stay rested. We would check daily for footprints encompassing the fresh water source and the small wooded area near the property where Ian taught me how to handle a gun. We were lucky in that we found nothing. We were more certain every day that whoever had come previously was just passing through.

Ian and I flirted quietly every opportunity we got, careful not to bring any attention to ourselves, and it was effortless. I discovered over those few days that my heart felt fuller and I was falling in love with him.

Every time I approached a door, he would speed ahead and make sure he was there to open it for me. Every time I made the slightest mention I was hot, he was there with shade. If I was cold, his arms circled around me. If I was tired, he was there for me to lean on. He was sweet and attentive yet didn't overwhelm me. He was subtle.

He once told me how strong he found me and how he thought I could do anything, how the only reason he helped me was because he wanted to, because he was purely selfish, he said. It was incredibly flattering. He proved it constantly by letting me decide when and where I needed him. I was learning the language and it got easier every day.

"It's Saturday!" Karina yelled over the din of chattering children at breakfast one morning and they all cheered in response.

"They're adorable," I told Ian and he laughed.

"And I've got a special surprise for you!" she told them.

"What's this?" Ian asked me, nudging his shoulder with mine.

I shook my head. "I've no idea."

"It's getting warm again!" Cheering. "So we're going swimming at our favorite spot." Louder cheering.

Ian clapped his hands once and rubbed them together. His brow raised slightly and he leaned into me. "Price, get your suit."

And that's all he said before skipping out and heading toward our huts.

Kids started eating quickly and taking their bowls to Kate before running off to their rooms to get whatever swimming gear they had. I wondered what they had before a thought occurred to me. I'd only brought a bikini, never thinking I'd actually use it. I knew this wouldn't fly with Karina because Ugandan girls weren't even allowed to wear pants let alone expose their stomachs. I couldn't imagine Karina would approve.

I stood up and made my way to her. "I don't think I can swim, K."

"What! *Why*?"

"I didn't actually bring a decent suit."

"Oh, well, do you have a t-shirt? Shorts?" I nodded. "You can wear those over whatever suit you did bring. The kids will think nothing of it since you wear jeans every day anyway."

"If you think so," I told her and made my way to my half of the hut.

I could hear Ian scrambling around in his room and I smiled. I changed into my suit and felt practically naked. It wasn't considered outrageous back home. It wasn't a string, just a standard bikini, but it was *definitely* not Ugandan appropriate.

I considered myself in the mirror for a moment. I'd lost any remotely fleshy part of my body to the hard work Masego had put me through. My fingers ran down my stomach and across each raised muscle. My parents had graciously paid Raul, my personal trainer, tens of thousands of dollars to try to get me to look like this because I was determined to have it, but he could never accomplish it, not like that anyway. I wanted to burst out laughing thinking how all I'd needed to do was volunteer at an orphanage in Uganda to earn it and now I didn't even care that it existed. Suddenly, my caring about what I looked like was trumped by the health of little kids instead. Irony, I suppose.

I let my hair fall free for once and smiled secretly to myself at how it would drive Ian crazy. I pulled a band around my wrist for later, tossed on a tank and a pair of cut-off denim shorts that cost three hundred dollars back home. I remembered thinking how I'd gotten such a great deal on them, which made me roll my eyes at *myself.* I forwent the boots for once and put on my old running shoes, the ones I'd brought with no intention of bringing back because they were "last season." I grabbed a drawstring bag and put a t-shirt to swim in, a bottle of sunblock, and my small radio. I tore open a new package of new batteries for it, agreeing with myself that this occasion warranted it. This was a time for celebration. P.S. I'm going to throw an absolutely mind-blowing fact your way. I'm not kidding, either. The country of Uganda is *obsessed* with Celine Dion. They dedicate entire days to broadcasting her music.

They love her that much. Five words. My. Heart. Will. Go. On. *Yeah.*

I heard a soft knock at the door and opened it to Ian. I got to see his legs for the first time since I'd met him and couldn't believe a man's calves could be that developed. I stood gape mouthed like a buffoon staring at them.

When I finally caught myself, my gaze raised to Ian's face and I was shocked to find he was equally as engrossed as I was. My laugh startled him and he shook his head.

His mouth worked a bit and he swallowed. "You-you ready?"

"Yes," I told him.

Karina took Charles' truck and we took the jeep and filled them both with the smaller children. The older kids would walk the quarter mile to the swimming hole with Katie and Charles. Mandisa moved to sit on my lap immediately, and I let her, kissing the top of her head as Ian started the engine.

When we unloaded the last of the jeep and truck and the kids started running for the water, I impulsively raised my face and hands, palms up and let the rays of the sun wash over me. It was bright and warm and felt so good against my skin. I sighed. There was just something about the sun. I drank its heat deep and breathed easily, closing my eyes and wondering to myself why I never really saw it for what it was before I'd come to Uganda.

I'd discovered that the sun equated happiness. Its bright and lovely existence was hope incarnate. It exposed the dark, brought forth the light and showed you that no matter how strong or oppressive the night was, that it was infinitely stronger, exponentially more substantial and just because you couldn't see it with your eyes, didn't mean it wasn't still with you, that you couldn't feel it or that it wouldn't come back for you. It was stalwart and constant. It was infinite.

I followed the sound of boisterous laughter to the water's edge.

"We're going to keep the smaller ones here on the shallower edge," Ian told me.

"That's fine with me."

He raised his left hand and placed his palm on the back of my neck, sending a tight heat barreling through my body only for it to settle in my belly. I smiled at him. He flirtatiously smiled back and I bit my bottom lip to keep from laughing. He squeezed a little bit and dropped his hand. I felt a little sad for the brief moment his skin had touched mine. It never seemed long enough. It was incredible to me that I felt that way.

Every time I'd ever let a boy touch my body felt suddenly wrong, suddenly heavy on the heart and soul and I found myself regretting my past life. I'd never really felt that before. I steeled myself against the guilt though, knowing how sorry I was for it. I stood taller, lighter, knowing that although the grief of regret laid heavily on my heart, it didn't mean I couldn't move forward, that God wouldn't forgive me. It also meant that I could forgive myself, especially since I then knew *exactly* what it meant to be treated with respect. And *that* was a heady, heavy feeling of euphoria.

A few minutes passed and the older children joined in the raucous. I'd never seen such purely happy people in my entire life. They screamed with joy, jumped and dived, splashed and played with one another. They had this moment and they were ecstatic. They had this simple joy and it was free. Another something I never thought possible. To me, the only time I'd ever convinced myself I was happy was when I could whip out my credit card and charge it.

I'd come to Uganda to fulfill a mandatory sentence but was being fulfilled in a completely unexpected manner and happily, with my full consent. I'd come to help teach these children but instead they were teaching me.

"What are you thinking about?" Ian asked me, his eyes roaming the water's edge and his mouth silently counting heads.

"Nothing," I lied.

"That's an untruth," he teased, glancing my direction and prodding his shoulder with mine.

"Fine, if you have to know," I happily pushed back, glad for the brief contact. "I'm thinking that I'm very happy I came to this place."

His eyes widened briefly and he studied me intently. "What brought on this revelation?"

"Them," I said, pointing to the boisterous laughing orphans sloshing about.

"And why, Sophie Price, have they made you so happy, do you think?"

"They are funny little representatives of simplicity, of awareness. No one is more aware of themselves as these children are. They have nothing, have no one but us, have seemingly no reason to be hopeful...yet they are. They choose to be happy even though the obviously easier choice would be to be frightened or sad and they have real reason to be those things as well. But they have life and faith and hope and love and they choose those things. Their innocence is addicting, their hope is catching and I'm happy to be surrounded by them."

Ian didn't answer, didn't even acknowledge what I'd told him. Instead, he looked at me. Really *looked* at me. It was a deep, penetrating stare, one that a few months before would have left me quaking in my metaphorical boots but not then. Then, I found myself opening the window further for him. I leaned over the ledge and reached my hands out to him to bring him even closer. I was inviting him to see me as I was because I was no longer ashamed. I'd tossed the heavy, bleak curtains, removed the grime coating the view and opened myself up.

His tense shoulders relaxed and finally he nodded but only once. We both turned back toward the water and did our jobs.

Three hours later and the kids were exhausted and starving. We loaded everyone up again, half of our jeep was already full of sleeping children and I couldn't help but laugh a little at how adorable I found that. Ian and I jumped into the front seats and started the engine but Charles unexpectedly ran up to Ian's window.

"Karina and I thought you two may want an afternoon break?" he asked. "I could drive the jeep back and you two could stay and swim for a while, as long as you're okay with walking back."

"Seriously?" I asked Charles.

"Don't act so surprised, Sophie. You and Din have done a lot the past few days. Everyone needs a little break now and then."

CHAPTER NINETEEN

We watched the dust from the trucks settle as the jeeps bumbled through the dusty field and toward Masego. My heart leapt in my chest instantly knowing Ian and I were alone for, really, the first time. There would be no children ready to jump out from corners or Masego adults with their watchful eyes, memorizing our every move.

"We're alone," Ian whispered, startling me.

I turned toward him, my lids feeling a bit too heavy from the heat of the sun. Or was it the heat of his stare?

"Very," was all I could muster.

Ian's eyes traveled from my face down my neck and over my shoulder, the searing fiery gaze branded as it trickled over my skin and soon his hand found that very neck, shoulder and arm until it wrapped itself around my own hand. He brought me closer to him and whispered in my ear.

"Run," he said quietly before a slow-burning grin split him from ear to ear.

My heart leapt into my throat when I took in the sparkle in his eyes. He winked once, as if in slow motion, and that was my cue. I took off running toward the water, my lungs pumping air in and out of my chest as I hurdled plant life and rock. The only sounds I could hear were the rhythmic pounding of blood in my eardrums on beat with each drop of Ian's boots behind me. Adrenaline raced through me knowing he was so near. He seemed to be getting closer and I couldn't fight the grin spreading slowly across my face in anticipation.

A slight giggle escaped my lips imagining the prospect of what was to come. I caught the sound of Ian's breath hitching before I felt him move even faster, his heat giving away just how nearby he was.

A burst of laughter fell from me when his hands scooped me up around the waist, dragging me to him. His arms enveloped my entire body when he knew he had me, his hands wrapped my shoulders and we tumbled to the ground just short of the water. We were both laughing hysterically despite the fact we were sides deep in mud.

"You almost made it," he teased in my neck.

"I slowed on purpose," I lied.

He laughed loudly.

"Liar."

My wide smile met his.

He stood and dragged me up with him. "Care to join me?" he asked, toeing his shoes off.

I gulped.

"Turn around."

He stopped mid-bend to remove his shoe and studied me. "Whatever for?"

"I-I only had this bikini thing I'd brought from home and I-uh-I'm not exactly decent, but I don't want to get this t-shirt wet."

"You can't be serious, Soph."

"Deadly," I teased.

"You do know this water is fairly clear, right?"

"Not that clear, Ian."

He did that thing boys do where they pull their shirts over their heads with one swoop. I felt drunk with too much eye consumption. My stare roamed his incredibly chest and stomach and my mouth gaped. I tucked my tongue back into my mouth and bit my lip to keep it from falling back out. He winked and I laughed out loud.

"You're ridiculous," I told him, setting up my little iPod station and turning up the volume to *American Daydream* by Electric Guest.

"Your turn," he teased.

"No, no, no, Ian. Go ahead and put your fine self in that water."

He leaned in and kissed my cheek before diving in

quickly. His head bobbed up, water sluicing down his neck and shoulders, his wet hair dark as night. Butterflies swarmed.

"Stay facing that way, " I told him.

He visibly sighed but kept his back toward me. I bent to remove my shoes and shimmied from my shorts and t-shirt. My arms instinctively covered my stomach knowing what Karina would say if she saw me in that moment.

"Hurry up!" Ian yelled.

"I am! I am!" I smiled.

I toed the water and hissed at how cold it was. I hated that part. I edged my way in, cringing with every step until my body became accustomed to the temperature just as Agnes Obel's *Avenue* began to play.

When I was shoulder deep, I called out to him. "Okay, you can turn now."

He turned and smiled. "It was a futile effort, you know?" he said, stalking me slowly.

"What was?" I asked, backing up as he edged my direction.

"Making me turn. It was a pointless effort," he said, closing in.

"How's that?" I asked, gulping down a giddy giggle.

"Because," he said, rushing me playfully and wrapping his hands around my waist. My hands rested on his wet shoulders. "Tsk, tsk, Miss Price, skin to skin. What would Karina say?"

I pushed at his chest. "*Ian.*"

"I'm only playing." He ran his hands up my back and settled them on my neck. "There. Comfortable?"

I jokingly pushed him a little in answer.

It got quiet for a moment. He reached both hands up and ran them over the top of my head and gathered the rest of my hair, twisting it in a fist at the back of my neck. "I'm going home," he told my brow.

My heart dropped.

"*What*?" I asked, suddenly confused, my stomach mixing space with my heart.

"My brother Simon wrote me last week asking if I'd come home for a two-day visit. It seems he has something to tell me and he'd prefer to do it in person."

"Oh, I-I-I mean, that's-that's great, Ian. When do you leave?" I asked, swallowing back my uneasiness.

I didn't want him to go. I realized in that moment that I equated Ian with security. The idea of him gone made my chest press and feel tight.

"Day after tomorrow," he told me, running his thumbs across my forehead and down my cheeks.

"So-so soon?" I gulped.

"I realize it's short notice and all..."

"It's okay."

"But I was wondering if, maybe, you might be interested in going with?"

My eyes shot open. "Seriously?"

He smiled. "Seriously. It's only two days. Karina already said yes. She'll keep that out of the report she is sending back with you for court," he winked.

My heart started pounding but this time in excitement. "Oh my word, yes."

He picked me up and swung me around in the water. "Good," he simply stated.

"What do you think Simon wants?" I asked when he set me back down.

He shrugged his shoulders. "No earthly idea, but I'm glad you'll be meeting my family."

"You-you are?" I asked, stunned. No one had ever willingly wanted me to meet their parents before.

"Of course," Ian explained, looking at me like I was making no sense. "Simon especially will adore you."

"Is Simon older or younger?" I asked, curious.

"He's older, twenty-five, the charming one. My parents adore him. He's also the one who always gets the girls."

I balked at that. "My God, *he's* the one who gets the girls? What? Is he made of chocolate or something? I can't imagine anyone would be interested in anyone else but you, no matter who you're pitted against."

Ian tugged me closer and kissed my neck. "No need to flatter me, Miss Price. I believe your bait worked. I'm hooked. Line and sinker."

I eyed him, one brow raised. "I keep reeling you in, Ian Aberdeen, but you're proving a difficult catch."

"Nonsense. Utter crap. You snap your finger and I jump from water to boat."

"Is that so?"

He nodded. "I'm still flopping at your feet, like a pathetic fool, awaiting your next move and severely out of breath."

I inched closer, resting my forehead against his. "How about I put you out of your misery then, hmm?"

Ian narrowed his eyes at me. "It's such a delicious agony though."

CHAPTER TWENTY

Karina took us to the airport where we hopped on a plane for a short *twelve-hour* adventure from Uganda to Cape Town, South Africa, with layovers in Nairobi and Johannesburg. It hardly seemed worth the two-day stay, but I quickly reminded myself that it was totally worth seeing Ian outside our daily lives at Masego.

I was so relieved to touch down in Cape Town that I didn't take in the startling differences between classes on the fifteen-minute drive into town right away. Five minutes in and my view on the right and left side of the highway was a stark contrast to say the least.

"My God, look at that," I sighed through the window.

"What?" Ian asked, scooting up in his seat next to me, leaning over me to see what I was looking at.

On our right were decent, clean homes, well maintained and obviously inhabited by more affluent owners. On our left was what I could only describe as a slum. Homes, if you could call them that, made of tin roofs, dirt floors, a makeshift town really. It looked like a haven for disease and I was willing to bet lots of crime.

"This," I said, gesturing to both sides of the road with my hands.

"Ah, yes," he acknowledged, sliding back into his seat, obviously accustomed to the sights.

"It's sad," I admitted.

"Very sad," he agreed.

"It's such a stunning contrast in living conditions it feels like a punch to the gut." I studied row after row of slapdash homes.

"As an American, I can definitely identify that my country has little to no idea what poverty really is. The worst living conditions I'd ever been exposed to back home pale in comparison. It's literally embarrassing that we complain at all."

"They just don't know, Soph."

"They just stay ignorant, Ian," I answered in kind to which he could only smile.

"And I was probably the most dense of all of them," I whispered.

He slid his hand over mine and squeezed softly.

"No longer."

"No longer," I repeated, squeezing back. I took a deep breath. "Why don't those in charge do something about this?"

To this Ian laughed suddenly and hysterically.

"*What?*"

"Oh, Sophie Price, you'll get the opportunity. Just wait," he told me, still laughing.

"I feel like I'm missing something," I smiled back.

"My mother is the executive mayor of Cape Town."

"If I was familiar with your politics, I'd probably know how grave that declaration was, but I'm not, so..."

"The executive mayor of Cape Town is essentially the big dog on the block. She's the equivalent of the governor of an American state or the mayor of New York City."

My mouth went dry and I desperately tried to swallow something that wasn't there.

"The executive mayor. Why the hell didn't you explain this to me before?"

"I did. I told you they were in politics down here."

"I figured they were council people or something equally mundane."

"Soph," he said, brows furrowed, "why would the son of a councilman have top billing in the newspapers here?"

"I figured news was a little slow here."

Ian laughed again. "Cape Town is one of the biggest towns in Africa, let alone South Africa." He sobered. "I can relate to you more than you could possibly know."

"Apparently," I told him, thinking of the gossip rags back in L.A. and how they all bit at the opportunity to expose the Price "darling, trust fund baby" as a whorish coke head when Jerrick died and how they'd followed me for months, tripping over themselves to catch me falter again.

They relished in the drama, in the darkness that was their profession. They were little slithering snakes, their forked tongues extended to catch the slightest bit of gos-sss-ip. I shuddered.

"Don't worry," Ian said, breaking me from my revelry, "they know you're coming and more than likely have done their research."

"Don't worry," I told him in return, "my father's aware they've done their research by now and has probably already figured out an opportunity to milk the acquaintance."

"Surely not."

I shook my head at him in mock sympathy. "Ian Aberdeen, you've no idea what he's capable."

"Well, he'll be in good company then," he said, wrapping his arm around me.

"Now you're starting to scare me," I teased.

Ian's parents' home was found in Clifton Beach, an area so wealthy in Cape Town even I'd heard of it, despite my not being familiar with much of anything concerning South Africa.

"You're wealthy," I stated as fact, watching the security guards check several cars as they attempted to pass the entry gates.

"No, my parents are wealthy."

I smiled at him. "I see."

"Does this change your opinion of me?"

"Hardly," I told him, hoping he'd never get the opportunity to absorb the cold monstrosity that was my own parents' estate.

The house was massive considering how tightly situated the neighborhood was. Crowded but extremely luxurious homes threaded up the side of Table Mountain, winding and conforming to the mountainside. Ian's home was a modern multilevel home that adapted to the rock face it set itself within.

When our little car pulled into the drive, Ian had to get out to open the cedar sliding gate. I watched as we wound up a dark rock drive all the way to the towering house that settled so ominously within the cliff face.

"Home sweet home," Ian deadpanned.

He grabbed my bag as well as his and we climbed the steep walkway to a wide cedar door. Adrenaline inundated me. I glanced down at myself and felt suddenly nervous. My father would not approve of my choice of outfit. In fact, there would be serious consequences if he ever found out I met the executive mayor of Cape Town, South Africa, in anything other than Chanel.

I could just imagine him. "Sophie, this is unacceptable. I require so little of you. Keep up appearances, Sophie Price. Keep up appearances. *Keep up appearances*."

"You okay?" Ian asked, dropping his bag and using his free hand to caress the side of my arm.

I plastered a fake smile on my face. "Of course, just nervous, I suppose."

He smiled genuinely in return. "No worries, love. My brother will love you at least and that's the only one we need to care about."

"How encouraging," I joshed.

He dropped his bag next to mine and held both my shoulders in his wide hands. "Trust me, Soph, even if my parents end up loving you, it should mean very little to you. They're impressed only with what others can do for them. They run their campaigns on serving the poor here, just as so many before them, but the slums are still here. You saw them. They almost encourage government reliance. It's sickening."

"They're politicians."

"Very much so."

"You weren't kidding when you said they'd get on well with my dad then."

"I really wasn't." He sighed. "Let's get inside. They're probably watching us on the cameras," he said, waving sarcastically at the discrete camera tucked behind a crevice.

He pushed open the heavy door and revealed the interior. Seventy-five hundred square feet of modern art and it could only be described as dark. Dark slate, cool brushed nickel railings surrounding the entire five-level, tiered property. The floor plan encouraged lots of open outdoor living and it didn't disappoint. Living spaces opened up to the outside by way of glass accordion doors. The architecture was a nod to classic mid-century modern and the furniture was no different. It was cold and perfect and everything had a place. It made my stomach turn.

"Simon!" Ian called out, startling me.

He dropped our bags just inside and walked with purpose through the picturesque living room to the glass wall. He slid one panel into another until they met the sidewall and exposed us to the rich sea air. The salt blasted my skin and I reveled in the tangible feeling. The ebb and flow of the incredible ocean at the base of the mountain settled my nerves almost immediately. It was then I knew Ian had done this on purpose.

"Thank you," I told him.

"It was the only thing that worked for me growing up here."

I hugged his side as we looked over our surroundings.

"Did you miss it?" I asked him.

"Not even one iota."

The tranquil-looking pool below us boasted an iridescent black tile floor and I found myself almost frightened of it. I imagined it would swallow me whole and I would sink into its dark abyss if I ever dared place a toe in that grim water.

"Ian!" I heard behind us.

We both turned and I took in an older, slightly taller version of Ian. He was more tan than my Ian with shorter, more clean-cut hair, though I think that was only because Ian didn't have a barber at his disposal as readily as Simon did. He sported impeccable clothing with a European flair. All in all, Simon was gorgeous, but he lacked a fire in his eyes that Ian possessed. Yes, Ian was infinitely more beautiful. Girls could keep Simon Aberdeen. I had Ian.

"Simon!" Ian shouted.

Simon scooped up Ian and tossed him around playfully. He greeted him in, what I assumed was, Afrikaans. They exchanged greetings and I stood awkwardly against the railing wishing to everything holy I could have understood them. I perked up only when Simon eyed me before gesturing and asking Ian another question in Afrikaans.

"Oh, I'm so sorry, Soph. Excuse me," he said, meeting me and wrapping my hand in his then pulling me over to meet his brother.

"Simon, this is Miss Sophie Price. Sophie, this is my brother, Simon."

"A pleasure to meet you," I said, extending my hand.

Simon bent and grabbed it with a wink my direction and kissed my palm cheekily. "A pleasure,

Miss Price, I'm sure." He righted himself. "Ian's told me so much about you. I feel like I know you already."

"He has, has he? What were these *things*?" I teased back.

"Not necessary!" Ian practically yelled. "Let's get inside, shall we? Mom and Dad are here?" he asked, practically pushing me back into the living room.

"Nah, shortly though."

My stomach dropped a little.

"Where are they?" Ian asked.

"Mom's at a press conference. Dad's at a meeting. They said they'll be home by four."

"So what's this news I had to travel half a day to hear?"

"It would sort of be anti-climatic, don't you think, if I just blurted it out there?"

"I suppose so."

"I'll tell you at dinner."

"Mom and Dad don't know then."

"No, you'll all find out together."

Ian eyed him curiously. "Where are we eating?"

Simon cleared his throat and looked at the ceiling. "Aubergine's."

"Dear Lord, this is serious," Ian stated.

Simon sighed, running his hands through his dark hair. He sat at the kitchen bar and sank his head into his palms.

He glanced up. "I had to. It's her favorite place and I need her to be *receptive* tonight."

I gazed from one brother to the other. "And what is Aubergine's?" I asked.

"Aubergine's is my mother's favorite restaurant," Ian explained. "The rest of us hate it. They serve ungodly things like trio of quail or abalone with spiced cauliflower mouse. Essentially, disgusting food."

"Ah, I see," I answered.

"We only go there when we *really* need mom to see our side of things."

"Oh, now I'm dying to know."

"You wait like the rest of them," Simon told me. He looked at me like he'd only just really noticed me. "Wait a second. You're a girl."

"Astute, this one," I told Ian, gesturing toward Simon.

"No, no. I mean, I knew you were a girl. You'd be hard-pressed not to notice with a figure like that," he said and I rolled my eyes, "but that's not what I meant."

"Careful, Simon," Ian gritted.

"You're the first girl Ian's ever brought here."

"Surely not," I balked Ian's direction.

"No, you are the very first. Once, in high school he had a party and naturally girls came but he has *never* brought a singular girl here...ever. This-this is good. You'll take some of the heat off me."

Ian ran a hand down his face and blew out a breath. "Simon, must you always humiliate me?"

"I am sorry, little brother," he said, standing and hooking his arm around Ian's neck.

Ian shook him off but smiled. It was the first time I'd ever seen Ian really vulnerable, almost child-like, and I liked it. I supposed Masego was a "forced to act mature" kind of place. I was glad to see him young, to see that creased brow relax, even if it was just for a small amount of time. Ian so obviously carried around Masego's worries on his strong twenty-year-old shoulders and they were more than capable of handling the weight, but everyone needs a break now and then.

Just then the front door handle began to turn and we all faced the door. I couldn't help but notice Simon and Ian exchange a glance before it opened, but I couldn't fully read it. All I caught was anxiety, but there was a very good chance that was all me.

I was so overwhelmed in that moment. I wanted to run and jump off the balcony and sink into that abyss then. Anything sounded better to me than meeting Ian's parents. I didn't know how much they knew of me, or what to expect of them. I wanted to kick myself for not preparing as my father had taught me to do.

"Always be aware, Sophie. Never let anyone take you by surprise," he would say.

I shook the thoughts away.

Ian came next to me and wrapped his hand in mine. "No worries, Soph," he whispered in my ear, soothing me almost immediately.

The door opened and two imposing figures emerged, talking shop, it seemed.

"No, Hendrik," the woman, who could only be Ian's mother, said.

She was tall, very. Dark black hair and fair skin just like Ian's. Her hair was stylishly short and met just below her ears. She was lean and striking and unbelievably intimidating. She was exquisite and I could see where Ian had learned "imposing" from. She invented it with the way she carried herself.

She'd stopped talking and stood staring at us. She'd mastered an expressionless face and she was wearing it then. It was no matter to me, because in that moment I remembered my breeding and immediately exuded my own brand of imposition.

The invisible projection hit her like the atom bomb and you could tell she was taken aback.

She and Ian's dad, Hendrik, laid their bags down on the rich, brown velveteen sofa sectional before approaching.

"Simon," her velvety voice purred. "What have I told you about rolling up the sleeves of your dress shirts. You'll crease. You'll have to change before dinner tonight."

"I'll do no such thing," Simon said, smiling at her, "but I've made reservations at Aubergine's, so I figure you'll forgive me?" He oozed charm and I could suddenly see why all the girls gravitated toward him.

"Fine," she said, a tight knowing smile gracing her lips.

Simon kissed his mother's cheek before collapsing on the sofa.

"Ian," his mother breathed. "It's nice to see you again."

"Mom," Ian said dryly, kissing her cheek as Simon had before turning. "Dad!" he exclaimed with more feeling and slapped his dad on the back. "So good to see you!"

"Happy to see you, my son," Hendrik said, kissing his son and bear hugging him.

"And who is this vision?" Hendrik asked, motioning toward me.

"Dad, this is Sophie Price. Sophie, this is my father, Hendrik." He turned toward his mother. "Mom, Sophie Price. Soph, this is my mother, Abri." He pronounced it Ay-Bree.

I stuck my hand out and shook Hendrik's. He shook it vigorously in return and with warmth. I turned toward Abri and extended my hand as well. She took it and something passed between us.

She knew.

She knew who I was and who my father was and, for whatever reason, she wanted *me* to know it.

"A pleasure," she said, her perfectly coifed hair sliding forward slightly as she dipped her head in a thoroughly practiced gesture.

"Likewise," I told her in my most uninterested voice.

She may have had a few inches on me, but it was obvious to everyone in that room that I was the bigger presence. It felt good. I turned toward Ian, glancing Simon's way as I did, and caught their bewildered stares.

"So," Abri interrupted the thick moment, "*Sophie*, Ian's told me you work with him at Masego?"

"Yes."

"And I also understand that you were caught with narcotics back home and that was what earned you that privilege?"

This lady wasn't pulling any punches.

"Ma!" Ian shouted in Afrikaans, coming to my side, "Ongevraagd!" *Uncalled for*.

I coolly leaned into the countertop behind me, briefly examining my nails as I did so.

"It's okay, Ian." I met her gaze fully. "Yes, Abri, unfortunately I was, but it's of no matter now."

"That's rather cheeky," she added, looking on the verge of laughter. She thought she'd won.

"You misunderstand," I answered. "If my bad decision led me to a place like Masego and exposed me to what life was really about, I wouldn't have had it any other way. Occasionally, some have to hit rock bottom to understand themselves fully, don't you think? I plan on using mine to launch myself further than I ever could have had I never known Masego...or your son."

"Well said," Hendrik told the quiet room, nodding toward me.

"Thank you," I told him directly with a soft smile.

"Some know themselves without having to hit rock bottom," Abri said, desperate for the last word.

I let her have it with a nod. She was right after all, but she was also was transparent to everyone in the room and her small statement only helped my cause.

"Shall we dress for dinner?" Simon asked everyone, attempting to break the tension.

"Let's," Abri said, her brows pinched as she examined me.

CHAPTER TWENTY-ONE

I'd had the foresight to pack a little Monique Lhuillier tulle cocktail dress in champagne back home but didn't feel it practical to pack heels so I'd stuffed in an odd pocket of my bag a simple pair of black Fendi ballet flats with a ribbon that wrapped the ankle. I was so grateful I'd done all that but forgot that it took days for tulle to "de-wrinkle" for lack of a better word. I had little under an hour and I was freaking out a little.

Abri had set her sights on me the minute she'd walked in the door and it made me, to say the least, a little uneasy. The last thing I wanted was to look unkempt when being scrutinized so closely. I wasn't sure her motive but I knew without a doubt that Abri Aberdeen did not trust me. I didn't think I could blame her, though her interrogation style left a little to be desired, because, well, she was the executive mayor of Cape Town and I do believe she'd set her sights on loftier political positions. I was a potential liability.

I unpacked my dress and hung it in the bathroom, took a steaming hot shower courtesy of their guest quarters and kept the room warm and humid by keeping the door shut while blowing my hair out and curling it with the wand oddly kept in a drawer next to the dryer. It was thoughtful of Abri to keep the instruments available to her guests but also felt like two points were added next to a dash by her name when I'd used them.

By the time my makeup and hair were done, the room had cooled. The wrinkles had disappeared significantly but not entirely. I thought about running the shower again but knew the water hadn't yet reheated. I'd just started to panic when I heard a knock on my door. I threw on the silk short robe conveniently hanging from the hook on the back of the bathroom door, one more point for Abri, and answered.

Simon.

"Hi," I said, my brow wrinkled in curiosity. "Can I help you?"

"Yeah," he told me, "I wanted to say, while I have the opportunity in other words, while my mother's not around, you're in."

"I'm *in*?"

"Yes, you're in with us already. The guys took a vote and you're in."

"Guys?"

"Well, my dad and I."

"And I'm in?"

"Yes." He looked me up and down. "Why aren't you dressed? We're leaving in twenty minutes." The way he was so comfortable with me, I supposed I really was "in," as he called it.

"I'm in a bit of a bind. The wrinkles in my dress won't fall out."

"Not a problem. Check the closet in your room. You should find a hand-held steamer."

"Dammit! Two more points," I gritted, my fist slapping an open palm.

"Huh?"

"Nothing. Thanks. I'll be ready." I shut the door behind him.

The steamer was where he'd said it would be and it worked beautifully. The dress looked like I'd just picked it up from the store, maybe even better.

"Darn you, Abri Aberdeen, and your thoughtfulness," I whispered to the steamer.

When I was done, I unplugged the steamer and returned it to its rightful place in the closet. I slipped on my dress and shoes, and spritzed myself with one of Abri's assorted choices of flowery perfumes. I brought my wrist to my nose and inhaled. Apple, peach and tuberose filled my senses. It smelled beautiful and my lips quirked. I spritzed a little more behind my ears. I owed her big already, what was one more point?

I stood at the full-length mirror a little shocked at my own appearance. I hadn't taken this much time getting myself ready in months and it was, needless to say, slightly disconcerting. I wasn't sure if I liked what I saw in the mirror. My reflection looked a little too much like my old self and that made me uneasy.

I looked closer.

There are differences. My skin was tanner, my muscles even more toned, but the biggest difference was in my eyes. Before when I saw myself, they revealed nothing but hollow. They were empty. But now, *now*, they were full of life, full of understanding. Suddenly, I didn't mind my own scrutiny. Suddenly, I saw a completely different person standing before me. Suddenly, I reflected love, hope and patience.

A knock on the door once again startled me. I grabbed my tiny pocketbook, checked my lip gloss one last time and swung it open to a breathtaking Ian.

"Jesus, Sophie Price," he told me at once, raking his eyes from the top of my head to the tip of my toes and back again.

He entered the room and closed the door behind him. "I had no idea," he told me, edging closer.

The toe of his shoes almost met mine and I wanted, no, *needed* him to swallow me whole. He was incredibly delectable, everything about him. I could feel his breath fan across my face as he examined me, could smell the spicy, clean scent of his soap, could practically count the hairs on his head. I searched his eyes and waited for it, waited for the declaration, but it never came. *Say it*, I silently begged.

I didn't have time to be disappointed though because his hands found my bare shoulders instantly. They bit into my skin and pushed me a little away from him so he could soak up another look.

"Sophie Price, you are devastatingly beautiful."

"Thank you. So are you," I told him honestly.

He hadn't heard me though. "I-I'm just-I knew you were beautiful, knew it so very well, but it's like I just woke up to the idea. There's something about you now, Soph. You exude something and I can't quite place my finger on it. You practically glow with it. You *devastate* me," he said, clutching at his heart.

I inched closer to him and rested my hand over his. "Thank you," I told him.

"You're welcome," he said, smiling at me.

"No, you don't understand, I'm not thanking you for the compliment, Ian. I'm thanking you for giving me the beauty you see."

"I can't take credit for that, Soph."

I smiled at him and we stood quietly, our hands on one another as if we were both awakening to whatever it was that was surrounding us both then. It was written all over us. There was something practically tangible there, like a ray of sun, warming us through to our souls. You could see it, you could feel it, but you couldn't quite capture it in your hands. That didn't mean it wasn't there though. Oh, it was there and it weighed a thousand delicious pounds.

I let that pressure inundate me, let it tether me to him.

Understanding. I was in love with Ian Aberdeen. So deeply, so incredibly. And it was true and it was sublime and it was mine.

Nothing could take that away from me and that was absolutely freeing to me. I owned that love. I chose it. I owed no one for it because it couldn't have been purchased. It belonged to me free and clear. I had never felt more empowered.

Ian's breathing deepened as he frantically searched my face. *Say it.* He had to have known. He had to have felt it as I did...but no words came.

A rap at the door came just as he'd begun to open his mouth and the moment died at our feet, never to resuscitate. It was gone and my heart tumbled beside it. I knew my expression was one of pain, of disappointment, because he furrowed his brows and slid his hands to my face, trying to force it to right. I was no longer going to mask myself. I was a different person from then on. Vulnerability was acceptable to me because it was real. He shook his head as another knock resounded.

He cleared his throat. "Co-Coming," he spoke, still attempting to smooth my skin.

"We'll be down at the cars," Simon said and we heard his footsteps fade away.

Ian turned his head away from me and toward the door. "We can take my car, for privacy."

I was hurt and no longer capable of hiding how I felt, so I turned toward the bathroom, feigning I needed something. "That's fine," an unfamiliar broken voice sounded from my lips.

I picked up the pocketbook I'd set down on the bed at some point and made my way toward the door.

"Soph," Ian whispered, grabbing at my arm. I let him stop me, but I refused to face him.

"Yes, dear?" I said, trying to sound lighthearted.

"Don't," he begged.

I looked his way but still refused to turn. "Don't, what?" I asked, a fake, polite smile plastered across my lips.

"We should talk," he said.

I ignored that. "We should probably leave, Ian. I don't want your mother hating me any more than she already does."

I slipped my arm from his grip and opened the door, following the short corridor out into the living room and through the front door. I could feel Ian's heavy presence right behind me, close yet so very far away. I wanted to run to him and away from him all at the same time. I was so confused. I loved him. I swore he loved me back, but he'd just stood there.

I descended down the winding pebble-paved drive and found my way to the cars. Standing beside them all was Ian's family. I smiled at them despite my heavy heart.

"You're a vision, Sophie," Simon said, reaching for my hand and kissing my cheek.

"Very lovely," Hendrik added with a jovial smile.

I looked on Abri in her sleek black dress and met her gaze. "Very beautiful, Abri," I told her sincerely. She simply nodded.

No one, from what I could tell, knew what had transpired between Ian and me in that room. No one, except for Abri. She studied me closely, then her son, and back to me. Her eyes narrowed on us both.

Hendrik opened the passenger door of a silver Audi for Abri and she got in, her gaze still plastered on Ian and me. Simon let himself into the back of the sedan and Hendrik walked to the driver's side. I watched all of them before Ian's hand found my lower back.

"I'm over here," he whispered in my ear, sending shivers down my spine despite what had transpired.

He led me to a black Mercedes G-Class. "This is yours?" I asked him.

"Not really. It's just the car I used when I lived here. My parents bought it."

"I see."

He opened my door for me and I slid in. I reached for my belt but he beat me to it, wrapping me with it and buckling me in. He kissed my neck unexpectedly, perplexing me, and shut the door. "What was that?" I asked him when he got in on his side.

"What was what?" he asked, buckling himself in. "The belt? The kiss?"
"I needed to do it, wanted to be close to you then, I guess."

He shrugged his shoulders as if that explained it and started the engine, bracing his hand on my headrest as he backed out of the driveway. We followed his parents to Aubergine's in silence. He never took his hand off the headrest and the warmth from his hand kept permanent butterflies fluttering. It felt bittersweet though because, at the same time, my heart pounded in hurt.

Just because he didn't say he loved you doesn't mean he doesn't care, Sophie.
I was being a little bit pyscho. I knew it. It's just, the whole love thing was new to me. I'd never loved anyone like I'd loved Ian before.

Cut yourself some slack then, but move on. Own your feelings but don't expect reciprocation. Let that come if it comes.

I let the bitterness melt off my chest and slither to my feet.

"I couldn't say it," he blurted.

My head whipped his direction. "I know."

"You don't understand," he said.

"I do," I told him, resting my cheek against his hand.

He looked at me briefly and I tried to convey to him that there was no pressure. He turned back toward the road.
"No, you really, really don't." He took a deep breath.

"The truth is, I'm so deep in love with you, I can't see straight. The truth is, I've been afraid to admit it to myself, let alone you. The truth is, I'm terrified."

"*Why*? Am I really so frightening?"

He smiled at me. "Shockingly so."

"Ian."

"You have no idea what you do to me. I've felt things for you these past few months that don't seem healthy. I've wanted you so desperately I'm afraid it may not be natural. You consume my thoughts, Sophie," he confessed, seemingly forgetting I was there. He spoke to the windshield, a sort of haze drifting over him. "You've arrested my senses and I can't seem to get enough of you. That's what scares me. I'm so deep there's no getting out for me. You own me, you know?"

I fixed myself so I faced him. "No, I'm afraid I don't, Ian. Embellish for me. Pretend I'm one of your students and I don't comprehend the lesson. Go into great detail...painstaking detail," I flirted, my heart pounding in my chest at his proclamation.

He fought a smile. "I don't know why I opened this floodgate. I'm tired, that's why, and you look so damn bewitching right now." He sighed. "At Masego, the way you roll the sleeves up your forearms, highlighting your beautiful skin with the perfect wrists that meet those incredible hands. I've imagined those hands on me so many times," he continued, shocking me and drifting further into his own thoughts.

"That might be when I first became aware. Possibly it's the way your jeans hug your thighs every time you take a single step though. All I can think of when you're around me are those damn legs, how they'd feel in my palms, how they'd feel wrapped around my waist." He lightly tapped a fist against the wheel and I sat up a bit. "They're distracting. Or maybe it's when your hair is loose and wild and down your back. I'd give anything to see it across your bare shoulders," he swallowed, "or coiled around my fists," he declared. He shook his head back and forth slowly, eyes still trained on the road ahead. "It's actually all those things," he said suddenly, "but mostly I think it's your face."

I squirmed quietly in my seat, praying to God I didn't break his seemingly unaware trance. My pulse beat erratically at the confession. I felt my throat dry, my stomach drop and it was everything I'd never experienced before but knew was exactly as it should have always felt. My hands gripped the leather beneath my fingers to keep from throwing themselves at him and wrapping themselves around his shoulders.

"Sophie Price, you are the most beautiful girl I've ever met," he stated before turning my direction and staring me dead in the eyes. "You are so gosh damn beautiful in here," he said, tapping my chest, "that what's here," he spoke, running the side of his hand down my face, "is magnified tenfold and that is a sight to behold."

My mouth gaped open. I was at a complete loss for words, all rational thought had left, so I did the only thing I could think to do. I leaped across the seat and pulled the collar of his shirt toward me. The next second, I felt the SUV pull over and slam to a stop before being dragged onto Ian's lap and he was exploring me with his mouth like no one ever had.

His hands found my neck and mine threaded through his hair. "Soph," he whispered against my lips.

"Yes?" I asked, a smile tugging the corners of my mouth.

We kissed for God knows how long before he answered.

"Say it," he asked, plucking my earlier plea right out of thin air.

"I love you," I told him.

"Again," he said, moving to my neck.

"I love you, Ian."

"Again," he asked, pulling my face away from him.

I looked at him, winded and twitterpated. "I'm in love with you, Ian Aberdeen."

He attacked my lips with an unparalleled ferocity, swallowed my breath and tasted my tongue with his. I wrapped the crook of my arm around his neck to bring him closer, furiously melting my mouth with his and confusing where I started and he began.

"Mercy," I said, briefly breaking contact before marrying my lips with his once more.

Suddenly his cell began to ring and we both groaned.

"Your parents," I spoke into his mouth.

"Man, do you know how to spur a guy on or what?"

I laughed against his swollen lips. "Shut up. That's them, has to be."

"I don't care," he said, his hand searching the cupholder beside him for the phone. "Unless it's Simon."

We both turned to see it was, indeed, Simon.

"Hello?" he answered, smiling up at me. "Yeah, we got separated. We'll be there soon."

He pressed end and I sank back into my seat. "To be continued," he said, kissing my temple.

Aubergine felt like a continuation of Abri Aberdeen's home. It screamed elegance and contemporary and there wasn't a moment it didn't make you painfully aware of yourself, of where you placed your hands, where you looked, what you said and even how you felt. If Aubergine was a person, it would be Abri Aberdeen.

"Welcome to Aubergine. Name?" a clearly uninterested young woman asked us. When she glanced up, though, her tune changed a little. She smiled at Ian.

"We're here with another party," Ian told him. "Aberdeen?"

Her eyes grew round as saucers. "Of course, pardon me for not recognizing you. This way," she said, scurrying in front of us. "Again," she said over her shoulder, "forgive me. I'm so sorry."

"Not a big deal," Ian told her, shrugging his shoulders.

The young girl led us up a flight of stairs that stemmed from the main dining room to the mezzanine. Ian's family was the only seated there. The perks of being the executive mayor, I supposed. An unexpected surprise awaited us when we finally met the table. Instead of the three Aberdeens, a fourth patron had joined the dinner. A young, exquisitely beautiful girl with butterscotch hair and bright blue eyes. She looked stunned and wide-eyed. Already, I'd decided to like her.

"If I were to guess," I whispered Ian's direction, "I believe this may be Simon's topic of discussion."

He nodded. "Strap yourself in, Sophie Price. I believe things are about to get unpredictable 'round here," he said, his accent thicker than I'd heard it in a while.

Simon and Hendrik stood when we approached the table. Ian held my chair out for me and I sat. The boys followed suit. We all sat quietly and awkwardly, awaiting something, anything to happen. Rather, we all stared at Abri on edge.

"You're being rude, Simon," Abri finally spoke. "Introduce your *friend* to Ian and Miss Price."

Uh-oh. Not looking good.

Simon sighed audibly and pressed his lids closed for a moment before leaning into his date toward us.

"Ian, Sophie, this is Imogen. Imogen, this is Ian and Miss Sophie Price."

"A pleasure," I smiled and offered my hand.

Imogen's tense shoulders relaxed an infinitesimal amount and she took my extended hand, shaking it. "Nice to meet you as well."

Simon presented his own hand and did the same.

Formalities over with, we all eyed Abri, but she gave no indication it was okay to speak. I astonished myself. I couldn't believe I was bending to this ridiculous woman and her outrageous intimidation. I decided to ignore her. She already felt insane disdain toward me, what further damage could I possibly do?

I turned Imogen's direction. "You're English," I stated with a smile. "What part do you hail from?"

"Manchester," she said, smiling back, her shoulders relaxing another inch. "Have you ever been?"

"I have," I told her. "It's lovely there."

"You're kind," she laughed.

"I actually stayed in Chester," I corrected.

"Oh, yes, it's very charming there."

"Agreed," I said, taking a sip of my water.

I took the opportunity to study the table and noticed an almost too well put together Abri staring our direction. I smiled softly as if I was unaware she was secretly seething inside before turning back Imogen's way.

"What brings you to Cape Town?" I asked her.

"Simon does," she said, laughing. "We attended graduate school at Oxford together."

"Really?" I asked, leaning her direction more, her shoulders relaxed another inch. "How did you meet?"

"In our Stochastic Analysis class," she said before looking at Simon.

"Goddard!" they said in unison before breaking into laughter.

It died quickly when Abri cleared her throat before taking a sip of her own water.

"Fascinating," I said, turning toward Ian. "You never told me Simon went to Oxford."

"Simon went to Oxford, Sophie."

I rolled my eyes. The table seemed to be getting more comfortable by the moment. Imogen's shoulders were almost completely at ease and Ian placed his arm on the back of my chair. Hendrik and the four of us continued with our conversation until the waiter took our drink orders.

"We'll have four glasses of your best red," Abri ordered.

"Oh, just bring the bottle," Hendrik said.

Abri's hand rested on her husband's. "Hendrik," she said, tossing her eyes my direction.

Imogen looked at me, but I just rolled my eyes and shook my head. She nodded in understanding.

Hendrik narrowed his gaze at his wife then back at the waiter. "Bring the bottle," he said, handing him the wine menu.

When the waiter walked away, Abri sat up in her chair. "Why don't you just come out with it, Simon?"
The entire table got quiet.

Simon cleared his throat and took Imogen's hand underneath the table. "All right. Mom? Dad? Imogen and I are going to be wed."

I knew it! This news made me giddy inside. I narrowly escaped my own beheading though when Ian stayed me with a hand to my shoulder, preventing me from shouting the congratulations balanced at the tip of my tongue.
Abri quietly lifted her napkin from her lap and laid it across her plate. I guessed correctly that was a bad sign.

"And you thought bringing me here would be the perfect venue for such an announcement?"

Simon sank in his chair, running a hand over his face. "This is hardly the end of the world, Mother. Most people rejoice when their children announce their engagement."

Abri leaned in closer toward him, balancing herself over the table. "We are not *most* people," she gritted between teeth.

"Lovely impression you're giving our Sophie."

I subtly shook my head at him. A silent *Don't bring me into this*!

"Maybe I should go," I said, when Abri's chilling stare sank through me.
I made an attempt to get up, but she locked me in place with a single look.

"No, it would be blasted all over the papers tomorrow if you left our table before we'd even gotten our wine."

"What?" I asked.

"You seem to be under a mistaken impression. Look around you, Miss Price. There are two paparazzi waiting by the valet as well as a Cape Times journalist in the main dining hall."

"I see," I said, not looking to rock the boat. I sat back in my chair, placing my napkin in my lap once more.

"Yes, so even though I'm loathe to have you privy to *my* family's discussion, one that, I might add, could be extremely damaging if leaked," she drilled me with another disparaging look, "you stay."

"Staying. Got it," I said, sinking into my chair.

Abri faced Simon once more. "Why now?" she asked, narrowing her eyes. "Your half a term away from graduating. Why now?" she repeated.

"Because I love her and I don't want to wait," he stated as fact.

I barely bit my "aww" back.

"Something's amiss," she said, her nails tapping at the stem of her water glass, the only sign she wasn't completely in check of her emotions.

Imogen fidgeted in her chair, glancing down at her lap, avoiding eye contact.

Uh-oh.

Simon's jaw clenched. "I know what you're implying."

"And?" Abri asked, considering an obviously nervous Imogen.

"Not that one has anything to do with the other but, yes, Imogen is expecting," Simon said, dropping the bombshell like he was announcing it would rain on Tuesday. "The only influence that had on my decision was when we would marry, not if."

Yowza. And aww.

This time even Hendrik lost his ever-present "It's all good" facial expression.

"Not again," Abri said, falling into the back of her chair.

I turned toward Ian and his face was devoid of color. I placed my hand within his, reminding him I was there. He squeezed my fingers.

"She's only six weeks right now, Mom," Simon continued. "We can marry at an undisclosed location and soon. We were thinking somewhere tropical, give the impression we've been planning a secret wedding for months. No one will think differently since Imogen has been a fixture in my life for more than two years. In fact, they'll be expecting it. And in a couple of months, we announce her pregnancy."

"Well, you've thought it all out, haven't you, son? It's all nice and tidy, isn't it? Except you forgot one thing."

"What?"

"Re-elections are this month and it would need to be immediate. No one would believe we were planning a wedding this close to the end of my campaign."

"Jesus, Mom. You know what? You're right. Let's wait. Yes, we'll wait and announce it when Imogen is showing and then you'll really have a scandal on your hands. Listen, we're only doing this for you because we don't want to compromise your career. If it were up to us, we'd wait until school was done and the baby was born, then wed in London at the church Imogen grew up in."

"Do you expect me to be *grateful*?" Abri whisper-yelled, startling Imogen. "God, this is Ian all over again."

"Abri," Hendrik said, "*enough*."

"It's," she began, but Hendrik silenced her with a hand on hers.

"I said, *enough*, Abri."

Abri looked appropriately chagrined and it made me have a little more respect for Hendrik. He wasn't quite the easy pushover I'd first thought he was. The table got quiet once more when the waiter brought our drinks and took our entree orders.

The meals had arrived and still not a word had been spoken. Surprisingly, none of us were that hungry and we all pushed our food around our plates.

I cleared my throat, inciting the potential ire of Abri, but I didn't care. "My father's company owns an island," I announced to the table. "I can offer you discretion."

CHAPTER TWENTY-TWO

Long Street in Cape Town was busier than the French Quarter at Mardi Gras. The street seemed littered with people, a sea of heads donning every inch. Cape Town reminded me so much of America it was scary. The only real difference was the accent. Occasionally someone would throw out a vibe that was typically Afrikan, but other than that, if I'd captured the scene when I'd first arrived and pitted it next to a picture of Fat Tuesday, NOLA style, you wouldn't be able to tell the difference. Even the Long Street architecture was reminiscent of New Orleans.

I was unexpectedly hit with a wave of homesickness in the moment and sidled closer to Ian as we meandered our way through the crowds. I didn't know how you could miss a place that utterly defined a horrific life, but there you had it. I was overwhelmed with a need to sleep in my bed, amongst my down pillows and Frette sheets. To have Margarite bring me my breakfast in bed. To have Katy, Peter and Gillian over for massage, hair, nails and makeup.

"Do you miss Mandisa?" Ian asked me, interrupting my thoughts.

"What?" I asked, shame heating my chest.

"You looked sad for a minute there. Do you miss her?"

I thought about the baby back at Masego and felt a crushing desire to hold her. Home and comfort quickly seeped from my conscious and my mind made a beeline toward Mandisa.

"I miss her like mad. She's my miniature sun." Ian wrapped his arm around my shoulder and kissed my neck.

"Stay within these arms all night?"

"You couldn't pry me away."

"The street can get a little wild though. Hold tight."

"That really won't be an issue," I toyed.

Ian ushered me like a bodyguard down the street until we arrived at the entrance of a building labeled with an imposing vertical sign that read *Goes the Boom*.

"This is where my old friends and I would go on Saturday nights. This was pure, unadulterated fun for me. I loved to dance."

I arched a teasing smiled his direction and wrapped both my hands around the back of his neck. "I have a feeling I'm in for lots of surprises tonight."

Ian twisted his hands through the hair at the top of my head and stayed them there. "Prepare yourself, Price, 'cause I'm about to rock your world."

Too late.

Goes the Boom wasn't your typical dance club. It was fit within a beautiful two-story Victorian with refurbished interiors of recycled dark wood and brick walls but contemporary concrete floors. And the bass was positively bumping, something you'd never expect in the low-lit ambience of the sophistication it exuded, but it was inviting. I found myself drawn like a magnet to the dance floor, but Ian dragged me toward the bar instead.

"What'll you have?" he asked.

I searched the bar and spotted what I wanted. A bottle of Glenlivet, single malt, aged twenty-one years. "Whisky, neat," I told him, "that bottle."

"The same," Ian told the bartender. "Damn, Sophie," he said, turning toward me, "I had no idea you drank like a fifty-year-old man."

I laughed out loud.

"You're sixteen," I told him, painting the picture, "your parents lock up their liquor cabinet, the kitchen is manned by people at all times, the only available liquor you can find is hidden away in a drawer in your father's desk and it's single malt whisky. What do *you* think you'd develop a taste for?"

"Coca-Cola?"

I laughed again. "Not if your name was Sophie Price."

"I see," he said as the bartender set down our drinks.

We both picked ours up, took a slight sip, then downed the entire contents, slamming down our empty glasses, an unconventional approach to finely aged whisky. We stood there, silently daring one another to cough. My eyes began to water. Eventually, I had to clear my throat, *had to,* it burned so badly. Ian only coolly stared at me, seemingly unaffected. I shook my head at him.

"You're a hoss," I finally relented.

"Thank you," he said, his voice faintly gruff from the whisky.

My hand reached for my glass and I turned it upside down, spinning the concave bottom around with my fingers. He edged in closer to me, *The Fear* began to spill from the speakers and we stood in silence, examining the other, until the bass line hit, subtle and resonating through our chests. His hand found mine, stopping the glass mid-spin. The heat of his fingers sent tingles up my arm.

"Another?" he whispered in my ear.

"No, thank you," I answered softly.

Ian watched me, running a hand down my cheek, continued down my neck to my shoulder and my side until it rested on the bone of my hip. "Come with me then," he said, tucking me into his side and leading me to the dance floor.

The song changed to Common's *Drivin' Me Wild*.

At the edge of the floor, he pressed me so close I could count each individual hard plane of his body with my own. My breathing labored, nearly hyperventilating at the proximity. He grabbed my neck with one hand and tucked his face near my ear, swaying my body against his. I took advantage of the nearness and took a deep breath, inhaling his incredible scent of woods and water and my eyes rolled into the back of my head. I pressed my lids closed, desperately trying to stay upright.

As if he knew I was struggling, the hand wrapped around my waist pulled me closer.

"Soph," he breathed in my ear, sending me toward an edge.

I sucked in a deep breath as his mouth found mine. He tasted sweet and earthy like the whisky. I moaned into his teeth and he kissed me even harder. His hands slid to the back of my dress and fisted the fabric there. This sent the butterflies flitting around my stomach into overdrive.

My arms tightened around his neck and my right leg wrapped around his calf. He bent me slightly as if he could bring us any closer and I pushed myself further against him. The kiss was frantic, borderline shocking even. I had never been kissed with such want before. We wanted so badly. We needed.

"God, Soph," he breathed into my smile. "You

taste incredible."

I corded my fingers with his hair and brought his head up. I needed to look in his eyes. "When we leave tomorrow night," I told him, suddenly afraid, "nothing changes?"

He smiled at me genuinely. "Nothing."

The song changed again to something with a faster beat and as we sang the lyrics to one another and practically lost our breath dancing. I realized that Ian Aberdeen was the most fun I'd ever had or ever would have.

We didn't leave until close to three in the morning. I'd removed my shoes by that time and Ian carried them for me, the ankle ribbons draped over one of his broad shoulders and me on his back. We sang the music being pumped into the streets and belly-laughed all the way to his car despite the fact that the only thing we'd had to drink all night was the single shot of whisky, burned off hours before.

"Oh, shit!" I said, remembering myself. "I need your phone," I told him, when he set me down near his car.

He removed it from the back pocket of his jeans and handed it to me.

"Can I call out of country?" I asked, when he opened the door for me.

"Yeah, I have an international plan for obvious reasons."

"Cool," I said, sitting as I slid the unlock button. "Huh."

"What is it?"

"There's fifteen missed calls from my sat phone."

"Seriously?"

"I'm not kidding. Must be Karina. Should we call them back?"

"Yeah, it's probably no big deal though. Go ahead and ring Pembrook first. Get that out of the way so Simon doesn't bombard me incessantly tomorrow."

"You really love your brother, don't you?"

He nodded seriously. "Like-like a brother."

"You think you're funny."

"I do. To both."

"That's sweet," I said as I dialed Pemmy. I did the math quickly in my head and nearly wiped the sweat from my brow when I realized it was a decent hour in L.A.

"Hello?" Pembrook answered.

"Pemmy!" I squealed.

"Sophie?" he asked.

I cleared my throat, my skin flushing at my unusual outburst. "Sorry, uh, I have a favor to ask you."

"Where are you? Are you okay?" he interrupted.

"I'm fine. In fact, I'm in Cape Town," I answered.

"*What*! Sophie, you were under court orders not to leave Uganda!"

"It's not a big deal, Pemmy. Karina and Charles approved it. It's only for two days. I'm going back to Masego tomorrow evening."

He was breathing deeply on the other end, obviously trying to keep himself under control. "If the courts get a whiff of this, you're done, girl."

My stomach dropped a little at his declaration, but I insisted to him that everything would be fine.

"And what was your purpose in calling?"

"Oh! Right! I need to let Ian's family borrow Dad's island in Belize. Can you let me know what dates it's available."

I heard papers shuffling in the background. "I'm very busy, Soph. Are you planning on escaping through Cape Town."

I immediately felt offended but knew Pembrook was only looking out for me. "No, I assure you. It's all very innocent. Is it doable or not?"

"Yes, it's fine. The island is completely open this entire month. Feel free to offer it. Just let me know the date and I'll arrange the staff."

"Thank you, Pemmy. I appreciate it." Silence descended over the line and I was afraid I'd lost him. "Pembrook? Are you there? I think I lost him," I told Ian's questioning face.

"No-no, I'm here. I'm here. You've just never said that to me before."

"What?" I asked, confused.

"That you appreciate me."

"Well, that's a shame," I told him sincerely, "because I do. I always have. I'm sorry."

"It's fine, Sophie. Thank you," he said, but I could tell his heart was the teensiest bit lighter.

"Okay, I'll ring you when we figure out a date.

Thanks again, Pemmy."
And with that, we hung up.

"Simon and Imogen have their pick of dates."

"Thank you for that," he said, kissing my temple and starting his engine.

Ian dropped me off at the guest suite door with a gentleman's kiss. Okay, maybe not a *gentleman's* kiss, but I did eventually shut the door with him on the other side. It counts!

I hung up my dress and hopped in the shower, desperate to get the smell of smoke and outside off my skin and out of my hair. Humming *Drivin' Me Wild* under my breath, I rinsed the conditioner and turned off the water. My hand shot out for the towel rack to grab my towel but it wasn't there. I felt around the metal for it but figured it must have fallen to the ground.

I rolled the door back a few inches and stuck my head out to find it but was met with a hand holding it instead.

"Agh! Oh my God!" I panted. "Abri, what are you *doing* in here?"

My hand whipped out for the towel, wrapping it around myself before stepping out of the shower.

"I'm here for a chat," she said, weirding me out.

"This couldn't wait?" I asked, gesturing toward the room.

"No," she said, exiting the door and settling herself casually across my bed.

I thanked God I had the sense to lay out my pajamas before I'd showered. I gathered them and went back into the bathroom to dress.

When I came back out, Abri was still there, proving it wasn't a bad dream. I awkwardly rested against the guest wardrobe and towel dried my hair.

"I talked to Pembrook, my father's lawyer, and he let me know your family could have any day this month on Ribbon Caye." I thought this would help the clumsy silence that lay between us but it didn't. "Dinner was nice," I added, so desperate at that point I was reaching.

"When do you leave back to America?" she asked, stunning me.

"Excuse me?" I asked, confused.

"When do you return? *To America*? When is your sentence over?"

I was taken off guard. "Um, January thirtieth, a month after Christmas. I leave February first."

"Another six weeks then," she said, studying her feet briefly before making eye contact again.

"Yes," I said, drawing out the word.

Without another word, she left the room, shutting the door behind her.

"What was that?" I asked no one.

I stood there, waiting for something, but Abri never returned.

I settled into my covers and laid my head down before getting up and locking the door.

I woke to Ian yelling in Afrikaans.

"Fine! Miskien kom ek dan net nooit weer terug nie!" *Fine! Maybe I won't be coming back here ever again!*

"Moenie dit sê nie," Hendrik pleaded. *Don't say that.*

"Ek is jammer, pa, maar sy is verby onredelik!" *I'm sorry, Dad, but she's beyond unreasonable!*

Loud footsteps resounded through the living room.

"Simon?" Ian said. There was no response. *His cell phone.* "Can you come pick up Sophie and me in half an hour? Yes. Thanks, bro."

The footsteps inched near my door. I threw off my covers and ran to open it.

On the other side, Ian was in mid-knock and out of breath from frustration.

"You okay?" I asked.

"Can you be ready to leave in half an hour?"

"Of course," I said.

He came into the room and sat at the edge of the bed, in the exact same spot his mother did earlier that morning. I decided that information would only anger him more and I would keep it to myself. I knew Abri had pissed him off, I just didn't know why.

I opened the wardrobe and removed my bag, settling it on the bed. I set aside what I wanted to wear on the plane ride that evening and put the rest inside. I was packed in less than five minutes. Ian laid across the bed next to my case not saying a word and buried his head in my pillow.

I brushed my teeth, dressed and put on my makeup before plaiting my hair in a messy fishtail, laying it across my shoulder. I came out, put the traveling stragglers back in the case and zipped it shut.

"This pillow smells like you," Ian said absentmindedly.

He flipped over, tucking a hand behind his head, straining his shirt against the muscles in his bicep.

"You all right?" I asked him again.

"I will be," he said when I crawled next to him, my head laying on his shoulder. He brought his arm around and held me close. "I called Charles back this morning," he continued.

"Oh yeah?" I asked. "What did he need?"

"They've confirmed the presence of Resistance soldiers at the swimming hole and this time it seems a bit more dangerous."

My heart thundered in my chest. "What do you mean?"

"They found several bullets left by accident near their footprints."

"What do we do?"

"Get home."

My hand followed a messy trail of bedspread and met his fingers. They inched their way up my palm until they met my forearm and held there, his thumb rubbing the skin there back and forth, back and forth.

"I'm torn between wanting to keep you here with Simon and taking you with me so I can protect

you."
I shook my head at him.

"If you think for one second that I'm going to abandon you or Masego now, when they need as much help as possible, you are out of your mind," I told him.

He eased to a sitting position, his grip still on my forearm and leaned into my face. He kissed me softly. "I must be the most selfish person on this planet because I'm not going to fight you on that. I want you near me. Always." He kissed me once more, this time much harder before pulling away.

Knock. Knock.

I climbed off the bed and answered it. It was Simon.

"Ready when you are, princess," he teased, tugging once on my braid. He nodded at his brother before leaving.

Ian stood and grabbed my bag for me. I supposed lunch with his parents was out of the question.

When we reached the front door, we noticed both Ian's parents were standing at the bottom of the walkway, talking to Simon. They seemed to be in deep discussion but eased up when we neared.

"It was such a pleasure meeting you," Hendrik told me, hugging me and kissing my cheek. "I hope it's not our last."

"I hope not either," I told him, smiling. I kissed his cheek in return and turned to Abri.

"Thank you for having me, Abri."

She waved my comment away as if it were a gnat circling her head and avoided eye contact. I was willing to bet that's what she equated me with. I wasn't going to bust my ass to prove anything to her. I'd just let time do that.

Ian placed our bags in the back of Simon's little sports car. I lingered by them when Ian went back to say goodbye to his parents. He'd hugged his father but not his mother. He opened the passenger door and attempted to get in the small back seat but I stopped him and pushed my way through.

"Not about to make your tall ass shimmy in there. I got this," I told him but was swung back playfully instead and pushed aside.

"Not about to make your bony ass shimmy in there. I got this," he teased, squeezing his impossibly large frame in the tiniest little back seat I'd ever seen.

"You are crazy," I goaded, settling in beside Simon.

We went to lunch with Simon before our flight and Imogen met us there. She was impossibly adorable and we exchanged emails before we'd said goodbye. We'd also solidified that they wanted Ribbon Caye on January twenty-sixth so they could have more time to prepare and give their guests at least a month to make arrangements. I'd called Pemmy, that time at not such a decent hour, *oops*, and he'd confirmed they could have an entire week there and that my father, surprisingly, didn't care, probably because of who Simon's parents were.

CHAPTER TWENTY-THREE

Masego was as we'd left it yet completely different to me then, at that moment. Its gates represented something I couldn't quite put my finger on...

"It's good to be home," Ian told Charles, sighing.

...And like a lightbulb, Ian had flipped a switch. Masego felt like home to me. Everyone I had grown to love so dearly resided there. Ian, Mandisa, Karina, Charles, Kate, Mercy, the children, and the rest of the staff. I suddenly knew I would do anything to protect them, anything to keep them safe.

When Pembrook arrived with the

construction crew, I knew I'd get him to arrange for protection, for some type of security. That was instantly my number one priority.

When the gates opened, they revealed a smiling Karina and the baobab tree, as stalwart as always. I remembered once Karina explained that as long as the tree was at Masego that she would always be and that made me warm inside.

We'd arrived too late for the children to greet us but Kate and Mercy had stayed up with Karina to see us home. Once we'd parked, I jumped from the jeep and tackled Karina in the biggest hug.

She giggled out loud. "Stop, you silly girl," she said, but hung on to me just as tightly.

"I missed you, K," I said, smacking her cheek with a kiss.

"I missed you, too, Sophie."

She pulled me from her hold and inspected me over.

"What?" I asked, breathless from laughing.

"You look...I'm not sure," she said, cocking her head to the side. "You look ecstatically happy."

"So what if I am?" I teased, bumping my hip with hers.

Her eyes grew bright, reflecting the stars above. "It's a very good look on you, my love."

She grabbed me by the waist and we made our way toward Ian, Charles, Kate and Mercy so she could say hi to Ian as well. He grabbed her and spun her around and she squealed.

"What in the world has gotten into you two?" she asked, bewildered.

"Nothing," we both answered simultaneously.

"If you think this is bad," Charles said, "you should have seen how they acted when they saw me."

My cheeks flushed red and I was never more grateful for the night sky.

"Come to the kitchens," Karina said, smiling and waving us her direction. "I've made you a homecoming bread."

"What kind?" Ian asked, wrapping his large arm around her tiny little shoulders.

"Banana, of course. What other fruit do we get around here?" she laughed.

We entered the small kitchen together and all pitched in, getting plates, cups, etc. for our miniature party. Karina uncovered a pan of nice, thick banana bread and my mouth began to water.

We all sat and began eating in silence.

Homecoming, yes. But *also* a discussion.

"What are we going to do?" Ian asked Charles.

Charles swallowed. "Honestly?" His face was devoid color. "I don't know where to start. They've never come this far south before. They've undoubtedly been scouting us for several months. There's no mistake about it, it's a ticking time bomb now."

Kate burst into tears, getting up and retreating to her rooms. "Kate!" Karina called, standing to chase after her, but Kate shook her head and Karina sat back down.

"We need action then," Ian said, taking charge and making me incredibly proud of him. "We arm ourselves. Get the locals to help us take shifts." The table got quiet. "*What*?" he asked, tension rolling off him in waves.

"We've already asked them," Karina said, her eyes never leaving her bread.

"And they've *refused*?" Ian asked in disbelief.

"You can't really blame them," Karina tried to explain.

"The hell I can't!" Ian exclaimed. "We would do it for them. We *have* done it for them!"

"They have families, Din. They can't risk it."

Ian's neck and ears grew red with frustration. "Then we leave," he said.

"Where?" Mercy asked.

"Anywhere," he answered.

"We have nowhere to put the children, Din," Karina said, looking as exasperated as her voice conveyed.

"What are you suggesting?" Ian asked, his brows furrowed.

"That we stay right where we are and keep watch. Charles seems to think we can do it on our own."

"Charles," Ian said, turning toward him, "you know that is foolhardy. We can't risk it."

"Where would we go?" Charles asked in return.

"Somewhere. Anywhere but here."

"How far south does the property line go?" I asked.

"Just south of Lake Nyaguo," Charles answered, "but it's of no importance because we have no way of building camps, no way of caring for the children once we're there."

I breathed deeply. *Here we go*. "I-I need to tell you all something," I confessed.

"What is it?" Karina asked, tucking a loose strand of hair from my braid behind my ear.

"I had planned on surprising you all next week, but I've arranged for a group in America to come here and build you a new kitchen house, install a new generator, do the odd repair and create a concrete court for the children to play on as well as a play area. It was supposed to be for Christmas, but I can see it's a blessing in disguise. What say you if we have them build the new construction on the south side of Nyaguo instead? Nyaguo would be north of us and it would provide protection, we'd only have to worry about our east, west, and south borders."

The table stayed quiet, too quiet, and I wondered if I'd overstepped my boundaries. My face burned in embarrassment and I was close to explaining it all away, apologizing and offering to call it off, but Karina was first to break the silence.

"Our borders," she said, her eyes glassy with unshed tears. "*Our* borders."

"Our borders," Ian said, repeating her and smiling my direction.

"Our borders," Charles said, his hand landing on mine.

Realization dawned on me. "Yes, *our* borders."

"Thank you so much, Sophie," Karina said, covering my only uncovered hand with her own. "You've given our hopeless situation *hope*."

"You're thanking me?" I asked, flabbergasted. "No," I told them all, choking back a sob. "*I* need to thank *you*. You saved me." I smiled at each of them in return. "It was just my turn to return the favor."

Ian sweetly kissed me at my door that night. We all had a plan and there was hope. The next day, we all decided we would begin preparations to move the children. I'd called Pembrook and told him our plan and he promised to get the men together earlier with new plans of creating an entirely new compound.

We all decided that when the unexpected came, sometimes new arrangements could become that much more extraordinary.

CHAPTER TWENTY-FOUR

But with the new extraordinary you still had the unexpected...

That morning, we all woke anew, with a mission. We informed the children of their Christmas present, a new place to live. Many felt uneasy about the potential move, but we assuaged any fears, letting them know it would be safer and that they would have a playground and that seemed to liven them up enough to get them excited.

With that, we went about packing rooms in preparation. Our plan was to set up temporary camps within the new territory. Pembrook had somehow arranged for military CHUs or container housing units to be dropped off within three days, which would allow us to house and care for the children during the weeks of new construction. I didn't want to know how much that was costing my father and I hoped he didn't either.

By the time the CHUs had arrived, we were prepared to transport. Most of the children's things were packed and ready to go as well. There had been no additional sign that the LRA was near or nearing. We were confident and happy.

The night before we were set to transfer everyone and everything, Ian and I were making our way to the CHUs, twenty minutes south of the current Masego. We just needed to make a quick pit stop a mile outside the gates to gather one of the missing cattle and mend a broken fence.

"She's a stubborn jerk," I said, pushing the cow toward the damaged fence.

Finally, the old girl hopped it and moved as quickly as a heifer could move toward her meandering comrades.

Ian and I dropped to the ground right next to the fence and laughed, out of breath from pushing the cantankerous bovine. The lights from our jeep lit us from behind, bathing us in an ethereal glow. He leaned into me, wrapping his hand around the nape of my neck and tugging me toward him, kissing me softly on the lips.

"What a Christmas," he told me, gazing at me and brushing his thumb across my lower lip.

"Indeed," I agreed.

"I love you," he professed, running his fingers through my hair before meeting my nape once more. Earlier he had undone my braids for me and I never thought I had ever experienced anything as sexy as the way his eyes danced when it fell across my shoulders.

"I love you," I told him, my hand coming to rest on his forearm at my neck.

His face became serious and I searched his eyes, his furrowed brow.

"Stay with me," he whispered, the hand that had been resting on my hip moved to meet the other side of my neck.

I swallowed, forcing my gaze downward. I'd had no idea how I was going to answer that because it was a forbidden topic, a forbidden thought. I was scared.

"I don't know what to say," I told him truthfully.

"Say you'll stay. Give it all up, Soph. You have nothing really to go back to, you told me so yourself."

"Excuse me? I have plenty to go back to," I said, affronted.

"Yes, but none of it means anything."

He was right, of course, but I didn't like how he dismissed my old life so readily. Yeah, I was different since Masego, but I could still have a righteous future in the States. *But can you leave Ian? Really leave him? How about Mandisa?*

I shook my head of the thoughts.

"I don't have a choice," I told him.

"You do. Choose me, Soph."

But with Ian comes responsibility. Could I choose a Masego life for myself? For the rest of my life? Could I commit to it?

I hedged. "I'm due back in court at the completion of my sentence, though."

"Then I'll come with you and we'll come back together," he said, hugging me to his chest tightly. "It would probably be good to have a Masego rep there anyway."

I pushed at him slightly. "We don't have to decide now," I told him.

He widened the distance I'd created. "Why are you being so difficult about this?"

"I'm not," I said. "It's a really heavy decision, Ian. I want to be careful."

"What's to decide?" he asked, incensed. "If the situation were reversed, I wouldn't hesitate!"

"Of course you wouldn't! You already live here!"

His hands fell to his side and my skin felt bereft of his warmth. I missed his touch almost immediately. I just stopped myself from grabbing those hands and placing them back. My chest ached from our fight and I didn't know how to go forward with him. This was such a huge thing. I just wanted him to understand that it was such a huge decision I needed time to come to terms with it.

"I see," he said, dejected.

He stood and made his way to the back of the truck to grab his tools. I stood and hesitated reaching for him like my gut was screaming at me to do. *Don't lose him!* it nagged. I followed him to the back to help but he had already gotten what he needed and was making his way back to the fence.

I stood next to him holding up the loose plank and the quiet was a heady thing. It weighed on my shoulders like nothing else before, a million pounds of unrequested pressure. Whenever I'd ever been faced with a difficult decision, I ran. Always. I ran as fast as I could and never looked back, constantly distracting myself from making any kind of decision that would alter my life one way or another.

But Ian didn't deserve that. He was in love with me and was sad that he might lose me. How could I possibly get mad at that? How could I possibly tell him no? Masego made me happier than I'd ever been. Ian was the love of my life, I was certain, despite my young age. He was *it*.

"Ian, I-" I'd begun, but he stopped me.

"Do you smell that?" he asked, distracted.

"What?" I asked, taking a deep breath.

"Something's burning," he said, standing rigidly straight and peering Masego's direction. It was too far away to see it and if there was smoke, we couldn't see it in the dark of the night.

"I smell it, too," I said, worried we might be caught in an approaching grass fire. "What should we do?"

Suddenly, shots rang out from the direction

of Masego. I jumped, grasping Ian's arm. My heart dropped and a lump formed in my throat.

"What was that?" I asked Ian.

"Get in the jeep, Sophie."

Ian dropped his tools where they lay and hopped in the driver's seat so quickly I'd barely had time to register his command. I quickly obeyed, goosebumps rising on my skin when five consecutive shots rang out again. An unchecked sob came bursting from my throat.

"No!" I yelled as Ian started the jeep and peeled backward from the fence. We raced, the lights from the jeep showing a seemingly endless sea of stark grass. The only sounds were the blades slapping against the sides and our breaths as we blundered the length of the fence to get to the entrance.

"Please," I begged out loud, my knuckles white against the dash.

I glanced at Ian and panic was written over every line of his face. My stomach plummeted further at his expression. Six more consecutive shots spilled from Masego and Ian punched the gas, grabbing me by the arm and wrenching me into his side.

"Hold on," he said steadily, before charging through the fence to get to Masego faster. When the truck righted, he said, "The guns, Sophie."

I grabbed his assault rifle hung at the back of our bench seat and rested the butt against the floor near his leg then opened the glove box and removed the handgun. Instinctively, as Ian had taught me, I removed the magazine and checked the bullets before replacing it. I placed the gun in my lap. My hands shook as I wrenched my hair back into a ponytail.

Masego came into view and my heart clenched in the worst pain I could possibly imagine. She was on fire. It seemed not an inch of her went unscathed. More and more gunfire rang out and the adrenaline took over. I was ready.

Ready to defend her.

Ready to save others if I could.

Ready to die for them...especially Ian.

It felt like we couldn't get close enough, fast enough. The inches dragged.

Ten feet within its barriers, though, we could see obvious LRA soldiers opening fire on anything that moved, running toward buildings in attempt to get people, *children*, out.

"If we don't make out of this alive, Sophie Price, I want you to know that I've never loved anyone as much as I love you. You're *it* for me," Ian said, stealing my breath and my words from earlier. Tears streamed my face. He kissed me hard and quickly.

"Stay down," he said, shoving my head toward the seat.

He exited the vehicle before I'd had a chance to say anything to him. He created distance between himself and the jeep, probably to keep the bullets from straying toward me, before opening fire himself.

"*No*!" I yelled a million times, tears plummeting. "I didn't get to tell you!" I cried. "You were supposed to let me tell you!" I choked in pain. "No," I said again, when bullets seemed to fly toward the direction I thought he'd gone.

I didn't hesitate, didn't think twice. I flew up from my crouched position, crawled over and opened the driver's side door, fixing myself behind it as a makeshift shield. I placed my hands on the window's edge and assessed the grounds.

"Two soldiers at the back of our huts, three at the kitchen's door." My eyes followed back across. "Seven on Karina and Charles' porch. Two at the children's house door. Five at Kate's." All the buildings were on fire except for Karina and Charles' cabin and Ian's and my huts.

Ian was nowhere to be seen which comforted me. He wasn't lying in the common area and that was one more check toward keeping my sanity. I scanned the area once more and drank in the sight of our stalwart baobab tree, its entirety had erupted in flames. Unease began to settle through me.

I didn't hear any of the children. "Please, God. Just, please. *Please*."

Do something, Sophie. My feet seemed rooted where they stood though. *Save them*.

Motivation is a funny thing. It can come from out of nowhere. For instance, a child's scream. From my hut.

I sprang into action, edging the courtyard

fence unseen and approaching mine and Ian's huts. I raised my weapon and crept around the side, edging my way toward the two soldiers near the back, their weapons raised, ready to fire.

Slowly, very slowly, I angled myself for a good enough view. They were within range and weren't aware of me. I took three deep breaths, readying myself to kill two men I didn't know. Two men who were so ready to take part in the slaughtering of my adopted family.

For them.

I checked the safety, placed my finger on the trigger and aimed it at the first one's head. My finger was ready to squeeze, but out of nowhere the men fell to the ground without the aid of my own bullets. I plastered myself back into the side of my hut.

Suddenly, a hand came around my mouth. The hand spun me toward them. A finger on his own lips. Ian.

"I told you to stay in the jeep, Sophie."

"I love you," I blurted, frantic and a little rattled from the deaths of the soldiers. "It's the kind of love I never thought I would have, never thought I deserved, but it's forever, Ian. Forever."

He nodded once in acknowledgement. All business.

"The kids are safe. They're hidden on the east side of the property. Kate got them out somehow." I breathed a sigh of relief. "Follow me," he ordered, then stopped. "Closely."

We ran to the front of our huts, first inspecting Ian's then mine for the child who had screamed. A pair of wide eyes met mine underneath the bed.

"Shh, Mandisa," Ian whispered with a smile. "It's us. Stay right here, okay?" She started to cry in protest. "Mandisa," Ian said sternly. "Stay here, stay hidden, stay *quiet*. No one will come near this hut, you understand? Stay hidden, baby."

We stuffed my heavy down comforter with her, hoping it would stifle any noise she heard. I kissed her and ran outside with Ian. We followed the line of buildings and Ian stealthily took out the seven on Karina and Charles' porch without blinking an eye.

"Cover me, Soph," Ian said, sliding open a shallow window of the children's house.

I aimed my gun inside as he entered, my ears peeled for the slightest noise. Ian pulled me through the window as if I weighed a trifle. I bit back my surprise. He stuffed me behind him once more and we scaled the walls, listening before we entered each room with a flourish of raised weapons. Each room was empty, the soldiers loitering outside the front door were gone, probably fled.

We exited the same window we entered and approached the kitchen and cafeteria quietly. Ian peered through a low window at the back of the building.

"Shit," he said under his breath. "That same pair from the children's house have a handful of children being held hostage at the front of the building. Karina's with them."

I glanced through the same window to see for myself. Sure enough, five children and Karina stood huddled together. You could tell Karina was assuring them, attempting to calm them. My stomach tumbled the remaining length of my body to my feet.

"How do we get them out?" I asked.

"Stay here," he told me, standing.

"Wait. Wait. What are you doing?"

"I'm going to get them."

"Ian, no. Let's think about this."

"And while we think, they could be killed. There's no time. Stay here, or I swear to God, Soph..."

He molded himself to the wall, edging slowly and disappearing from my view. I raised myself just enough to see through the window to the other side in time to see Karina notice him. My breath stilled as the soldiers spoke to one another unaware of his approach.

I couldn't hear anything but saw Karina suddenly tuck the children into themselves, shielding them.

I waited for the gunfire but none came.

The breath I'd been holding rushed from me and the released adrenaline made my body shake. The soldiers laid down their weapons at their feet before kneeling with their hands above their heads and Karina pulled their guns out of reach.

I ran around the building to help and noticed Mercy had been among the huddled. She was so small we thought she was a child. Two children ran and hugged me, crying.

I sank down to my knees. "Shh," I told them as they wrapped their arms around my neck and waist.

Mercy grabbed the one wrapped around Karina and took the one already with her as well as mine. She ran with them to join the others who had already escaped and Ian escorted them. Karina took one of the soldiers' guns and held them at gunpoint. I raised my own gun to assure they weren't going anywhere.

While we waited, I drank in the two men. They were practically boys, seventeen at the most, with bodies only on the verge of becoming men, really. Their faces still exuded innocence. They were a walking dichotomy. Baby-faced assassins.

Back home, these boys would have been peers, with lives of their own. Lives unstolen by a psychopath and I almost found myself feeling sorry for them. Almost.

"Is anyone hurt, Karina?" I asked her, feeling out of breath.

"Not that I know of. Somehow, by the grace of God, the children came out of this unscathed. They'd opened fire on them almost immediately."

I released a shuddered breath.

"I'm so sorry we weren't here."

"You were doing your jobs, Sophie. We all were. We were just a day too late."

"It's okay, though," I told her. "We can leave tonight. Thank God the CHUs are there."

She nodded.

After a few minutes, Karina approached one

of the boys.

"What are you doing?" I asked her, nervous.

"I'm checking to see if he has any other weapons hidden."

I nodded, lowering my gun closer to their heads.

Karina patted the length of the first boy's legs and lifted the back of his shirt to reveal any weapons. She made him turn over on his back and did the same thing to his front side.

"Nothing," she said, relaxing a bit. "You," she told the other one, "Move onto..."

But she didn't get a chance to finish her sentence because the second boy lunged for the assault rifle around her shoulder, yanking it over her head. I raised my own to shoot him, but the first boy pitched forward for me. I didn't hesitate, shooting him in the head once and dropping him where he stood.

I turned to defend Karina, my friend, practically a surrogate mother to me, a surrogate mother to all the children there and someone I had grown to love so dearly...but it was too late.

The second boy had already shoved her to the ground, his rifle pointed at her chest and fired a single shot.

It was the only shot he would get because I raised my weapon and shot him twice in the head. I fell at her side, screaming but noticed she was still conscious. Absently, I heard stifled shouting come from the east.

"Karina?" I asked, more afraid than I'd ever been. "Hold on for me, okay?" I removed my button-up and pressed it into her chest to slow the bleeding but within seconds it was soaked.

My shaking hands fluttered over her. I had no idea what I was supposed to do. Karina's bloodied hands stopped mine as she cradled them in her own. She looked at me and smiled softly, shaking her head for me to stop and closing her eyes.

"No, no, no, no," I kept muttering under my breath, tears streaming down my face, waiting for Charles to find us. "Charles will find us. Charles will fix this."

I cradled her beautiful head in my lap, held on to her tightly, as if I could tether her to my earthly world. The fire from her burning baobab tree warmed our bodies with such heat that the tears felt cool against my cheeks and chest. "Oh, my lovely, lovely, Karina," I cooed, running my hands over her silky hair. "Oh, Karina." A sob burst from my chest at her name.

Her eyes drifted open lazily and her face reflected her age for the first time since I'd known her. "Don't cry for *me*, my love," she whispered, raising her tender hand and wiping my face. She smiled softly, and it relaxed me instantly, even at that obvious hour of her death. "I've lived the most extraordinary life and I can genuinely say that I would wish this life on anyone. Even now. Even as I lay here staining the ground beneath us..." she coughed, and I held her tighter "...because it wasn't what I had decided for myself.

"It was better. Better than anything I could have conjured on my own. So I'm telling you, my beautiful Sophie Price, don't cry for me." She coughed again and this time blood accompanied it.

"Karina, don't leave," I begged her.

"Promise me one thing," she requested. "Promise me you'll give it all to God and let Him decide it for you. He'll gift you no regrets."

"Shhh," I told her, brushing her hair back when she inhaled and choked on air. "Save your breath, Karina."

"You may have misery," she continued, ignoring my plea, "you may lose hope in the sorrow of an unplanned life but as long as you have faith and trust in adoration, in affection, in love, that sorrow will turn to happiness. And *that* is a constant, dear." She breathed deeply and steadily for a moment, seemingly catching her breath.

"No one can know sincere happiness, Sophie, without first having known sorrow. One can never appreciate the enormity and rareness of such a fiery bliss without seeing misery, however unfair that may be.

"And you will know honest happiness. Of that I am certain. Certain because it's why you are here and also because *here* is your inevitability."

I hugged her, crying into her shoulder and silently begging God to save her, silently screaming out for Charles to be there. I worried for him.

Her breaths sounded wet and labored and I stole a moment away from the embrace to look at her. I shook my head at how pale she'd become.

"Tell him he was my greatest adventure. Tell him I love him," she rasped.

I nodded. She sputtered her last breath and died in my arms.

"*No!*" I screamed at her. "*No!*"

A noise approached and I raised a trembling gun at it, bawling openly. It was Ian. The gun forgotten.

He stopped short at the sight, shaking his head back and forth in disbelief. His eyes reflected glassy in the light of the fire. He ran to us, sliding before us. He raised his hands before me, words escaping him. I couldn't explain. I'd lost my voice as well. I could only offer him tears in explanation. I watched his unsteady hand smooth Karina's hair from her face and a sob broke from between his lips.

"Karina?" we heard come near us. "*Karina*?" Charles desperately inquired and my heart already ached severely for him. "Karina!" he exclaimed, finding her bloodied in both Ian's and my arms. "*Karina*!" he bellowed, hysterically grabbing for his wife. Ian and I gave her to him and he held her closely. "Oh my God! My God!" He clutched her to him fiercely. "Karina, my love. Karina. Karina. Karina." He could only repeat her name over and over.

We could hear children's voices approaching and I ran over to stop them from getting any closer. I kept them at the fence, preventing them from seeing anything. I looked upon each of their unsure faces and was close to bursting. *How are we going to tell them*?

I checked on Ian and Charles and noticed Charles had begun to carry his wife to his cabin, struggling in his older age to take all her weight. When Ian attempted to help, Charles refused, lifting her up the porch steps and closing the door behind them.

Ian watched the door for a moment before turning my direction. The sun was beginning to rise, the buildings were but smoldering, charred remains and the gray morning cast a murky pall over Masego.

I studied the hopeless state within its walls, my eyes falling upon the still burning tree, no longer the imposing, comforting soldier I'd come to rely so heavily on.

As long as the baobab tree is here, I will be...

CHAPTER TWENTY-FIVE

We buried Karina at the new property within twenty-four hours because there was no way to preserve her body. It was just as well; none of us would have grieved her properly even if we had been able to keep her for a few more days.

That night we took the children to the CHUs, pairing the older kids with the younger kids so they had someone to watch over them as well. None of them took the news of her death well, but a handful of children were beside themselves and it took days to get them to feel they were out of harm's way.

Charles fell into a deep depression, tending to keep to his CHU a lot. We would take him trays of food but they only sat near the edge of his cot. It seemed we were going in just to replace the old untouched food, but I was diligent. Eventually, he would need to eat, and I wanted it to be available to him when the time came. Poor Charles, every time I'd knock and enter, he'd be still on his cot but would always roll over to smile at me, pat my hand and tell me I was good girl. I would keep a brave face for him but the second that CHU door fell closed, I'd have to stifle a sob.

Pembrook arrived two days before he was originally scheduled, which helped a lot. The second their plane touched down in the field next to the new community he'd asked where Charles' room was. They'd disappeared inside and I'd only gotten to see him when I took them both dinner that night.

Pemmy hugged me tightly and I returned the hug, a little piece of security fitting back into place. I knew it would take awhile for it ever to go back to rights and I wasn't even sure if it ever would completely. My whole world had been knocked off its axis. When I thought I could find solace in Ian's arms, I'd discovered that he was entirely too busy, too exhausted and too frayed for me to expect anything out of him. In fact, I worked tirelessly to appease any burden I possibly could for him. Selfishly, I admit it also made me feel closer to him. He was so closed off he felt unattainable.

He was running Masego by himself, while overseeing construction, arranging for meal preparations, and so on and so on *and so on*. He was stretched thin–very, very, *very* thin.

Which is why I hadn't mentioned his mom ringing me a few days after we'd buried Karina...

"Hello?" I asked, not recognizing the number on my sat phone.

"Miss Price, this is Abri Aberdeen."

I was perplexed. "Hello, Miss Aberdeen. How are you?"

"I'm fine. Thanks. I need to talk to you."

"I figured as much since you've rang my sat phone. It must be fairly important for you to be calling now," I nettled, "seeming as we just buried Karina. Did Ian let you know?"

"Yes, yes," she flippantly acknowledged, "I'm very sorry and all that, but..." *And all that?* "I needed to speak with you." My blood boiled in my veins.

"I can see that it must be urgent then. Is there something the matter?"

She cleared her throat. "I, well, I need to be blunt with you, Miss Price." She paused.

"Go on." *What? Do you need an invitation? Or are you hesitating because you know you're about to do irreparable damage?*

A lazy, curling unease settle throughout my entire body and I tensed, preparing myself.

"I need to know the extent of your

relationship with my son."

"I'm sorry?" I guffawed.

"Are you with him? Together?"

I choked on my own words. "Why would you need the clarification? What is it any business of yours?"

"Because!" she exclaimed, all politeness evaporated. "Do you know who I am? Know my political aspirations? If the media caught wind that *you*, of all people, were with him, they would have a field day with it! I can't afford this right now. I need all media outlets in my corner. I'm the leading candidate right now!"

I barely smothered the scream ready to erupt from my throat. "Abri," I said in the most collected voice I could conjure, "I don't have time for this right now. We just buried Karina. Do you know how much she meant to your son? And we're relocating the entire orphanage, Abri. Excuse me if I'm not able to see how important this election is to you. Truly, I hope the best for you, but the fish in my fry pot are so big, the oil is spilling over, burning everything in its path."

"What if I could fix it for you?" she asked, her voice tinged with desperation.

"What could you possibly do?" I asked, curious.

"I have political ties in L.A. I can arrange for you to come home early. Would that be enough?"

"You're kidding me. You must be." I laughed. "Abri, I'm sorry but I don't need nor do I want your 'help.' I would stay here regardless if you got me a reduced sentenced. I need to go. Have a good day."

"One more thing, then," Abri said, her voice seething. "Leave Ian be, or I will cut him off. He will never again see a dime from me." Then she hung up.

I'd hung the sat phone up, shaking from how angry she'd made me. *Bribery! Threats!* I'd hung up with her that evening trying very hard not to feel the restlessness our conversation had given me. I wasn't joking with her, I had about a million things on my plate.

Little did I know, her unreal request would be the loose thread that would unravel my entire world.

The day before Christmas Eve, things felt to be steadying out and looking hopeful again. We would surprise each child with a new outfit, new shoes and two toys Christmas Day, the construction was moving forward seamlessly, and even Charles had come up for air to help every once in awhile. Yes, I, we, had every reason to be hopeful.

I woke that morning to a knock on my CHU.

"Pembrook? What's up?" I asked, smiling.

He looked visibly put out. "May I come in?"

"Of course," I said, swinging open my door for him. He sat at the little chair at the little built-in desk and I sat across from him on my cot.

"Just spit it out," I said, burying my head in my hands. "I don't think anything you say could make our situations any worse." He shook his head in answer and my stomach dropped. "What is it?"

"Somehow the courts became aware of your unscheduled trip to Cape Town. A warrant for your arrest has been issued and you have until January second to turn yourself in."

I stood, my hands going to my head. "There's no way," I said, beginning to pace. "She wouldn't."

"Who wouldn't?" he asked.

"Abri Aberdeen. Ian's mom?"

"Yes?"

"She called a few days back and essentially threatened me to leave her son alone. She felt the match imprudent considering both our background stories, felt it would be detrimental to her current political goals. She wanted me to promise to leave him alone."

"Preposterous!" Pembrook exclaimed.

"She'd admitted to having political ties in L.A. There's no other person I could think of who would do this. Would my father have done this?" I asked Pemmy.

"No, he knew of the trip, was ecstatic about the potential connection."

"Figures," I said, laughing. "So that leaves Abri. I just can't believe she would do this. What should I do?"

"You have no choice, Sophie. You'll return home and face Reinhold."

"I can't leave them now, Pemmy. I just can't," I said, straining not to break down. "It would make things so much worse."

"If you don't face Reinhold now, your legal troubles will compound. It would be wiser for you to appease them now."

I looked at Pemmy. "He'll throw me in jail."

He shrugged his shoulders in reply.

I smiled at him in disbelief. "I'm paying for my past sins, Pembrook."

"Oh," he said, taking my hand, "I believe you've already paid for them tenfold, Sophie."

"When will you tell, Ian?"

Ian! "I can't tell him. Not now, Pemmy. News that his mother did this would send him over the edge!"

"He's going to know you're gone, love."

"I know. I think I'll try slipping out with you tonight when your plane arrives." *I'm a coward.*

"You won't even entertain the idea of letting him know his mother did this?"

And risk her cutting him off too? Never!

"No, I can't, it would kill him, Pembrook."

"So you'll let him believe you betrayed him? Is that really a better fate?"

I nodded, sure revealing the blackmail tactic would only hurt. "Betrayed by someone he's barely known six months or his mother?" *Not to mention her little threat.*

"But why be the fall guy? Why allow her to escape this intact?" he asked, suspicious.

"Because I love him, more than you could possibly imagine," I confessed truthfully. *Let him take that however he wishes.*

Pembrook smiled at me but his expression was sad. "How unselfish," he told me, wrapping me in a hug. "Who would have thought such an unselfish act would, in turn, cause you so much pain."

"Not me," I confessed candidly.

Pembrook left my CHU and I looked around me, certain I didn't need to take back a single thing. I discreetly gave away all my things, leaving Mandisa my comforter. I would return home with only a single pair of jeans, shirt, boots and toothbrush.

Which is why Ian hadn't thought it anything weird when we went to say goodbye to Pembrook together.

"Are you coming?" Ian asked as he passed by my CHU.

I nodded, a queasy feeling residing in the pit of my belly.

I followed closely, listening to him fill Pembrook in on whatever they would need soon. Pemmy dutifully dictated it all on his pad. I had no doubt Pembrook wouldn't hesitate in accommodating them. I would ensure it was my money that paid for it all though.

I watched Ian's hands as he gestured when he spoke and even they looked tired. Calluses on his palms and fingers screamed out they needed tending to, but I knew him well enough he would ignore the plea. His own needs never came before

Masego and that was unfortunate because Masego would always be needy.

I looked at him knowing I would be saying goodbye to him soon and that familiar hollowness began to creep within, making me feel cold and alone already. My gut twisted at the thought of how he'd react, how he'd interpret my leaving. I was determined though. I wouldn't be responsible for his mother making his life miserable, not when she so callously and easily made my current life a living hell.

When we reached the plane, I yelled at him to stay back with me. He obeyed without thinking much of it, hugging Pembrook goodbye. Charles, whom I'd tearfully said goodbye to earlier, waited for Pemmy below the hatch and they spoke to one another briefly before Pemmy boarded the plane.

"Ian," I said softly, fighting tears.

He turned toward me, his concerned expression wounding my already wounded heart. Something in his eyes lit in understanding.

"I..."

"Don't you dare, Soph," he said. A muscle ticked in his jaw. "I swear to God, Sophie Price."

"Ian," I said, the unshed tears giving way.

He edged closer, but I stepped back, unable to handle his touch without breaking down completely. He recognized this and grabbed me by the upper arms, bringing me close to him. "You owe me," he gritted. "Why?"

"I-I've been given an opportunity to go home

and I decided it was for the best."

"Bullshit," he said, shaking me a little in his frustration. "You're lying. I know you and you're lying."

I avoided eye contact, focusing in on the tips of my worn boots. The same boots that worked tirelessly with me day after day caring for Masego. The same boots I wore while falling in love with him.

"Look at me, damn it!"

I raised my gaze toward him.

"Answer me," he demanded. "*Why*?"

"I-I told you already. My answer won't change. I think it's for the best," I lied.

He shook his head back and forth. "You can't go," he begged, hugging me to him like he could hold me there forever.

"Why?" I whispered in his ear.

"Because I'm in love with you."

I clenched my lids and kissed his tanned cheek. "I love you, too," I confessed...and walked away.

"Soph," I heard behind me.

"Sophie," he pleaded, softer.

"Soph," he barely whispered.

But I didn't answer. I just kept on walking, the tears cascading forth in a sea of excruciating pain.

"Sophie Price," he yelled, agony and animosity lacing each word. I turned to face him. "You leave me like this, alone here, and I'll never be able to forgive you. Don't bother trying to come back. You get on that plane and I'm done with you!"

My breath hitched in my throat, warm tears spilling anew. I nodded, choking back another sob, and stealed myself. *For him. For him. For him,* I kept chanting. A large bellowing roar rumbled behind me, shattering my heart into a million pieces. I gulped back my own cry, placing one heavy foot in front of the other, refusing to turn back around. I knew if I saw him, took even a second to gaze on him, I'd forego all threats and ruin any future he may have had if he ever left Masego.

For him, I breathed internally, shutting the hatch behind me.

CHAPTER TWENTY-SIX

My cell phone buzzed and woke me.

Disoriented, I surveyed my surroundings. My room. In L.A. It was quiet and cold. Quiet, cold and empty. No sweet, baby voices woke me. I would never wake to the sight of Mandisa's angelic face or the stalwart baobab tree, never eat the odd dinner with Charles or Karina again. My heart thudded harder in pain.

Karina.

The singsong voice of my gorgeous Karina would never greet my ears again. I would never stand in line at lunch with Ian and talk to our students, teasing or playing with them.

Ian. Ian. Ian.

My heart sputtered with exceptional misery. I'd never known such sorrow before, never would be able to convey fully just how badly I was willing to be stretched and torn into pieces if it meant it would stop the heartache, just keep me from never knowing the pangs of missing Ian again.

I rolled onto my side and my cell buzzed once more. My hand stretched before me and I picked it up.

"Hello," my voice cracked.

"Sophie fucking Price!" a male voice howled over the phone. Spencer.

"Hi, Spence."

"Hi, Spence? *Hi, Spence*? That's all I get?" he teased. "I think I at least deserve an *Oh, Spencer!*" he crooned in mock falsetto. "Come on! I haven't seen or heard from you in five months, Sophie."

I sat up, wiping the sleep from my eyes. "Oh, Spencer," I deadpanned.

He laughed heartily and breathed deeply. "God, it's good to hear your voice, Sophie."

"How are you?" I evaded.

"I'm fantastic now that you're home," he said. "I'm in your drive, actually. Come to pick your beautiful ass up. I'm taking you to lunch, baby. A celebration of sorts."

"I'm not really up for it," I told him.

"Sophie, I'm not taking no for an answer. If you'd like, I can honk my horn until your dad calls the cops."

"Fine," I relented. "Give me five minutes."

"Five?"

"Yes, five minutes, please."

"But didn't I just wake you?"

"Yeah, so?"

"Sophie Price only needs five minutes to get ready?"

"Hush, Spence. I'll be right down."

I lay there for a minute just to spite him then sluggishly brushed my teeth, threw on a pair of jeans, a t-shirt and some black Converse. I grabbed a hoodie out of my closet after putting on a little bit of makeup. I ran a brush through my bone-straight hair. My eyes burned thinking of the waves Ian liked to run his hands through when it would dry after being plaited. I spritzed a little perfume and didn't glance twice at my reflection.

I exited my front door and followed the dramatic path down to his car. I stifled an eye roll at Spencer's reaction.

"Who the hell are you?" he asked me.

My hands rose to my hips. "What are you saying?"

"I want to know what you've done with sex goddess Sophie Price?"

The title made my stomach roil. "I'm not that girl anymore."

He studied me intently, his head cocked to one side. "Apparently," he stated, and I wasn't sure how to interpret his reaction until he'd scooped me up into his arms and spun me around. "I like this Sophie. You look relaxed and able to have fun. You're still as beautiful as ever but add carefree to the mix and that's the new Sophie. I like it. It's a good look on you."

I inclined my head. "Thank you."

He opened his door for me and I got in. "How'd you get off early?" Spencer asked, sliding into the sleek driver's seat.

I snorted. "You don't wanna know." I sat up a bit in my seat. "How did you find out I was home anyway?"

"Pembrook texted me."

I didn't know what to be more stunned at: The fact that Pemmy contacted Spencer, or the fact that he'd done it by text. I smiled knowing he'd done it because he knew I needed a friend.

I hadn't been paying attention to where we were going until he pulled into The Ivy.

"Oh no, no, no. Not here," I told him, sitting rigidly. My fingers worried my lips, desperate to leave.

"Why not?" he asked, puzzled.

"I'm not prepared to see anyone we know here."

"Shit," he said suddenly.

Sav knocked on my window, startling me. I turned Spencer's direction and gave him the dirtiest look. *Sorry*, he mouthed.

I got out and she eyed me with obvious disdain at my appearance. "*Sophie*?" she asked, obnoxiously raising her sunglasses as if that would change what I'd worn. A snicker left her lips before she checked herself. "Um, how are you?" she asked, letting her glasses fall back down on her plastic nose.

"I'm all right. How are you?" I asked.

"I've never been better," she said, not disguising the obvious pleasure she got out of seeing her mighty queen fall so hard. Little did she know how much I couldn't care less what she or any of the others thought of me. I just didn't want to be kicked while I was already down.

Savannah led us into the restaurant and Spencer fell in beside me. "If I had any idea, I never would have done this, Sophie."

I wrapped my arm within his to reassure him. "It's okay, Spencer. I'll survive," I told him, offering a smile.

His eyes grew wide for a moment before he checked them. "I'm still very sorry."

I squeezed his arm to reassure him it was okay.

We sat at two tables pushed together. Two by two they all came flitting in, dramatically announcing themselves with flourish by flaunting their ridiculous material. Everywhere I looked, an Hermès scarf, a Fendi bag, a Patek Phillipe watch would flash in my face. Before, all I could think of when I saw these things was that I wanted or needed to have them as well, but after Masego? All I could think of was if I pawned these items, I could buy them food for a year, purchase a new generator or even a new building.

I was met by all of them with disbelieving eyes and snobbish contempt. I wanted to scream in their faces, "It's your parents' money! Not yours!" but it would have done no good. To my right sat Graham, Sav and Brock, apparently reunited, then Spencer and Victoria. They'd kept to conversation within themselves, excluding me on purpose. The icing on the cake was when Ali arrived with Brent.

My face flamed bright red when Brent nodded at me instead of speaking his hello. Ali wrapped her arm through Brent's in a palpable attempt to show ownership. I wished to God everyone would disappear except for them so I could have apologized. Glancing around the table, I realized I'd wronged every single one of my lunch patrons. Suddenly, the urge to flee was discernible.

I sat quiet, praying it would end quickly for me. The waitress came and took everyone's orders skipping over me by accident. Spencer had to call her back. I felt like I'd been punched in the gut when they all sneered under their breath at me, hiding their laughs behind manicured hands.

But then I reminded myself that I deserved it, even from a group as selfish and unaware as that one, because I'd created them. I'd never really regretted anything I'd done before Masego, but I certainly regretted many after.

"So, Africa?" Victoria asked, her valley girl accent laughingly pronouncing it *Africaw*.

"Yes," I told their riveted stares, hoping one-word answers would suffice.

"Did, you, like, see lions and shit?" Graham asked.

"Occasionally," I told them.

"Which one, lions or shit?" he added as if he was clever.

"Both."

"Is that, like, why you look like you do right now?" Sav asked, making the table erupt in laughter.

"What? Comfortable? Or without a nauseatingly noticeable amount of couture on?"

"Did your dad lose all his money?" Sav needled, ignoring my own questions.

"Not that I know of," I stated.

"You're in serious need of a makeover," Victoria added, her fingernails outlining a box around my face.

"I've just had one," I implied, referring to my heart and soul.

They each looked amongst themselves and pretentiously and silently acknowledged with single looks exactly what they now thought of me, except for Spencer. Spencer seemed blissfully unaware what jackasses they all were, but he was clearly aware of how uncomfortable I was.

"Sophie and I have to go, guys."
He stood abruptly laying a few bills on the table and escorted me from my seat. As we left, a burst of repugnant laughter resounded from the table all at once. My shoulders sank into themselves, but Spencer wrapped his arm around me and righted me.

"You broke the cycle," he whispered in disbelief, his eyes bright with admiration.

CHAPTER TWENTY-SEVEN

I'd been home two days and I had yet to see my parents. I couldn't tell if it'd been because I was practically living in my bed, more depressed than I could have ever imagined missing Ian, or because they couldn't be bothered to come by and see me even though I'd been gone for months.

My heart felt heavy the morning of the second, knowing I would have to appear in court, in front of Reinhold. I woke, dressed in jeans and a t-shirt, not giving a crap. I knew I would be thrown in jail that day. This was the moment Reinhold had been waiting for.

The courtroom was exactly as I remembered it. Cold and desolate and devoid of hope. It felt as if my breath was sucked from my chest the second I placed a foot inside. I met Pembrook as his table and sat.

"This is a simple hearing," he told me, arranging his satchel on the table. He poured me a glass of water and set it down in front of me. "The judge will state what you're accused of and you will enter a plea, which, of course, will be a 'not guilty.' I advise you not to say a word."

"Pembrook," I told him, taking in his stark appearance, "for once, can you not act as my 'attorney' here?"

He smiled gently. "Stay quiet, love. I'll take care of everything."

This made my heart ache, but I nodded my consent. *Take care of everything. Everything but the everything I want back.*

Reinhold stepped into the room, his robes billowing out from behind him. Immediately, I wanted to vomit.

"All rise," the bailiff said. "This court is now in session, the Honorable Judge Francis Reinhold presiding."

Reinhold sat and we followed suit. He began to filter through paper documents behind his bench and the quiet was deafening. My hands began to shake, so I tucked them into my sides and stared at my feet. I glimpsed behind me when the doors opened and Spencer walked in, waving and sitting on a bench directly behind me. He was the only presence there, but it was comforting enough that it allowed my body to calm a bit. I was still shaking, but the nausea was gone.

"Sophie Price," Reinhold's voice boomed. He looked right at me and pierced me with a penetrating gaze. "You're accused of violating the terms of your sentence. How do you plea?"

Pembrook and I stood. "My client pleads not guilty," Pembrook announced.

"I see. What say you, Prosecution?"

"Your Honor," the prosecutor said, addressing the court, "we move to dismiss Miss Price as time served."

My breath whooshed from my lungs all at once and I began to choke. Pembrook comically slapped at my back to get me to breathe, shrugging toward Reinhold. Reinhold pinned me with a look that screamed *check yourself!* I coughed back my choking and pinned my lips together.

"Would you care to explain?" he asked the prosecutor.

"Yes, we'd like to call a witness to the stand, Your Honor."

"Were you aware of this?" he asked Pemmy.

"No, Your Honor."

"And do you object?"

"If the prosecution moves to dismiss, then my client and I are comfortable with their witness." Reinhold was quiet for a moment, contemplating whether he would allow the witness, and I held my breath.

"Proceed," he said. "You may sit, Defense." Pembrook and I sat.

"Pemmy, who is it?" I asked under my breath.

"I've honestly no idea," he said

Just then, the doors opened and I thought my eyes were deceiving me. I blinked slowly before wiping my eyes. When I reopened them, I discovered what I'd only thought was an illusion.

Ian.

I'd stood and begun to run toward him, but Pemmy stayed me with an arm. He shook his head back and forth and I was forced to sit. Seeing him for the first time since I'd left felt incredible yet overwhelming. I needed his touch but simultaneously, I was so afraid he still meant what he'd said. I didn't want to know, but I was desperate to know at the same time.

He moved toward the witness stand with only a brief glance my direction, spearing me in the gut. When he approached the witness stand, the bailiff approached him, Bible in hand.

"Place your right hand on the Bible," the bailiff ordered and Ian complied. "State your name," he said.

"Ian Aberdeen."

"You do solemnly state that the testimony you may give in the case now pending before this court shall be the truth, the whole truth, and nothing but the truth, so help you God?"

"I do."

I gulped audibly.

"Mister Aberdeen," the prosecutor began, "what is your position at the Ugandan orphanage Masego?"

"I'm technically a teacher there, but I suppose you could also consider me a jack of all trades. I mend fences, birth the occasional calf, assist in medical emergencies, that sort of thing."

"Were you present at Masego for the length of Miss Price's stay?"

"I was."

"And are you an authorized representative of Masego?"

"Yes, I am."

"Tell the court then, Mister Aberdeen, your experience with Miss Price during her stay at Masego."

"The day Sophie came to Uganda," he began...

For the next hour and a half, Ian told our entire story to the court leaving out the part where we fell madly for one another. It was an incredible story to hear all at once, and I found myself crying at the tale. I peered around me and noticed there didn't seem to be a dry eye in the room. But he never once made eye contact throughout the entire thing and that wounded my already bleeding heart. He was going to help me, yes, but he wanted nothing to do with me beyond saving my hide.

When he was done, the prosecution

dismissed him and he sat on the opposite side of the courtroom to await Judge Reinhold's decision. I looked at him, begging him to glance my direction, but his stare at the front of the courtroom was unmoving.

"*Sophie*?" I heard.

I turned to Reinhold. "Uh, I'm sorry, did you say something?" I asked him.

Reinhold breathed deeply. With a brief tap of his gavel, "I dismiss your case as time served. You're free to go, Miss Price." Reinhold stood and the rest of the courtroom followed suit. He made a move to go but stopped himself. "Before I leave, Miss Price," he said, turning toward me, "know this, yours is the most satisfying punishment I've ever given." He inclined his head out of respect and I nodded once in return.

When Reinhold was gone, I turned, ready to run Ian's direction. I sprinted around the table, pushing chairs out of my way, my heart jumping into my throat without ever taking my stare off his heavenly face.

Everyone rushed me at once, congratulating me and attempting to hug me. Spencer bombarded me, kissing my cheek, and picking me up. I struggled to get down, still staring Ian's direction. Finally, he made brief eye contact before walking through the double doors and out of my eyesight.

I broke free and ran for him.

"Ian! Ian!" I kept shouting before a passing officer ordered me quiet.

I ran the length of the corridor, but he was nowhere to be found. I pressed the elevator button for the first floor but was too impatient watching it slowly ascend for me, so I ripped open the fire exit door and ran the four flights to the ground floor. I was panting when I burst from the door on that floor. My eyes searched for him throughout the marble lobby. He wasn't there. I rushed to the wide, wood entrance doors and out onto the descending steps. I discovered him just as he entered a taxi. I sprinted down the steps calling out his name and waving my arms over my head but he was gone. My disappointment was crushing. I fell hard to the bottom of the steps and sobbed into my hands.

"Why did he just take off like that?" Spencer asked coolly beside me, looking the direction Ian had fled. I peered up at him. His hands rested in his pockets.

"Because he thought I betrayed him," I said.

He tore his gaze away from the street and observed me below him. "You didn't?" he asked.

"No, I-I was blackmailed."

"Scandalous," he said, bending to sit beside me. He leaned back on his elbows. He looked back out toward the street, avoiding eye contact. "You're in love with him," he stated as fact.

"Yes."

Spencer sighed, turning toward me. "Then what the hell are you doing here, Sophie Price?"

"I don't know where he's staying," I explained.

"And when has something as small as that ever stopped a whirlwind force like you, girl?"

I smiled at him.

"Never," I told him truthfully. His smile faltered a bit. "I'm sorry, Spence."

He shook his head. "Don't, babe," he said, winking. "They're all lined up. They're waiting for me as we speak," he said, extending his arm.

He teased but the sadness there troubled me. I loved Spence so much but knew I couldn't say as much, that it would be cruel. So I just smiled at him, shoving my shoulder into his.

He picked himself up and dusted the back of his pants. I stood and threw my arms around him. "Sophie Price, you'll be the one that got away, I'm afraid," he spoke into my ear. He pulled away. "You know how to solve that problem?" he joshed. I shook my head no. "With bigger problems."

He kissed my cheek and stalked off, twirling his keys in his hand and whistling as he made his way to his car.

CHAPTER TWENTY-EIGHT

I knocked twice but there was no answer.

Impatient, I headed back down to Ian's lobby.

"Excuse me," I told the concierge, "but can you check to see if a guest named Ian Aberdeen is still here?"

"Of course, miss." His fingers cracked the keys of his keyboard. "I'm sorry, but Mister Aberdeen has checked out."

My heart raced. "Thank you," I told him before hauling back out to my car, hopping in and racing toward home.

I dialed my cell.

"Pemmy?"

"Yes, dear? Fantastic job today in court," he said. "I was just telling your father so."

A lump formed in my throat. "I-Pemmy, listen, I need you to do me a favor." I weaved between two semis, almost clipping one. *No wonder you aren't supposed to talk or text while driving.* "Can you find out if Ian is flying back out tonight?"

He sighed. "Come home first, your father needs to talk with you."

"Pemmy!" I yelled, exasperated. "*Please*, Pemmy, can you just check for me?"

"Come home, love. I'll see what I can find out for you."

"Thank you!" I said, pressing end and tossing the phone on the passenger seat.

Fifteen minutes later, I whipped my car into my parents' drive and pulled into my garage space. I turned off the ignition, attempted to get out but realized I'd left my phone. I bent back in to retrieve it.

"You're wealthy," I heard behind me, staying me in place.

My mouth instantly went dry, my hands trembled, my breathing labored. I climbed out of my car and shut the door, leaning against the frame.

"No, my parents are wealthy," I told him, mimicking what he'd told me outside his own home in Cape Town.

He smiled at me. "I see."

"Does this change your opinion of me?" I asked.

"Hardly," he told me, a rogue smile playing on a mischievous face.

We stood there staring at one another.

"My mom told me everything," he said.

"I'm sorry."

"No. I'm sorry. For what she said. For what *I* said. I'm just...sorry."

"What you did for me in court. That was...incredible. Thank you."

"I'd have done it again and again if it meant freeing you."

I smiled. We stood, staring again.

"Who was that guy at the courthouse?" he asked, his fists unwittingly tightening at his sides.

"That was Spencer."

"Spencer. The Spencer who took you dancing that night?"

"Yes."

"He's in love with you, ya know."

"No, I-"

"He is. I could see it," he coolly replied, inching closer, "but that means nothing."

"Oh?" I asked, one brow raised in question.

"Yes, because you belong to me, Price." I opened my mouth to confirm just that, but he cut me off. "And before you argue with me," he continued, grabbing me quickly and clutching me closely to his chest, sucking the very breath from mine.

He brought both hands up to my neck. I could feel the thumping of his heart against my own. "Would you like to know how I know this?"

I simply nodded, unable to speak.

"This," he said before slamming his mouth on mine.

EPILOGUE

Ian tumbled atop me on the mattress, languidly kissing my shoulders and collarbone and then, as if he couldn't wait, his lips trailed up my neck at a furious pace to my mouth. I smiled into his lips.

"It works better when the dress is off," I teased him.

He sat up before dragging me off the bed and standing me in front of the mirror. "You know, I usually hate weddings but this one...," he said, trailing off, brushing my hair to the side and over my shoulder.

"It wasn't so shabby," I completed the thought. "Plus, Ribbon Caye is beautiful this time of year."

"Mmhmm," a distracted Ian replied, unzipping me from behind. "It was nice of your dad to donate it to Masego."

"He's really come around," I said, thinking on how my father had changed.

He'd donated Ribbon Caye to us and it had become a way to provide a steady source of income as we rented it out regularly. He also agreed to a one-hundred-thousand-dollar annual stipend. It allowed us to bring children into a safer environment as well as help us afford twenty-four-hour armed guards, something he insisted upon, which surprised us. Within six months, my father had also completely rebuilt Masego. It was the finest home for children we'd ever encountered in Uganda, in Africa, really and could house more than two hundred children at once.

When I'd told my father my plans to move to Uganda permanently, he didn't fight it as I had anticipated. Instead, he said he only had two requests. The first was that I let him support my cause however he saw fit. He had an incessant need for control. But if he was the one being generous, I wasn't going to begrudge him that. The second was that he and I would start over, that I would help him become a good father because, and I quote, I'd "turned into a magnificent daughter and magnificent daughters deserved good fathers."

Ian tossed my white silk gown to the side and gazed at my reflection. He ran his hands down my shoulders, sides and rested them on my hips, smiling wickedly.

Suddenly, I was swept up and tossed back onto the bed, making me laugh. My hair fanned around his face. The moment quickly faded from amusement to something urgent.

"I love you, Sophie Aberdeen."

I kissed his lips softly. "I love you too, other half."

He smiled at this then rolled us both over once. He reached over and turned up *Between Two Points* by The Glitch Mob playing on our iPod.

He kissed me deeply, our tongues intertwined and said my name, bringing my ear to his mouth. He bit my earlobe and whispered, "The shortest distance between two points is the line from me to you."

He was good on his word.

BETWEEN TWO POINTS

BY THE GLITCH MOB

WE'VE GOT FOREVER
SLIPPIN' THROUGH OUR HANDS
WE'VE GOT MORE TIME
TO NEVER UNDERSTAND

FALLING FOOTSTEPS
WEIGHING HEAVY ON ME

BEHIND DARKNESS
BENEATH CANDLES
WHISPERS WALTZ
AROUND OUR DREAMS

THE SHORTEST DISTANCE
BETWEEN TWO POINTS
IS THE LINE
FROM ME TO YOU

FEET TURNING BLACK
IS THIS THE PATH WE MUST WALK
NO TURNING BACK
WISH I COULD JUST HEAR YOU TALK

CAN SOMETHING LIKE THIS BE PULLED
FROM UNDER OUR FEET
LEAVING OUR SKIN
AND BURNING COALS TO MEET

TELL ME NOW

THE SHORTEST DISTANCE
BETWEEN TWO POINTS
IS THE LINE
FROM ME TO YOU

VAIN'S

PLAYLIST

HTTP://WWW.FISHERAMELIE.COM/YOURESOVAIN

ACKNOWLEDGEMENTS

Thank you to the editor who tolerates me. Hollie Westring. You're officially my life twin and it's a little scary. November 27th will never pass by without my thinking of you. Love you so much for all that you do. Thank you so very much for being so easy, breezy, lemon-squeezey, too.

Thank you to the most fabulous South African I know, Natasha Mion. Though you might be the only one I know, I'm willing to bet my life savings I'd be hard pressed to find anyone more incredible than the likes of you. Your generosity in taking the time and effort in helping me correct my terrible Afrikaans mistakes is so humbling! I'm so grateful. Thank you, again. P.s. Look for that book in the snail mail.

Leighton. M. Leighton. You're so shaken, you're not stirred. Thank you for being so incredible. You're my thick when I'm running thin. Love you so much.

Court "is in session" Cole. You're my beacon when I'm floundering inside that preserver and that seems to be too often. If you were a game of Rock, Paper, Scissors, you'd be my perpetual rock. I'd win every time. Thank you for everything. Love you so much. P.s. Kiss B for me.

Nichole Chase, Tiffany King, Shelly Crane, I'm in awe of you three. Success comes in some incredible packages and I dig what you're selling. You guys are always there for me when I need you. Always. You're my personal baobab trees. Love you so much.

Plumes, I'm still waving that purple feather and every time I do, it gets a little shinier, a little brighter, a little "plume-ier". Love you all so very much.

Hubs, I always save you for last and it's because nice guys finish last but also because I think great things are worth waiting for. Great things like, proclamations of my undying love. Cheesy, I know, but *I breathe just to be near you.* This has been one of the roughest years of our lives and we trudged through the sucking mud better than anyone I could possibly imagine. When life pulled me in, you were always there to get me out. When I look at our future, all I can think of is "We got this. Bring it." So hook your arm with mine, dude, because although adventure seems to find us at the oddest times, we're awfully damn good at tiding the storms and screaming "Yee Haw" at the tall swells.

Fisher Amelie is a member of The Paranormal Plumes Society.

http://theplumessociety.com/

SIGN UP

FOR FISHER'S NEWSLETTER

HTTP://WWW.FISHERAMELIE.COM/NEWSLETTER

FEEL LIKE GIVING TO A FEW IMPOVERISHED UGANDANS?

COME VISIT BEAUTIFUL RENEE'S SITE AT

SERVINGHISCHILDREN.ORG

AND DONATE IF YOU CAN.

EVEN IF IT'S JUST A DOLLAR...

EVERY LITTLE BIT HELPS.

"BESIDES," SOPHIE SAYS, "A DOLLAR CAN BUY A LOT OF RICE."

Enjoy the first chapter of Fisher Amelie's *Callum & Harper* just ahead.

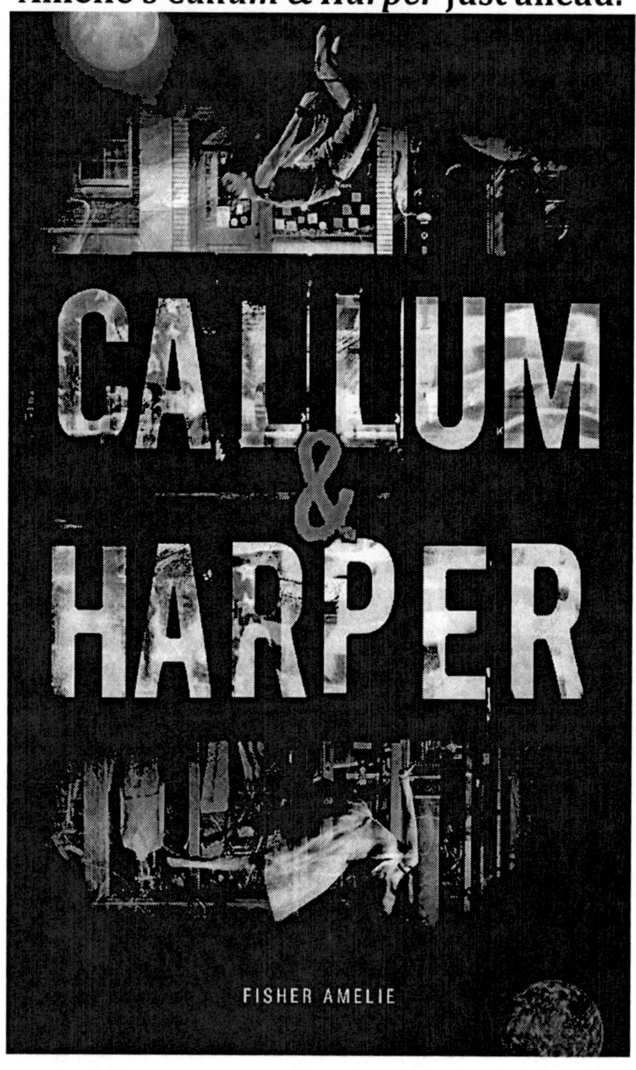

Fisher Amelie
http://www.fisheramelie.com/
First Edition: December 2011

Printed in the United States of America

To C.Z.P.
This is for you because you need
to know that you're worth
dedicating a book to and
because I think you've forgotten
who you are. Simply put, you're
incredible and I love you.

Chapter One
Where is My Mind?

Callum

I was sitting next to one of the most beautiful girls I'd ever seen in my entire life. She was so intriguing, I could actually feel the sweat dripping down the back of my neck at the effort it was taking to keep from staring at her. I hoped to God she couldn't tell...or smell.

If I were to guess, I'd have said she was about five foot, five inches, she had wicked long coppery hair and hazel eyes that looked more gold than green. Her eyes killed me. I believed I could peer into those eyes all day long, maybe on a blanket on the grass, in Central Park, that we could've *shared.*

Get it together, Callum, I thought. *You're probably making her nervous. You've too much shit on your plate, dude.* I paused, mid thought, remembering where we were. *She* is *sitting in the same office you are, bro. Yeah, Callum, she is,* I debated with myself, with only a fleeting thought toward how mentally unstable people who talked to themselves were. *But the last thing this lovely probably wants is to mess around with someone with as much drama as you own.*

She tucked her chin into her chest and glanced my direction but when she caught me staring back, she quickly fixed her eyes onto the floor. *Then again....*

"Harper Bailey!" A social worker yelled out. Gold eyes stood up. *Harper Bailey. What an appropriate name.* She even *looked* like a Harper and that made me want to smile for some reason. Harper Bailey looked back at me and flashed a perfect row of white teeth making me melt a little into my seat.

Harper

Oh my God, I think I just melted a little bit into the floor. The guy I'd been sitting next to that entire time was bona fide swoon worthy. If I'd showed a picture of this guy to a hundred girls and asked their opinions, they'd all, without fail, would've said, 'swoon worthy'.

If I were to have guessed, he was probably six foot two or three. He had brown hair, piercing green eyes and a jaw line that screamed 'I might just let you kiss me here'. There's something about strong jaws that sing to me but his shoulders and back didn't look so shabby, either. Yet another feature he owned, I could say I wouldn't mind running my hands across.

I could feel his eyes on the back of my head, heating me up from the inside. I shivered involuntarily. Never had someone affected me like that and I was stupefied because I was Harper Bailey, self-professed bachelor and lover of singledom. 'Rely on no one because people inevitably fail you' Harper Bailey.

"Callum Tate!" A social worker called. I whipped my head around and watched him walk to their desk. Callum Tate. I liked the sound of that. It sounded sweet, like, 'Hi, my name is Callum Tate and I'm going to take care of you, Harper Bailey', which is exactly what I'd always openly confessed as stupid but also *always* secretly wanted. *Yikes, Harper. Crazy much?*

He looked over his shoulder at me. We stopped pretending and smiles ensued. He had a slightly crooked smile which somehow looked amazingly adorable on him.

"Miss Bailey?" I heard. *Oops.*

"Yes, Mrs. Carson?"

"If you can trouble yourself to pay attention to me, baby, I can give you some information. Now, when did you turn eighteen?"

"March seventeenth, ma'am."

"Alright, did you finish high school?"

"Yes, ma'am."

"Alright, why did Mrs. Drawing ask you to leave her

home?"

"Isn't it obvious?" I said, dropping my arm over the back of the chair next to me. This was my attempt at feigning indifference. I don't think I was fooling anyone. Truth was, I was scared, no, terrified of being alone. "She won't be receiving benefits for being my foster mother any longer since I've turned eighteen. Her free lunch ticket expired, if you catch my drift."

"Harper, you're always so cheeky, maybe if you'd bite your tongue you wouldn't have been asked to leave."

"Oh, Mrs. Carson, that's why I love you. You make it seem as if it's my mouth that got me kicked out of all those homes when in truth, it was my fists." *And a little bit my mere existence.*

"There you go with that mouth, young lady. You're telling me, of all the fights you were in, not *one* of them was your fault?" Her eyebrow arched over one eye. That brow screamed 'bullshit'.

"I know it's hard to believe, Mrs. Carson, but when someone calls you a variation on the word orphan enough times, it does something to your heart and there's only so many occasions where a person is expected to endure it before they end up punching that someone in the face."

"Hmm," she said, "maybe you're right, baby."

We both laughed loud enough to draw Callum's attention and that tickled my stomach slightly. *That's smart, Harper. Focus your attention on mister perfect and forget all about how pathetic your situation really is.*

"Okay, well," she sighed. "There are homes for those in your situation but this is New York City and they're full up, not an opening in the foreseeable future."

Of course. "That's fantastic news, Mrs. Carson. Well, that was invigorating, I think I'll leave now." I stood.

"Sit, Harper!" I sat. "Calm down now. I've got some other options for you." She frowned at the mess of papers in her hands. "Harper, the best we can do for you here is to put you on the waiting list for a few homes but until then, you'll just have to make do with the night to night facilities in the city."

I'd heard all sorts of stories about these places. If you didn't get there early enough, you missed your chance to stay and when Mrs. Carson said 'night to night' she meant you literally had to fight to stay there from one night to the next. I'd recently read about two homeless men who'd gotten into a fight vying for a chance at an open spot in line and one of them killed the other for it.

"Alright, put me on the list then and jot me down a few places I can stay until then."

"Already have a printed list." She said, handing me a piece of paper that had been Xeroxed so often it looked solid black. "Here ya' go. You call me in two weeks and I'll let you know the progress of your name on the permanent housing list."

"Thank you, Mrs. Carson."

"No problem, honey. I'll see you in two weeks."

I stood to leave and gathered the bag that housed every belonging I owned. So essentially, inside my small canvas messenger, were two pairs of jeans, a few button up fitted flannels, one striped dress, and a pair of flip flops. Also inside, was my signed copy of 'To Kill A Mockingbird' by Harper Lee, my namesake and hero, which I'd won at a county fair when my foster family at the time, traveled there to visit their own extended family. I wore my only other pair of jeans and a fitted t-shirt that read, 'Save The Drama For Your Mama'.

When I turned around, I saw Callum heading for the door and my stomach clenched in anticipation.

Callum

Oh dear Lord, we're leaving at the same time. If she hadn't stopped attempting to hide her smile, I would've been forced to reveal my plans to toss the stranger outside against the brick and kiss her face until the sun set.

She passed ahead of me and I caught a whiff of her shampoo, involuntarily sending my eyes into the back of my head. This chick was a walking version of the Pixie's "Where Is My Mind?". Sexy. As. Hell. Though, now that I think about it. is hell *sexy*? I'm guessing not. I continued to watch. Her hips could have kept time with the damn beat.

"Here, let me get that for you," I said, throwing open the door. The sun cascaded down her copper hair and made her eyes feel transparent.

"Thank you," she shyly said but offered up a cute lopsided grin as if to say 'good boy'. *Thanks for the bone, buttercup.*

She took the wrought iron steps down to the sidewalk two at a time, which told me she was in a hurry and since it was nearly sunset, I was willing to bet that she and I were heading in the same direction. I scrambled at what to say while her feet scurried along the pavement.

Say something! "Where you headed?"

Clever.

She stopped and turned.

"Uh," she said, seeming embarrassed. She thought twice for a moment before stiffening her body and raising her chin. "I'm headed to..." Confusion set in. She glanced down at the same piece of paper I, as fate would have it, held in my own hand. "Hope House, on One Hundred and Second," she finished.

"What a coincidence," I teased with a slight grin.

"You too?" She asked, one eyebrow raised.

Cynical, a product of the system.

"Yup, what can I say? Looks like we share the same amount of luck."

"Which would be?" She asked.

"Nil, if you're going to Hope House."

She laughed at our dire situations which was pretty much all you could do.

"Want a ride?" I asked. She didn't answer me, obviously not willing to trust me, so I offered, "Listen, by the time you walk there they'll be closed and definitely won't have any spaces open. If you ride *with me*, at least we have a chance of getting a spot for the night."

She sighed. "A valid point," she said, looking around for my car.

I'm embarrassed by this. "Uh, " I said, scratching the stubble on my chin with the backs of my fingers. "I don't actually own a car." I point to my vintage nineteen-fifty Indian motorcycle. "Come on. It's better than walking, right?" I stuck my hands out in offering.

She smiled slowly in appreciation, her mouth curling

up at the sides and her eyes squinting into the sun. Her head bobbed slowly up and down on her neck. A silent yes. "I'd probably pick this over any car on this street." She stood back and admired it. "Solid black," she said. I nodded, intrigued. "Nice," she simply added.

"*You think so*? I plan on fixing her up when I get the time and, of course, the money. She's been good to me, though," I said, patting the handlebars. "She's pretty much all I have in this world." Harper looked at me as if in pity or maybe it was understanding. I really hoped it was understanding because if a girl that beautiful pitied me, I didn't think I could stand it. "Hop on," I said. She straddled the back of the leather seat and slid her duffel across her chest to sit behind her. "Uh, you might want to, uh," I said awkwardly, struggling with how to ask her to push her hair back so I could fit my helmet on her.

Instead, I set the helmet on the seat between her legs and brazenly ran my fingers through her hair. It flowed off her shoulders and settled onto her back. The scent of her shampoo bombarded me one more time and I swayed slightly at the assault but regained my stance. I grabbed the helmet off her lap and fit it onto her head. She giggled at the awkward familiarity of it.

"Sorry," I said. "But I wouldn't dream of putting you on the back of my bike without this."

"It's alright," she said, but paused. "*Why*? Are you an unsafe driver?"

"No, uh, my parents died in a car accident when I was four," I said matter-of-factly.

"Oh, I'm so sorry." She had the decency to look sincere. That was pretty refreshing, actually.

"It's alright," I sighed, shrugging my shoulders. "I barely remember them."

"I don't know *anything* about mine," she said, studying her feet, then realized what she was doing. "Harper Bailey," she said cheerfully, holding out her hand, revealing a dimpled grin.

I buckled the clasp around her delicate chin, resting my hands on the top of the helmet playfully. "My name is Callum Tate and I'm going to take care of you, Harper Bailey."

Her extended hand dropped into her lap. Her eyes went wide and her mouth dropped open. "Wh...*what* did you say?"

Shit. Was that was too forward? "I'm sorry," I said, shaking my head. "I'm Callum Tate. It's a pleasure to meet you, Harper Bailey." I grabbed her thin hand and a shot of warmth crept up my veins and shocked my heart into a frenzy.

The smile that had so quickly faded before came back with a vengeance. She squeezed my hand in greeting and whispered, "It's very nice to meet you, Callum."

I climbed on to the front part of the seat and started the engine. Harper settled her hands on the side of my ribs and I couldn't think of anything I wanted more than her arms wound tight against my chest. Suddenly, I couldn't get on the road fast enough.

Harper

I think Callum Tate can read minds. It's either that or there was something seriously *strange* going on between the two of us.

He started the motor and pulled the bike up on its wheels, lifting it off its stand and balanced our combined weight effortlessly.

He turned slightly to face me, exposing a flirtatious off-kilter grin, "You might want to hang on."

My stomach flipped in circles as I tightened my hands around his chest and I could feel his heart beat furiously against my palm which only served to make mine race faster.

"You okay?" He asked over the purr of the motor.

More than okay. "Yeah," I try to say as coolly as possible.

He revs the motor before placing his left hand over mine. "Hold on tight," he said as if I'd ever let go. As if I *could* ever let go.

Heat coursed through my arm and when he removes his hand, I felt a lacking I'd never known I could possess.

The wind whipped my hair behind me as I breathed in the warm summer air, letting it fill my lungs. With each breath he took, his chest expanded tightly against my stomach and hands and I can do nothing to stifle the tingling electricity that came with each one, sending my heart into violent trembles.

The Hope House is nothing like I thought it would be because it was worse, which is incredible as I expected awful. The building, though old and beautiful in architecture, was dark and extremely dirty, lines of sickly, equally filthy people huddled against the frame of the structure waiting and desperate to hear they have a place to rest their own heads in a cot for the night rather than the alternative and that was more than likely a cardboard box or a bench. I heard three gunshots go off as well as a woman's screams but the hundreds queued paid no heed, obviously accustomed to the harrowing sounds.

"Hold on," he said loudly before popping the curb and settling the bike near a lamp post.

He swung his leg over the seat and unbuckled the strap to my helmet before lifting it from my head. He grinned mischievously.

"My hair is stuck to my head at weird angles, isn't it?" I asked, a blush already descending upon my cheeks.

He studied me carefully before bursting out laughing. "Maybe," he teased. "Here," he said, smoothing out the unruly mess. The contact he makes with my skin gives me an involuntary shudder. "Are you cold?" He asked, raising one eyebrow.

"Uh, no, just...just got a glimpse at where we were and gotta' admit, I'm a bit un-enthused but beggars can't be choosers, right?"

"Poor Harper," he said with a slight frown. "You most certainly are not a beggar but I will admit we've not any choices," he playfully winked, sending me into yet another frenzy. "Come on." He placed his hands on my waist and lifted me off the seat.

"Good gosh, Callum!" I say, lifting my voice to the level of my now boiling blood pressure. His touch is intimidating, making me choke on the sharp inhalation its spark gives to me.

"What?"

I'm flustered. "I just wasn't expecting you to lift me is all."

"I'm sorry," he apologizes. "I'm acting too familiar with you and I just can't explain why. I'm usually more polite than this. You just affect me differently than most."

Don't read too much into that, Harper.

"Alright," he says, wrapping a large, thick chain around his bike and the post beside it before attaching the largest lock I've ever seen made. "Shall we?" He gestured toward the rows of people.

We walked toward the end of the line and sat in uncomfortable silence, each probably wondering if we knew what we were doing.

Callum

I don't know what I'm doing. I think I might have offended her by grabbing her waist without asking. I don't know why I did it either because the last thing I want is to offend this incredible girl.

"So, tell me, how were you orphaned?" I asked. Shock colors her face. Nice start there, goofball. Really sensitive. "I'm sor...," I start, but before I can even finish, she bursts out laughing.

"I've never actually had anyone ask me that so blatantly before yet it doesn't seem like such an unnatural question, seeming as we share the same plight."

"And what plight is that?" I ask.

"Oh, I don't know. The one where we meet in the lobby of social services after being kicked out of our foster homes for being afflicted with the 'eighteen disease'. Not to mention the part where we're standing in line together at The Hope House, a relief center that can't accommodate the demands being asked of it."

"God, you're plucky," I blurted out.

"You know it, but to answer your question..."

"What question?"

"The one where you asked me how I became an orphan?"

"'Kay."

She took a deep breath, readying herself to spew the prepared speech all us orphans kept at the tip of our tongues. "I'm not truly an orphan. My mother is alive and I'm hoping well somewhere out there but I've never met her. She left me at the hospital she gave birth to me at, slapped the name Harper on me, before peacin' it out and wishing me the best.

"I was adopted almost immediately into a young family who thought they could handle the demands of an infant. When they discovered that they couldn't handle one addicted to drugs, they passed me over. At three, I began the tireless process of being passed around once a year in the foster system. I assume my dad is some deadbeat crackhead, probably doesn't even know I'm alive. Anytime I pass a dude beggin' for change, if he could be my father's age, I slip him a buck or two in hopes he sees something in me he could recognize."

"Has it worked?"

"Nah, but my fingers are crossed," she teased.

"Wow, that is a sad, pathetic story," I prod.

"Tell me about it."

"My story's better than your story, though."

"That so?" Both her brows are raised in challenge.

"Yeah, double the pathetic, *quadruple* the sad."

"No kidding."

"As I said before, my parents died in a car wreck

when I was four. I barely remember either of them. From what I can gather from my limited memories, though, they were loving. I think my father may have been an attorney because he was always on the phone and I remember the words brief, client, and evidence were at the top of his vocabulary.

"I remember my mother was sweet and kind and that we'd always bake cookies on Sunday after church. It's my only distinct memory of her. I would sit at a kitchen island on a stool and we'd mix all the ingredients, then she'd ask me questions about whatever difficulty my four year old life could conjure up while they baked and when the bell tolled, no pun intended, we'd grab hot cookies, dip them in our milk and life would be peachy.

"I don't remember the day they died. I suppose I may have blocked it out but I *was* in the car with them and the car seat they paid a freakin' fortune for may have saved my life but left me utterly alone."

Her breathing got deeper.

"My mom was an only child," I continued. "My dad had a half-brother who was only ten at the time of my parents passing. He was raised by his maternal grandparents. So, basically, there was no one to take care of me."

"Damn, Callum. That's tragic," she said, the teasing losing its potency.

Suddenly, our attempts at trying to make light of our misfortune lost their charm. I hung my head against my chest and breathed deeply, exhaling acceptance with each blow. I was no longer interested in acknowledging my lot in life. I was in line, begging to stay on a revolting cot, that'd had probably slept a thousand others before me. The worst part was I had no idea if I'd get to have even that.

Sensing my discomfort, Harper took initiative and wrapped her hand within mine, squeezing reassurance into my heart. I looked over at her and smiled as lightheartedly as possible. She squeezed harder. It's funny how this total stranger could relate to me better than anyone else I'd ever met. It was as if I'd known her my entire life.

"It's like I've known you my entire life," I stupidly admit.

But she doesn't rebuff me as I anticipate. No, instead, she says, "I think, in some ways, we have. Only you could know what I've been through; the humiliation, the judgments, the unwanted pity and none of it at your doing. We may not have known each other our whole lives but we've definitely lived them in parallel."

We waited in line for three hours, marking the time with idle chit chat that held no meaning whatsoever, but felt strangely vital to have at the time.

"Your favorite color?" I asked.

"Green," she said. "Yours?"

"Same."

"Liar."

"I'm not lying."

She eyed me disbelievingly, "Mmm-kay."

"I'm not! Seriously, it's always been green."

"Alright, I believe you, I guess."

"Favorite food?" I continued, changing the subject.

"You first," she says.

"Afraid of an unoriginal answer?" I teased. She raised both eyebrows. "Okay, my favorite food is Tex-Mex. Good, authentic Tex-Mex though and as you may not know, that does not exist in this city."

"Have you ever even been to Texas?" She mocked.

"Yes, I have, miss. When I was sixteen, I went there for a Latin competition for school. So there."

"A Latin competition!?" She scoffs.

"Don't make fun!"

She attempts to straighten her face, "I'm sorry. Really."

"Yeah, that burst of laughter your hiding is really convincing."

She sobered up, after some effort I'm unhappy to report. "I didn't even know they taught Latin anymore," she said. "I thought it was considered a dead language."

"It is *not* a dead language! Your language is based in it, Harper."

"I'm sorry. I can see that this subject is a sensitive one for you."

"Obviously, I'm insane. I'm defending myself as if I was Roman. Listen, I took the language in high school because I thought it would give me a good foundation vocabulary for my intended college major."

"Oh, I'm dying to know what major you've chosen that *Latin* could possibly create a good foundation for," she teased.

I feel the corners of my mouth twist up. "I'm going pre-med."

Her eyes bug wide, "Seriously?"

"I know it's a lofty goal, even for people who come from money but I'm determined and it's been a dream of mine since I was small, so..."

She's staring at me.

"It's not lofty Callum. It's brilliant that you have

dreams. You should do it."
I was taken aback.
"I wasn't expecting that," I grinned. "I mean, my teachers were always supportive but I got conflicting messages growing up. My foster parents constantly told me I'd amount to nothing."
"But you didn't listen to them, did you?" She asked with a twinkle in her eyes.
"Stop looking at me like that."
She shook her head. "Like what?"
"Like I'm already a physician," I grinned.
"What kind of doctor do you want to be?" She asks, ignoring me.
"Uh...a pediatrician."
"How ya' going to do it?"
"Well, there's this thing, see, it's called a university. You apply..."
"Very funny. Seriously, how are you going to pull it off?"
Before I could answer though, a woman came out. Harper didn't know it, but we were about to get word that we were sleeping outside that night.
"I'm sorry," the woman callously announced, "but we're full tonight!" And with no other explanation, she shut the door behind her. The veteran homeless scrambled to the nearest restaurant dumpsters in hopes of finding new cardboard, resigned to their evening's fortune. Others stood gaping, unsure of what that exactly meant. I turned toward Harper, ready to speak but instead found myself studying her. She brought her hands to her mouth, her fingers trembled against her lips. She felt lost, I could tell, her tough outer facade was beginning to crack.

"Come with me," I said, quickly grabbing her hand, leading her through the dispersing crowd toward my motorcycle.

"Where are we going?" She whispered.

"Away from here."

Tears threatened the corner of her eyes and I caught one with my thumb before it slid down her cheek. I pushed her hair out of her eyes and strapped the helmet to her head without another word, before plopping her small frame toward the front seat of my bike, afraid she was too dazed to hold on to me. I got on and straddled the seat behind her, her lovely back against my chest, kicking on the motor and driving off the curb onto the street.

I leaned in closely to her ear, hoping she'd be able to hear me through her helmet, "You know everything's going to be okay, right?" She shook her head. "Trust me," I said. "I'll figure it out. Promise."

She slowly nodded her head, but I wasn't sure she really believed what I'd told her.

I stopped at a nearby gas station, narrowly avoiding a cab who cut me off but it didn't seem to faze her.

"Stay here, Harper. I'm going to call my friend Charlie, see if he'll let us crash on his couch." Her reply was a soft grin.

I held the receiver to the pay phone a few inches from my ear, nothing is grosser than a New York City pay phone. It rang three times before I got Charlie's voicemail. *Hey, Charlie here. Leave a message and I'll ring you back.*

"Charlie," I sighed, "I'm in need of a couch tonight, dude. Maybe you can call me back in the next five? I'm at 555-9876," I said, eyeing the number on the payphone. "I'll stick around for a bit. Also, I've picked up a stray. She's cool, you'll like her, just, *please*," I begged, "ring me back soon."

It was hit or miss with Charlie, he was a roadie for a mediocre band and he had mentioned a few weeks back that he'd be going to Japan with them soon. I just hoped he hadn't left just yet. The phone rang before I even got an opportunity to turn around.

I placed my hand on the receiver. *Please, God, let this be Charlie.* I picked it up.

"Hello?" I asked.

"Yo, Callum. It's Charlie."

"Oh ,thank God!" I exclaimed a little too loudly.

"Calm down, dude." He laughed. "Got your message. I've got some good news and some bad news. I'm not in the city tonight." *Damn.* "And I left my spare key at Cherry's and she's doing some waitressing job in the Hampton's this weekend for some extra cash so she's nowhere near you *but* if you *want*, you can crash at my studio tonight. There's a random shower in the back of the shared common space, if you remember, not ideal but all yours."

I breathed out an audible sigh. "Thank you so much, dude, seriously."

"No problem, man. I'll call Henry, let him know you're coming, he'll let you in, just mention my name."

"Thank you so much, Charlie. I can't thank you enough."

I hang up, invigorated.

I turn and slap my hands together. "Okay, Harper Bailey, you're comin' with me."

"I am?" She said, looking hopeful.

"Yeah, it's not going to be ideal," repeating Charlie's words, "but it's going to be better than staying the night outside in this heat."

We arrive at Charlie's studio around eight thirty in the evening. I ride my bike over the curb and onto the sidewalk, next to the entrance. Harper takes her helmet off and I get assaulted by her fragrant hair again and almost lose my balance.

"Where are you going to lock up your bike?"

"I'm not." I smile.

"Aren't you afraid it'll get stolen?"

"Nah, because I'm taking it inside."

"Can you do that?" She asked.

"Yeah, I've done it a million times, all the floors are concrete where we're going and I always promise Henry, the owner, to keep a mat beneath it to catch any oil." I point to the second story window above the door. "That's his apartment right there."

"Will he be cool about all this?" She asks, skepticism leaking from her tone.

"Yeah, I think so. Henry knows my situation. He never lets me stay more than one night, though. I suppose he's afraid I'll move in and that's against some sort of tenant code city thing. He's not licensed for that and a real stickler for the rules. The city has it out for the rockers, I guess." I winked, like a dumbass. I immediately regretted the cheese move.

I pressed the buzzer in awe of my total loss of cool. This girl seeped the 'smooth' outta' me.

"Henry," Henry announced in a static voice.

"Henry, it's Callum. Did Charlie call you?"

We hear another buzz for the door and I opened it. I clicked the buzzer again and hear the other end connect but Henry says nothing.

"Thanks, Henry."

"No problem, Callum. See you in the morning, dude."

"And that was Henry."

"How old is he?" Harper asked.

"I don't know, like thirty?"

"Cool."

"Alright, hold the door for me?" I ask.

She whips inside the covered alcove and holds the door as wide as it will go. I give my bike two hard shoves and it lurches over the step to the alcove and into the building foyer. I lead Harper to Charlie's studio in the very back.

"It's the last door on the right."

She jumped ahead of my bike and opened the door for me as I wheeled in the bike. Charlie's studio space is large and it should be, because it costs him a small fortune but apparently it paid for itself when he recorded for random bands when he wasn't on the road.

Harper let out a low whistle.

"Incredible," she said, turning around.

I set my bike up in an open corner of his instrument room and opened one of the only closet doors near the entrance. I pulled out a large rubber pad that Charlie kept inside for my motorcycle and tossed it underneath the motor.

I turned around and caught her watching me. It reminded me that I was alone, with an unbelievably beautiful girl, and that no one was around. I tucked my hands in my back pockets to keep from seizing this stranger and kissing her until she gasped for air.

"So," I said, rocking back on my heels. I grabbed my

bag. "Listen, I've done this a couple of times. It gets old fast but the one thing I've learned is to take advantage of anything you can while you can because you may not have the opportunity to do it for awhile which means I recommend we shower, then take any dirty clothes we have to the laundromat close by."

"This isn't your first rodeo then?"

"Not by a long shot. I'll go first, ensuring you'll have privacy later."

I grabbed my towel, something noticeably missing from her "luggage", also something I plan on addressing later, and head for the shower with my soap and shampoo in hand.

The "shower" was a drain in the floor, a poorly pressured spout, and a thin plastic shower curtain in the corner of what at one time must have been a pre-war locker room. The water was lukewarm at best but better than I'd had for the past two days, which was sponge baths in subway restrooms. Even though the water temperature was crummy, I had never been in such a good mood and was positive it was from meeting Harper. There's nothing more thrilling than meeting someone new for the first time, especially if that someone new was freaking gorgeous as hell.

I stepped from the shower feeling better than I had in a very long time and toweled off. *Shit,* I thought as I looked down at myself, *I forgot my clothes.* I wrapped my towel around my lower half and trudged along the hall back to Charlie's studio, already turning beet red at what I was about to do.

As I near the studio though, I can hear loud music trembling through the air and one miss Harper Bailey singing at the top of her lungs. I edged toward the slightly ajar door and quietly pushed it open, hoping to grab my bag next to the wall nearest me and holding my breath that she'd be too distracted to notice me but when I catch a glimpse of her, I become engrossed.

Forgetting my towel and my bag, I leaned against the door jamb just watching her dancing around, singing Aerosmith's 'Dream On'. I couldn't believe how remarkably entertaining it was to see her shuffling over the floor like she was, her hair falling over her shoulders and in her face. I can tell it was probably the most free she had felt in quite awhile making her face flushed and excited and her body swaying to each beat. I wondered if the words meant anything in particular to her and suddenly didn't know if I was intruding. If this was some sort of therapeutic ritual for her, I'd feel like an ass if she knew I was watching. I leaned forward and grabbed my bag just as she turned and saw me standing there.

"Agh!" She squealed, turning down the music. Her face a deep red. "How long have you been standing there?" She asked, her chest heaving from the effort of her song. Her eyes followed the lines of my body until they stop at the towel. "Why aren't you dressed?"

"Uh, I didn't mean to intrude," I said, the heat of a blush creeping up my neck. "I forgot my bag with my stuff and came back for it and, um, I accidentally saw you and..."

She looked like she was about to cry, her hands flew to her mouth and I reached for her, "I'm so sorry, Harper. I didn't think. I'm sorry."

But she burst out laughing, the tears streaming down her face her obvious attempt at holding it in and not from humiliation. I breathed a sigh of relief and my smile began to match hers. She sucked in air harshly and started laughing harder.

"Oh my Lord, Callum. This is so embarrassing!"

"You're embarrassed! Look at me! I'm in a towel, dripping water all over the effing floor."

She snorted, making her laugh even harder. My laughter harmonized with hers, tears streaming down both our faces now.

Harper sobered suddenly and we stared at each other for at least a minute. I made a cautious step toward her, my face inching toward hers. She laid a hand on my damp shoulder but instead of meeting my kiss, her eyes brightened and she turned her head in embarrassment.

"You have to get dressed, Callum."

"I'm so sorry, I forgot," I said, as I grabbed my bag and headed for the common room one more time. When I returned, dressed and slightly flustered, I found Harper playing an acoustic guitar in one of Charlie's recliners.

"Wow. You can play guitar too?" I asked.

"Nah, I just dabble."

"I noticed you didn't have a towel and although mine's a bit wet, I wouldn't care if you used it, if you want."

She set the guitar aside and stood, smoothing her wrinkled jeans down her legs and stood before me.

"Thanks," she whispered, grabbing her bag and throwing the towel over her shoulders.

She returned a few minutes later, her coppery hair wet and hanging at the middle of her back, already starting to dry in soft waves. Her eyes were brightened by the shower and her lips were plump and red. *What I wouldn't give to kiss those lips.*

CPSIA information can be obtained
at www.ICGtesting.com
Printed in the USA
FFOW02n0721020216
21056FF